THE
FATAL
FOLIO

ST. MARTIN'S PAPERBACKS
TITLES BY ELIZABETH PENNEY

The Apron Shop series

Hems & Homicide
Thread and Dead
Bodies and Bows

The Cambridge Bookshop series

Chapter and Curse
A Treacherous Tale
The Fatal Folio

THE
FATAL
FOLIO

ELIZABETH PENNEY

St. Martin's Paperbacks

NOTE: If you purchased this book without a cover you should be aware that this book is stolen property. It was reported as "unsold and destroyed" to the publisher, and neither the author nor the publisher has received any payment for this "stripped book."

This is a work of fiction. All of the characters, organizations, and events portrayed in this novel are either products of the author's imagination or are used fictitiously.

First published in the United States by St. Martin's Paperbacks, an imprint of St. Martin's Publishing Group.

THE FATAL FOLIO

Copyright © 2023 by Elizabeth Penney.

All rights reserved.

For information, address St. Martin's Publishing Group, 120 Broadway, New York, NY 10271.

www.stmartins.com

ISBN: 978-1-250-78774-3

Our books may be purchased in bulk for promotional, educational, or business use. Please contact your local bookseller or the Macmillan Corporate and Premium Sales Department at 1-800-221-7945, ext. 5442, or by email at MacmillanSpecialMarkets@macmillan.com.

Printed in the United States of America

St. Martin's Paperbacks edition / November 2023

10 9 8 7 6 5 4 3 2 1

To intrepid booksellers everywhere

CHAPTER 1

November had arrived in Cambridge, bringing with it crisp, cool air, the emergence of mufflers and wool coats from closets, and—new to me, as an ex-pat American—Guy Fawkes Day. Almost six months earlier, my mother and I had made the move from Vermont to Cambridge, joining my great-aunt Violet in running Thomas Marlowe—Manuscripts & Folios, one of the oldest bookshops in this historic city with its more than thirty colleges.

"Explain Guy Fawkes Day to me," I said to Kieran Scott, my significant other, while opening my laptop. "I want to be ready for tonight's celebrations."

We were in the library at Hazelhurst House, a once-moated manor and Kieran's childhood home, located in a village near Cambridge. His mother, Lady Asha, had offered me a side job cataloguing a five-hundred-year-old collection stuffed with first editions and eclectic subjects. With the usual dip in sales before the Christmas ramp-up, the bookshop could use the income, and as a former librarian, I relished the challenge and treasure hunt.

Leaning against the table beside my chair, Kieran folded his arms, brown eyes twinkling. With his mop of curly dark hair and the lean, strong build of an avid cyclist, he was ridiculously good-looking. "Do you want the long version or the short?"

I eyed the floor-to-ceiling shelves, a gnawing sensation warning me I needed to get to work. Today's task was to tour the library and decide how to approach the project. "The short for now." I pressed a few keys and logged into a cataloguing software program. Project name: *The Library at Hazelhurst Manor, founded in*—"When did your ancestors start buying books?"

Rubbing his chin, Kieran looked thoughtful. "Not exactly sure, but we have an illustrated *Book of Hours* purchased around 1500." He grinned. "That's not our most cherished book, though."

"What is?" I took the bait, realizing we were veering off our original topic but too fascinated not to follow up. Guy Fawkes could wait a minute. I entered *founded in 1500* to my project description, figuring that was good enough for now, until we uncovered a more accurate date.

"Have you ever heard of *The Fatal Folio*, as popular in its day as *The Castle of Otranto*?" Kieran asked.

I flipped through the library catalogue in my brain. *The Castle of Otranto* was considered to be the novel that launched the gothic genre in the mid-eighteenth century, soon followed by *The Monk*, *The Mysteries of Udolpho*, *Frankenstein*, and yes, *The Fatal Folio*, the story of a book that killed its owners. "Selwyn Scott," I said, the pieces falling together. "He was your ancestor?"

Kieran nodded. "Whoever *he* was."

"Selwyn was a pen name?" Not surprising. Horace Walpole, author of *The Castle of Otranto*, had first published under a pseudonym, "William Marshal, gentleman." Walpole, a member of Parliament, historian, and architect, had presented the story as a *found* manuscript, an interesting literary device. Like Walpole, the Scotts had been members of Parliament as well, a tradition that extended through the centuries to Kieran's father, Lord Graham Scott. Kieran's older brother, Alan, who was living and working in Hong Kong, was next in line for the title and the position. Before meeting Kieran, I hadn't really been aware that a functioning aristocracy still existed beyond Charles, William, and Harry.

"No one has ever identified the author," Kieran said. "Though many have speculated." He leaned close, whispering seductively, "Want to see the original manuscript?"

I laughed. "You sure know the way to my heart." I pushed back in my chair, eager to view the historic document, which was even more enticing due to its personal connection to the owner.

Kieran led me across the spacious room, which was carpeted with fine Persian rugs and furnished with gold brocade upholstered chairs and sofas and long oak tables. Faded red silk wallpaper and carved paneling adorned the walls, and hanging crystal chandeliers provided light along with deep-set diamond-paned windows. As a book nerd, though, the sliding ladders used to reach high shelves were my favorite feature.

Instead of guiding me to a bookshelf, he slid aside a hanging tapestry near the fireplace to reveal a hidden door. Pulling a ring of brass keys from his pocket, he said, "This is where we keep the family papers and records." He inserted the key and turned. "I'm warning you, it's a bit of a mess."

My heart skipped a beat at being allowed into this inner sanctum. As I'd experienced at the bookshop, nothing could beat the thrill of delving into family histories and mysteries. Still awed that our bookshop was established in 1605, I was as likely to come across an ancient bill of sale as a packing slip from last week.

Kieran twisted the knob and pushed the door open, revealing a larger room than the closet I expected. Wooden shelves lining the windowless walls held a jumble of faded ledgers, file holders, banker boxes, and in one section, several archival storage boxes. They drew my attention like a magnet.

"We'll take this into the library," he said, choosing one of the acid-free boxes. "The light is better."

I peered at the others with curiosity. "What's in those?"

"The *Book of Hours* I told you about, for one thing," he said. He tapped the largest box. "This is a family Bible with dates of birth, marriages, and death, starting in the early 1700s."

Interest leaped. "Including Selwyn's generation?" If so, perhaps we could identify some possible authors and dig into their background. What a thrill it would be to solve this long-standing literary mystery.

Kieran's eyes widened when he got my drift. "Yes, as a matter of fact." He stacked the manuscript box on the Bible box and picked them both up. I let him leave the room first, giving the family papers a lingering, longing look as I followed. To me, this collection of dusty documents was a window into history, a topic that continually fascinated me. Even more so here in England, where we were immersed in it.

I joined Kieran at the table, standing next to him as he opened the smaller box. "The author didn't sign his or her real name?" I sort of joked. If only it were that simple.

"No, unfortunately." Kieran placed the lid to one side and motioned toward the box. "There we have it."

A stack of pages lay inside, inscribed with flowing, curling script on creamy rag paper. "*The Fatal Folio*," I read from the top page. "By Selwyn Scott. This looks like the copy that went to the printer."

"That's what we think," Kieran said. "Every page is perfect, no cross-outs or blots."

We had it so good in modern times, when it came to publishing, at least. Using computers, we could easily make changes and spit out an error-free copy without spending days and hours trying to use our best penmanship. Even typewriters had been more difficult.

"There you are, old sweat." We looked up from staring at the manuscript as a tall blond man about our age strode into the library. With chiseled features and a flop of hair over his brow, dressed in a tweed blazer and jeans, he resembled many of the academics I saw around Cambridge. "Aunt Asha said I'd find you here."

Kieran gestured. "Oliver. Come meet my girlfriend, Molly. Molly, this is my cousin, Oliver. Don't mind him, he's a bit of a prat."

Oliver grinned as he thrust out his hand and shook mine. "Nice to meet you, Molly." Blue eyes studied my face, in a nice way, not creepy, and then lit with recognition. "You're from Thomas Marlowe, right? I pop in there now and then. Great shop."

Now that he'd mentioned it, I was fairly sure I'd seen him there. He was attractive enough to notice. "You live in Cambridge?"

"I'm at St. Aelred." One of Cambridge's smallest, oldest, and most charming colleges. "Professor of Literature."

"Dr. Scott, I presume," Kieran said and by the way they both laughed, I guessed it was one of their inside jokes. "How are things at the college?"

Oliver rolled his eyes and sighed, then seized on the topic of the manuscript. "*The Fatal Folio*. The Scott family's claim to literary fame. At least so far. Did I tell you I'm writing a novel?" He plopped down at the table and began tapping his fingers.

"No," Kieran said as we both sat. "What about?"

Oliver nodded toward the box. "A gothic, of course. Inspired by Selwyn, but updated. A modern gothic." He turned to me. "Ever since Kieran and I discovered *The Fatal Folio* here in this library, I've been fascinated by the genre. I wrote my dissertation on haunted objects, with *The Fatal Folio as* the centerpiece. About five years ago, a colleague and I founded the Gothic Literature Institute, which is why I swung by, Kieran. The symposium starts tomorrow, with a lecture by me, right here at Hazelhurst. Today I'm making last-minute arrangements with your mother."

"I'd love to sit in," I blurted. "If that's all right." Maybe it was invitation only.

"Of course you can, Molly." Oliver pulled out his phone. "Give me your digits and I'll shoot you the agenda. Many of the events are open to the public, like tomorrow's, so feel free to pass it along."

"I know someone," I said after giving Oliver my number. "George Flowers." I was referring to my aunt's friend, who often did small repairs around the bookshop. "He's a huge Brontë fan."

Oliver nodded, his fingers tapping the screen. "Part of the canon, for sure."

A soft throat-clearing caught our attention. Kieran's mother stood in the library doorway. "I hate to interrupt," she said, "but lunch is ready."

I was still slightly in awe of Lady Asha, who was gorgeous as well as impeccably elegant and well mannered.

Today she wore her long, glossy hair in a messy bun and half-glasses were perched on her nose, both touches that made her slightly more approachable.

"Coming, Molly?" Kieran asked as he got up.

"Well . . ." I glanced at the bookshelves awaiting my attention. I hadn't gotten anything done, unless you counted viewing the Scotts' most prized literary possession. One book down, only a thousand to go.

"Please feel free to join us," Lady Asha said. "I was counting on it."

In that case . . . I stood. "Thank you. I'd love to have lunch with you."

Oliver went ahead of us, slinging his arm around his aunt's shoulders and speaking into her ear. Judging by their laughter, I gathered he had said something amusing.

"I like your cousin," I said to Kieran as we made our way to the dining room. "He seems like a lot of fun."

Kieran smiled. "He is. We used to get up to all kinds of mischief when we were kids. We'd dash around here pretending to be knights or invading Vikings."

I pictured miniature versions of Kieran and Oliver rampaging around. Talk about a place to spark a child's imagination. Although growing up in Vermont had been wonderful. Woods, fields, lakes, and barns had been our playground.

"We're in the small dining room," Lady Asha called over her shoulder before she and Oliver turned a corner.

Kieran took my arm, then as the other two vanished out of view, halted me for a kiss. "Are you busy later?" he asked, his lips close to mine.

I wrapped my arms around his neck, enjoying this aspect of the cataloguing job very much indeed. "What did you have in mind?"

We grinned at each other, then he put his arm around

my waist and we continued on. "You were asking about Guy Fawkes," he said. "It all began in 1605."

"The year Thomas Marlowe was founded," I said, noting the coincidence.

Kieran nodded in acknowledgement. "The plot was hatched after King James the first disappointed the Catholics by refusing to support the religion after Elizabeth the first died. A group of dissidents met at the Duck and Drake in London and plotted to blow up the Houses of Parliament on opening day, the fifth of November. Guy Fawkes was one of them."

As we wandered toward lunch, he relayed how Guy had rented a cellar under Parliament—under a false name, Guido—and was sitting there, with matches and thirty-six kegs of gunpowder, when he was arrested. The Gunpowder Plot had been foiled.

"A day of thanksgiving was instituted in 1606," he concluded, "which soon became the holiday we now know, with bonfires, fireworks, and the burning of effigies."

"Kind of like our July fourth," I said. "Without the effigies. Sounds like a good time." We were attending the main event in Cambridge, held on Midsummer Common.

"It will be," he promised. We had reached the small dining room, which held a table seating eight or ten, in contrast to the main dining room, which sat upward of forty. A fire was crackling in the fireplace and thick velvet draperies made the space seem even cozier.

Along with Lady Asha and Oliver, Lord Graham was at the table, all politely waiting for us to arrive. "Good afternoon, Molly," Lord Graham said, a trace of a smile on his austere features.

I think he liked me, although it was hard to tell. "Good afternoon, Lord Graham. It's lovely to be here." Kieran's father had been ill and staying out of public view lately, so I was extra glad to see him. I sat, smiling up at Kieran, who was holding my chair. Not a typical courtesy of his but one that seemed appropriate here.

Once we were settled, Lady Asha picked up a ladle. "Red lentil soup?" Oliver was already passing around a plate of naan bread. In addition, assorted sandwiches were stacked on a platter.

"Please," I said, inhaling the mouth-watering mix of spices wafting from the soup.

Soon we were all digging in, the conversation focused on light topics, which thankfully didn't include my progress—or lack of same—on the catalogue job. After lunch, I'd insist that Kieran and Oliver leave me to it so I could get on schedule and stay there.

"Molly is going to figure out who Selwyn Scott actually was," Kieran said. He patted my knee. "If anyone can solve the mystery, it's you, love."

Everyone turned to look at me with curious interest. I put down my spoon. "Am I? I mean, I thought we could try . . ."

Oliver pointed a finger at me. "What an incredibly good idea. We can unveil Selwyn's identity when my book comes out. We'll get all kinds of press and publicity, maybe even a write-up in *The Sunday Times* book feature—"

"They'll want you for the talk shows," Lady Asha put in. "Everyone loves a mystery."

"You'd be compensated, of course," Oliver said, knocking aside another concern I was harboring. "Plus mentioned in my acknowledgements."

"Molly should be interviewed as well," Lady Asha said. "She can explain the steps she took to learn Selwyn's identity." Her eyes shone with certainty that yes, I would solve the puzzle that had eluded others for centuries.

Talk about being pushed into the deep end. On one hand, I really liked the project—and money was always a bonus; on the other, I was feeling a ton of pressure. In ordinary circumstances, I could hold my own, assertively tell pushy people to back off—tactfully of course, but this was Kieran's family. I didn't want to overpromise and let them down.

I also have to admit, the idea of media appearances where I wasn't the "Vermont beauty" Kieran was dating appealed to me.

"Um," I temporized. "How about this? I'll do some preliminary investigation and we'll talk specifics after that." Not only did I need time to determine the likelihood of success, I needed to estimate how much time it would take so I could charge appropriately. I didn't want to overcharge—or undercharge. "It is a fascinating project and I want to make sure I can do it justice."

"No worries, Molly," Lady Asha said. "From what Kieran has told me about you, I'm sure it will be a piece of cake." She twinkled at me, her expression so like her son's I was momentarily stunned. Then she moved on. "Speaking of cake, we have mini éclairs for dessert and I've brewed a pot of coffee."

Despite groans around the table, we all indulged. After lunch, shooed away by Lady Asha, who insisted on cleaning up, Kieran and I waddled back to the library. Oliver wandered off, saying he had to make some calls.

I was about to suggest that Kieran let me get to work when he opened the box holding the Bible. "Let's take a quick look," he said, setting the large, thick book on the table.

The cover was leather embossed with gold lettering, much of it worn. Kieran reverently opened the cover, gently leafing through the pages. "Woodcuts," he said, referring to the illustrations.

"What a great heirloom," I said, thinking of the generations of Scotts who had cherished this Bible.

He reached the family register at the back and we studied the faded, rusty entries. "Ah, here we go. Samuel Scott was born in 1812, so he would have been thirty when *The Fatal Folio* was published in 1842."

"What about . . ." I squinted. "Frances? His sister?" She had been born in 1820. I couldn't read the death date. "The Brontë sisters used male pseudonyms. She could have done the same."

"True," Kieran said. He studied another entry. "I can't quite make this name out. But it looks like they died young. Too bad this page is so faded."

I felt a pang of sadness. I'd noticed quite a few entries with birth and death dates close together. All the children who didn't live.

Kieran's expression was thoughtful. "You know what? We have portraits of Samuel and Frances. And their parents"—he looked at the page again—"Agatha and Alistair. They're in the upstairs hall, if you want to see them." He started to close the book.

"Wait," I said, pulling out my phone. I snapped a picture of the page despite its flaws, thinking to create a file for the Selwyn quest. Placing my phone on the table, I said, "Can we go look now?" What did another delay matter at this point?

"Of course. Then I'll get out of here and let you work." Kieran glanced at the camelback clock on the mantel. "I should go back to town anyway." Kieran ran a bicycle shop, Spinning Your Wheels, located in Magpie Lane beside the bookshop. That's how we'd met. At the time, I had no idea he was of noble birth, as they say. He'd just been the nice, good-looking guy who worked next door.

We left the library and made our way through the great hall, which was huge; the original keep, Kieran had told me. Stone walls draped with tapestries loomed overhead, black-and-white tiles lined the floors, and more than one suit of armor stood at attention.

Paneled in walnut, the stairs were wide, with a landing, and trimmed with an ornate railing and balusters. Every time I went up or down, I pictured myself wearing a sweeping gown. It was that kind of staircase.

Portraits lined the upper hall in a seemingly endless procession. "Where's yours?" I asked, only half-joking.

Kieran rolled his eyes. "It's in my mother's sitting room. A family portrait from when I was around five or so and my brother was ten. I'll show it to you sometime."

Almost every day, I found new proof of the social and economic gulf between Kieran and me. Good thing it really didn't impact our relationship. We had a friendly, easygoing, drama-free partnership. It helped that Kieran deliberately downplayed his heritage and, in fact, rejected it on many levels. That's why he was running a bike shop, not working in international finance like his brother.

We strolled along, pausing to read the brass plates attached to every portrait. Ladies with high-piled, severely parted hair. Men wearing uniforms and hats with feathers, hands on their sword hilts.

"Ah, here we go." Kieran stopped in front of a young couple, the woman seated and her husband standing beside her. The brass plate read, "Lord and Lady Alistair Scott, in 1790."

The woman wore a gold silk off-the-shoulder gown trimmed with lace at neckline and three-quarter-length sleeves. She had an oval face and dark hair worn up and adorned with a flower. Oddly, she was holding a bunch of grapes in one hand, the other poised to pluck a few.

Alistair wore a brown velvet coat and trousers over an ivory satin waistcoat. A cravat circled his neck and his sleeves were also trimmed with lace. He wore a white wig. They were attractive, with amiable expressions.

The next two portraits were of Frances and Samuel, both around eighteen or twenty years old judging by the portrait dates. Frances resembled her mother, and held a book in both hands as if interrupted while reading. Was the book a clue to her secret life as an author? Samuel had a rakish expression, his eyes twinkling in a way I recognized even across almost three hundred years. No book, but he looked the sort to enjoy pulling the wool over people's eyes.

"I see the family resemblance," I muttered. Pulling out my phone, I snapped pictures of all three paintings.

A male voice drifted down the corridor, preceding the arrival of Oliver, who was on the phone. He stopped a distance away, not seeming to notice us. "Yes, sir," he said. "I understand. Next month, then."

After hanging up, he lifted his chin and yelped in frustration. Then he stomped his feet a couple of times and growled. "Thad Devine, I'm going to kill you."

CHAPTER 2

I glanced at Kieran, not quite sure what to make of this display. Kieran threw me a smile before calling, "Great performance. What's your encore?"

Oliver jolted, literally rocking back on his heels. Then he composed himself and strode toward us. "Sorry you had to witness that. I just got some irritating news."

"So I gathered," Kieran said. He lifted a brow. "College politics?"

His cousin snorted. "Exactly. I've been up for a promotion from associate to full professor for almost the entire past year. Every time I think they're going to pull the trigger, there's a delay. And now I've got competition. Sophia Verona, who also runs the Gothic Institute, is in the running."

"That must be tricky," I put in. "Competing against your friend."

He ran a hand through his hair. "It is, but that's not the worst of it. I've got a student trying to make trouble for me." Oliver grimaced. "Thad claims I didn't rank him fairly. I make it very clear that all my students are treated the same."

Thad Devine, I'm going to kill you. I put two and two together. "If he complains, it might affect your promotion?"

Oliver's expression was grim. "Might? Definitely. Dr. Cutler is a stickler. His favorite aphorism is, 'You faculty *are* St. Aelred.' If he could, he'd have us living like the monks who founded the place."

"St. Aelred is rather traditional," Kieran said. "Didn't you say there are endowments that ride on the college's reputation?"

"Uh-huh," Oliver said. "Some donors monitor our every move. Nowadays, with social media, a scandal can blow up out of nowhere, as you know. If there's a risk of that, well, Dr. Cutler certainly won't promote me." He sounded bitter.

"Tough break, old man," Kieran said. "I know how dedicated you've been."

Seeming to shake off his bad mood, Oliver smiled a thank-you. "Hence the need for Plan B. After I get a book published, I'll retire from teaching and pen novels." He glanced at the portraits. "It's a family tradition, after all."

Having known a few writers, I was aware that venturing into publishing was never a slam dunk. Although Oliver did have a few things going for him—namely, being a Scott. His blond good looks and connections to the nobility would certainly be attractive on a book cover, I thought somewhat cynically.

He gestured toward the portraits. "Getting started already, Molly?"

"Part of my preliminary work," I said. "Let's talk in a day or two, okay?"

"Sounds good." Oliver turned back to Kieran. "Are you going to town for the festivities tonight?" When Kieran said yes, he asked, "Want to grab a bite to eat first? I'm thinking we could meet around six thirty."

Kieran looked at me, so I answered. "We'd love to. If you don't have any preference, how about the Magpie

Pub? It's one of our favs." The pub was right across the lane from the bookshop and bike shop, which would be easy for us. From there, we could walk to the common.

"Magpie Pub it is." Oliver nodded at me. "I already have your number, Molly, so I'll shoot over what I'm thinking on the research project. Then you can get back to me at your leisure."

If the offered rate was decent, I already knew my answer. I wanted to be the one to discover Selwyn Scott's identity. Not for fame, or even necessarily for the money, but because I loved using my research skills—and intuition—to solve mysteries.

The early winter sun was setting as I drove away from Hazelhurst House later that afternoon, towers and ramparts etched against the sky. After much practice, I was finally comfortable driving on the left in Aunt Violet's vintage Cortina. The retro ride handled well, so as I tooled along quiet country lanes toward the A14, I reviewed the afternoon's progress.

To my relief, I'd discovered that the library was organized by subject, loosely perhaps, but in some kind of order. It wasn't much good having a list of books owned if they couldn't be located. The library had a wide array of fiction and poetry, including the esoteric, architecture and art, farming and veterinarian sciences, biology, history, law, and the physical sciences. And that was less than a complete listing. From a quick survey of their reading habits, the Scotts were inquisitive, dedicated to estate management, and lovers of the arts.

My heart warmed with joy as I approached my exit,

the college spires creating an enchanting skyline. We lived in the heart of the oldest section and it was very easy to imagine that I had stepped into the past. Automobiles were strictly limited in this area and I crept along the cobblestone streets, watching for pedestrians and cyclists.

I reached Magpie Lane at last: a short, narrow, hidden enclave, and bumped down the cobblestones toward our garage at the end. On the way, I passed the Magpie Pub and the Holly & Ivy Inn, both on the corner, Spinning Your Wheels, and Tea & Crumpets, my friend's tea shop. As always, I slowed to take in the bookshop, located in an iconic timber-and-plaster Tudor building. The bow-front diamond-pane window was softly lit, and the bookshop cats, Clarence and Puck, sat in the display, watching me go by. They knew the car.

When I walked into the bookshop a few minutes later, Puck, a young black stray I'd rescued, came running to greet me. Clarence didn't move from his spot. It was beneath him to show enthusiasm unless it involved his dish.

Instead of trying to leap into my arms, Puck meowed again, sounding alarmed. "What is it?" I asked, bending over and allowing my bags to slide to the floor. "Is something wrong?"

His answer was a hiss and an arching of his back. I followed his gaze to a dark corner of the bookshop, where a grinning white face seemed to hover in midair, its curved brows, curly mustache, and chin-strip beard making it even more eerie.

I jumped with a gasp. "What the—"

Aunt Violet stepped the rest of the way around the bookcase and pulled off the mask. "Did I startle you, Molly?" The way her blue eyes twinkled behind her glasses revealed that had been her intent. My tiny and energetic great-aunt, with her high-piled white hair that often hid a pencil or two, wasn't above an occasional practical joke.

"Yes, I was," I admitted, scooping up my things. "Puck didn't like it either." I'd seen that face before, I realized. It was a Guy Fawkes mask.

"Sorry. I couldn't resist." She studied the mask. "When I was at university, we used to wear something similar. Such freedom in being anonymous, although some took it too far."

"Someone always does, right?" I carried my bags around behind the counter and pulled out my laptop. "Where's Mum?" My mother, Nina Marlowe, who was a published poet, also worked in the bookstore.

Before Aunt Violet could answer, footsteps creaked along the floor from the direction of the kitchen, which was located behind the shop. I turned, expecting to see Mum. Instead our friend and handyman, George Flowers, appeared. A sturdy, broad-featured, and balding man about Aunt Violet's age, George was like an uncle to me.

"I fixed the leak," he said. "Needed new washers in the faucet."

"Thank you, George," Aunt Violet said. "I don't know what we'd do without you."

"Oh, go on with you," he scoffed, a protest belied by his obvious pleasure at the praise. George, who owned an apartment building nearby, was a whiz at almost any repair job. Happily, he always came right over when we called.

"George," I said, leaning against the counter, phone in hand, "I have something to show you." I had downloaded the agenda for the gothic symposium and now brought it up on my screen. Nothing yet from Oliver about the research project, I noticed. Not that I was expecting anything this soon.

George ambled over to stand by my side. "What's this?"

I handed him the phone. "You're a Brontë fan, I know, so I thought you'd like to attend this symposium. Most of the events are open to the public."

He studied the list, muttering under his breath. "A lecture series, the gothic in Film Series, Gothic tour of Cambridge . . . a costume dance . . ." He gave back the phone. "Can you send that along to me, Molly? There are one or two events I'd like to take in."

"Definitely." I forwarded the agenda to George's number. "Let me know which ones you're interested in. Maybe we can go together."

Aunt Violet was rearranging some books nearby. "How did it go at Hazelhurst House, Molly?"

"I made a good start," I said, not wanting to reveal I was already behind, at least in my mind. "Oh, guess what? Kieran showed me the original manuscript for *The Fatal Folio*. His cousin is lecturing on the book tomorrow for the symposium."

George, who was browsing the fiction shelves, paused to show us a book. "You mean the original of this?" He flipped through the edition from the late 1800s, a nice but not exceptionally valuable copy. "This is a real classic."

"It is." I sat behind the counter and flipped open my laptop, thinking to catch up with my email. "So exciting to think that Kieran's ancestor wrote it, although under a pen name. Kieran and I are going to try to find out who Selwyn Scott actually was by researching the family in that generation." Oh, who was I kidding by holding out for Oliver's offer? I was too curious not to continue the project. Besides, it was something Kieran and I could work on together.

Still holding the book, George wandered over to the counter. "It was one of the women, I'm guessing."

"Really?" I reached into my memory for the name. "Not Samuel? He was the only adult male Scott alive when the book was published."

George tapped the cover. "A man wouldn't write under a pen name. He'd be too proud for that."

"Well, they did sometimes," I said, warming to the debate. "Horace Walpole, for example. *The Castle of Otranto* was first published under the name William Marshall."

"That's true." George made the concession before swinging into his argument. "He was trying to pass off the story as a translation of a sixteenth-century manuscript written by a monk." He held up the book. "By the second edition, he came clean and included his name as author. William Beckford also used that device with *Vathek*, claiming it too was translated from an ancient manuscript. In contrast, *The Fatal Folio* is set in the contemporary time and makes no claim to a mysterious origin."

He was correct. *The Fatal Folio*'s main character was an English bookseller traveling in a mountainous and remote region of Italy. The story was in first person, told after the main character survived a beautiful book rumored to kill its owners. Objects that bring disaster are a gothic trope—for example, Wilkie Collins's moonstone.

"Good point, George," I said. "I'll keep it in mind during my investigation. With any luck, we'll find some hard evidence one way or another." Were there clues among Kieran's family papers? Or perhaps in other library holdings?

"That would be best," he said. "Otherwise it's all theory and speculation, right?" His smile was sly. "Not that many haven't made a career of such. There's a new theory about the Brontë family every time I turn around."

"They seem to be an endless source of fascination." While Selwyn Scott couldn't claim anything close to Charlotte, Emily, and Anne's popularity, new information could spark interest. Someone might even want to make a television series or movie based on *The Fatal Folio*. Or the life of Selwyn Scott. Hazelhurst House would make the perfect setting for a period drama. Letting my mind run away with me a bit, I wondered if the Scotts would allow filming there.

The front door opened and Mum breezed through, chased by a cold wind. "Brr. It's frigid out there." She set down a cloth shopping bag and plucked off a wool hat to reveal her pixie-cut dark hair. Smoothing it down, she wrinkled her nose. "People are already setting off firecrackers. One startled me as I walked out of Sainsbury's."

"The police will have their hands full tonight," George said. "You're not supposed to set off bangers in the street or public places."

I revised my expectation of Bonfire Night from us standing beside a fire while watching fireworks to something less tame.

"Bonfire Night has gotten wild at times," Aunt Violet said. "Remember when we were young, George? The drinking and carousing. Running through the streets."

His expression was carefully innocent. "That'd be telling, wouldn't it?" He tapped the copy of *The Fatal Folio* he'd placed on the counter. "Will you ring this up, Molly? Then I'll get out of your way and let you close up."

After George left with a promise to connect regarding the symposium, Aunt Violet and I tallied the day's sales and locked the shop door. Mum was in the kitchen preparing the evening meal. The three of us took turns shopping and cooking, an arrangement we all appreciated.

"What are your plans tonight, Molly?" Aunt Violet asked. "You aren't staying in, I hope."

"And miss my first Guy Fawkes Night? No way." I slid the bank deposit into a bank bag and zipped it. "Kieran and I are meeting friends at the Magpie for dinner and then heading over to the common for the celebration."

"I'd warn you to be careful but that would make me a meddling old woman," Aunt Violet said. Concern shadowed her blue eyes. "But I must say this—if things get violent, don't hang around. Run."

⚫◗❖

Aunt Violet's warning came to mind as Kieran and I made our way through packed streets toward Midsummer Common. Thousands of people were out tonight—families; groups of laughing teenagers; and older, more furtive adults. Dressed in black, they wore Guy Fawkes masks and wove through the crowd in swift silence.

I checked my coat pocket for my wallet and phone after someone brushed by a little too closely. Public mask-wearing was a perfect cover for pickpockets, especially when all the masks were identical.

Down an alley, something banged and a light flared. Acrid smoke drifted our way. "Someone put a firecracker in a trash can," Kieran said, shaking his head.

I edged closer to Kieran, scanning the throng for trouble. Oliver hadn't shown up at the Magpie, finally sending Kieran a text saying he'd meet us later, at St. Aelred, on the way to the common. To my surprise, Kieran took the change of plans in stride, although Oliver had asked us to dinner. "He's like that," he said. "Easily distracted." I would have called him unreliable, but didn't say anything. He wasn't my cousin. I did wonder how it would be working with him on the research project, if he did hire me.

Happily, we had connected with our friends Daisy Watson and Tim Ellis at the pub. Daisy owned Tea & Crumpets and Tim worked at the bike shop. They were walking ahead of us, Tim with his arm around Daisy's shoulders.

"This way," Kieran called. We had reached the intersection with St. Aelred's Way. Although I'd heard of the college, I hadn't explored this area yet. Cambridge had so many enticing colleges, parks, and historical sites, not to mention shops and events.

"Where are we meeting him?" I asked, hoping we wouldn't have to go inside the school tonight and track him down, although I wouldn't mind a tour another time. Founded in the fourteenth century, St. Aelred featured medieval architecture and gardens. "At the Master's Lodge Gate," Kieran said. "That's why we're going this way. The main gate is back there." He pointed south. "Students and visitors have to use that entrance. Faculty only at this one." A deep-voiced bell tolled beyond the wall. "That's the monk's bell, in the campanile."

At a better time, I'd bring up a map of the college on my phone and examine it more closely. Cambridge colleges were like worlds unto themselves, with classrooms, lodging, dining facilities, libraries and more tucked behind walls. Something about the cloistered nature of these establishments appealed to me, the notion that one could retreat from the world and focus on learning, often with distinguished instructors.

St. Aelred's Way was narrow and paved with cobblestones, tall stone walls looming on both sides. The sounds of the city dropped away before we'd even walked a block. Only an occasional pool of yellow light from a lamppost lit the way. Beyond the walls, bare branches swayed and rattled in the cold wind.

Daisy pulled her collar up with a shiver. "It's creepy back here." Like me, she wore a peacoat and jeans, her blond curls hanging loose under a wool beret. "How much further is it?"

"Right up ahead," Kieran said. "Promise." He picked up his pace, seeming as eager as the rest of us to return to civilization.

"This lane is actually a shortcut," Tim chimed in. He wasn't wearing a hat, and his short blond hair stood up in cute spikes. "It comes out near the common."

As if to verify his words, running footsteps came pounding along from that direction. Someone cutting through, perhaps, or maybe a St. Aelred student hurrying to the main gate. A tall, lanky figure soon loomed out of the darkness, feet flying and arms pumping. To my unease, I saw they were dressed in black and wearing one of those infernal masks. Not exactly someone I wanted to meet in a dark alley.

"Uh-oh," Kieran muttered. "This could be trouble." He pushed me behind his body, as if guarding me, and Tim did the same with Daisy.

But the runner kept going, not even glancing our way. As they passed under a lamppost, subtle silver designs on the cuffs and neck of a black neoprene jacket caught the light. Kieran had the same brand of jacket, favored by runners and cyclists.

On the runner went, soon disappearing from sight. Moving along even faster after the strange encounter, we soon arrived at the Master's Lodge Gate, a simple wooden door set under a stone arch.

"What's that on the ground?" Daisy asked.

Just beyond the glow of a light over the gate, a bundle of something lay in the street. Trash? Discarded clothing?

As we moved closer, I saw it was a person wearing a Guy Fawkes mask.

"Someone get a bit squiffy?" Tim asked.

"Possibly." Kieran glanced up and down the lane. "Not a good place to take a nap. Want to help me, Tim? We need to move them, maybe get them onto their feet and on their way."

"If they're a student at St. Aelred, we can call the porter at the main gate," Daisy said. "Get them inside to their room."

Speaking of St. Aelred, where was Oliver? Unless that *was* Oliver, drunk off his face already. I sure hoped not.

Tim went over and the two men arranged themselves, one on each side of the person. "Hey, mate," Kieran said, reaching down to gently shake a shoulder. "Wake up."

"Take off the mask," I suggested. "See who it is."

Kieran slid the mask up, revealing a young man with curly dark hair and beaky but attractive features. His eyes were closed.

Phew. It wasn't Oliver.

"Uh, Kieran?" Tim held up his hand. "He's hurt."

Daisy inhaled. "Is that *blood*?" She bent to take a closer look at the young man. "Yes, it is. His whole chest is soaked, see?" She scanned his torso with her phone flashlight. Darker splotches were visible against his black clothing.

"Does anyone have a tissue?" Tim sounded freaked out. "I have blood on my hand."

In the distance, a boom sounded, followed by a spray of gold and red high in the air. The fireworks were starting.

"We need to call nine-nine-nine." I yanked my phone

out of my pocket, a wad of clean tissue coming with it. I grabbed it off the ground and tossed it to Tim.

Kieran was on his knees, checking the young man's neck for a pulse. "He's still alive." He nudged his shoulder. "Can you hear me?"

My fingers fumbled at the screen although my mind was strangely still, as if emotions and thoughts were on hold for the emergency.

"I know who this is," Kieran said. "Thad Devine. His parents—"

Thad Devine? That name sounded familiar. "Nine-nine-nine," a woman's voice intoned in my ear. "What's your emergency?" As I gave the details, my name, the location, the incident, my words tumbling over each other, I realized where I'd heard that name before. He was Oliver's student.

"Thad, Thad," Kieran was saying. "Who did this to you?" Thad didn't answer.

"Someone will be there shortly," the dispatcher said. "Downtown is a mess tonight so it might be a few minutes."

"Send the ambulance right away," I said. "He's still alive." *For now.* After losing that much blood, I was afraid he'd die before help arrived.

"We'll find one," she promised. "Do you need me to stay on the line?" She sounded harried and I was pretty sure other calls were flooding in, due to it being Bonfire Night. Overhead, more fireworks exploded in the sky.

"No, though I'll call back if someone doesn't arrive soon."

Daisy gave a cry. "I've found the weapon." She shone her light on a slender metal object. "It's some kind of knife. Antique."

Footsteps scraped in the lane and I whirled around,

hoping it was a bobby on foot, sent to help. Instead it was Oliver. "What's going on?" he asked, striding toward us.

Here was Oliver, finally arriving at the meeting place he'd suggested. Exactly where the man I'd heard him threaten under his breath was lying unconscious, close to death. To say I didn't like the coincidence would be an understatement.

CHAPTER 3

No one had answered Oliver and he continued on, walking toward Kieran, who was still kneeling on the ground. When he saw Thad, he halted with a gasp. "What the heck? Is he all right?" He bent over. "Who is it?"

The light was poor here and Thad's face was in shadow. Despite those facts, I found myself listening very closely to Oliver's words and tone. Did he really not know? Was his casual manner feigned? To be fair, finding bodies sprawled on the ground probably wasn't a rare occurrence around the colleges, especially on weekends or occasions known for excess. A category I guessed Guy Fawkes Night fell into.

"It's Thad Devine," Kieran said crisply. "He's badly hurt and we've called the authorities."

"Injured?" Oliver took a closer look. "Hit his head, did he?" He started to kneel on Thad's other side. "He's one of my postgraduate students." He nudged Thad's arm. "Start the celebrations early, did you?"

"Careful," Kieran said, warning him back. "He's been stabbed. There's quite a lot of blood."

"Blood?" Oliver reared back, with the result that he ended up falling and landing on his bum. He scrambled backward like a crab, a horrified expression on his face. If he was acting, he was very believable.

"We think we found the weapon," Daisy said helpfully, before I could tell her not to share any information.

"Really? Where?" Oliver levered himself to his feet. "Did you know you're not supposed to remove a knife if you're stabbed? Makes it worse, they say."

Perhaps why the assailant had done that. They intended for Thad to die. Though then why hadn't they taken the weapon with them? I thought of the runner. Had that been the killer? Daisy shone her phone light on the object, guiding Oliver. He stared down at the knife, a hand covering his mouth and chin.

"Do you recognize it?" I asked, only a guess. Maybe he was transfixed with horror at seeing the weapon. I'd given it only a glancing look myself.

He shook his head. "Maybe. Not sure . . ."

"If you know something, you need to tell the police," Kieran said, his tone firm. He pressed his fingers into Thad's neck. "I hope they hurry up. We're losing him." He bent closer. "Hang in there, Thad."

Blue-and-white lights flashed in the alley, announcing the arrival of help. The panda car was first, parking so the ambulance could squeeze by. Doors opened and two officers approached, both male, both wearing black uniforms and fluorescent vests. They showed warrant cards and gave their names, Constables Derby and Lane. The medics were already assessing Thad, preparing to take him to the hospital.

"What happened here?" Derby asked. We all looked at each other and then began talking at once. He held up a hand. "One at a time, please."

Everyone looked at me now, probably figuring I had

more experience with the police. Unfortunately, this was true. "We were on our way to the common," I said. "Stopping at this gate to meet Oliver—Dr. Scott," I clarified. "He teaches at St. Aelred. We found Thad lying on the ground, wounded."

Derby's voice sharpened. "Thad? You know him?"

"I do," Kieran offered. "His parents are friends of my parents. And he's Oliver's student."

Oliver nodded solemnly. "Postdoc. Very talented. Brilliant, really."

One of the medics glanced up from his position next to Thad. "We need to get him out of here ASAP." Lane went over and they had a muttered exchange regarding medical stats.

"All right." Derby pulled out a tablet. "As you probably know, we're a wee bit busy tonight, so I'm going to get your names, addresses, and brief statements. We'll follow up later, probably tomorrow."

When it was my turn—Thad already loaded and on his way by then, Lane busy taking the knife into custody—I gave my information and verified what the others had said. "There is one more thing, though." Derby's brows rose. "I—we—saw a runner heading toward us in the alley before we found Thad." He looked interested until I mentioned the Guy Fawkes mask.

"Any details on the clothes?" He didn't sound hopeful. Black clothing was black clothing, right?

My gaze fell on Oliver, who was wearing a black jacket with silver trim. "It looked like his," I said. "See the logo and designs in silver? I noticed them when they went by."

As soon as I said that, I could have bitten my tongue. It wasn't nice to direct police attention to a friend. Or in this case, my boyfriend's close relative. Especially someone who had been angry with the wounded man, although he'd told the police that at the time of the attack, he'd been having a quick beer at the Headless Monk, a nearby pub.

Or was he lying? The suspicion was immediate and unwelcome. One of the most uncomfortable aspects of murder investigations—or in this case, attempted murder—was how everyone close to the victim became a suspect. Not that I was planning to get involved. Not this time.

When Derby took a closer look at his jacket, Oliver tugged at his jacket hem, then examined his sleeve, his expression disconcerted. "These are really popular right now," he said in a defensive tone. "Must be dozens, if not hundreds, around."

"They're a top brand," Kieran said. Was he frowning at me? "We sell a lot of them in the bike shop. Good for all sports or just as a casual jacket."

"I think I got mine at your shop," Oliver said. "You said you could barely keep them in stock."

Derby jotted notes. "Thank you, miss. As you know, it's a needle-in-the-haystack situation tonight. Every other person is wearing black and a mask."

Exactly why the attacker had dressed that way. I was more convinced than ever that the person we saw had stabbed Thad and then run away.

"We'll be back in touch," Derby promised as he and Lane got ready to depart. The radio in their car had been squawking, all in code but sounding urgent. Climbing into the driver's seat, Derby paused. "I'd stay away from the common. A stray rocket set a tent on fire."

"I'm sure it's insane right now," Kieran said. "All those people panicking." He gave the officers a polite wave as they pulled away.

Silence settled over the alley after the engine noise

faded. We all stared at each other. What now? Even if there wasn't trouble at the common, I wouldn't want to go there now, not after finding Thad so badly hurt. It felt wrong.

Oliver gave a rueful laugh. "I don't know about you, but I could use a drink." He started toward the gate. "Why don't we go in?"

"I think we're going to head home," Daisy said. "I've got an early morning." She was up at dawn almost every day, baking scrumptious delights for the tearoom.

"Are you sure?" I asked. When she nodded, I gave her a quick hug, inhaling her Jo Malone English Pear & Freesia scent. "Talk to you tomorrow."

"See you then," she said as I embraced Tim. He hugged me back tightly, all of us experiencing the surge of emotion common after a shared traumatic event.

"Take care, you two," Tim said, shaking Kieran's hand, then giving him a manly embrace with back pats.

"You as well," Kieran replied. "The streets are wild tonight." Unspoken was the truth that a knife-wielding assassin was out there somewhere.

Or, I thought, as Oliver unlocked the gate with his card, right here with us.

⁕

Inside the gate, the campus was dead quiet, the air cool and misty. With Oliver in the lead, we skirted the green on a flagstone path that led under arched cloisters.

In contrast to Daisy and Tim's warmth, Kieran was definitely being distant with me. That hurt, because he and I were usually very close, with the ability to practically read each other's minds. If I wanted to guess, I'd say he was angry with me for pointing out Oliver's jacket to the police. To be fair, he'd also heard Oliver rant about Thad earlier today. He might be worried about his cousin's possible guilt—the coolness could have nothing to do with me at all. Though I was having a hard time believing that.

"Where are we going?" Kieran asked Oliver.

"To my office. After a detour to Thad's stair."

My pulse bumped. Why did he want to visit Thad's room? Could he even get inside? Did he have a key or the code?

"What are you doing there?" Kieran sounded alarmed, as if he shared my concerns.

"I want to see if his friends are around," Oliver said. "His fellow lodgers on the stair. Someone needs to tell them that Thad's in the hospital." He lowered his voice. "They also might know something."

Kieran stopped walking. "Hold on, Oliver. Are you thinking one of them might have stabbed him?"

Oliver shrugged. "Maybe. Thad has the knack of making enemies wherever he goes. He's the type who likes to stir the pot and watch everyone else get upset."

I wanted to ask for more details about his conflicts with the other students but held back. I didn't want the crack between Kieran and me to become a crevasse.

The students lived in the next court, which consisted of three-story stone buildings with mullioned windows and ivy surrounding a spacious grassy area. Oliver went right to the closest building and scanned the lighted windows. "Looks like someone might be home."

As he said that, a shadow passed in front of a window that wasn't covered by shades or curtains.

Oliver pulled out his phone and sent a text. "Wesley is another student I supervise." After a moment, he said, "He's coming down to let us in."

The exterior door soon opened, revealing a young man with a mop of brown curls. "Dr. Scott. What's up?" He was bone-thin and awkward, dressed in a threadbare Sex Pistols T-shirt and faded jeans. Barefoot, despite the cold.

"May we come in?" Oliver asked. "Wesley Wright, this is my cousin, Kieran Scott, and his girlfriend, Molly Marlowe." Actually, it was Kimball, but I didn't bother to correct him. "It's about Thad."

Wesley jerked as if he'd been electrocuted. "Thad? What has he done now?" He glanced upward, as if at Thad's room. "I haven't seen him since this afternoon."

Interesting response. Did Thad have a pattern of misbehavior?

"He hasn't done anything," Oliver said. "He was attacked tonight. Near the Master's Lodge Gate."

Wesley's hands flew up and his round blue eyes practically bulged out of his head. "Is he okay? I told him earlier it was a bad idea to go out tonight. People are basically roaming around looking for trouble."

Inhaling, Oliver glanced at Kieran as if seeking guidance. From what Wesley had said—if he was telling the truth, I amended—he didn't know anything about the stabbing.

Voices rang out across the grassy court, and as they drew closer, it became clear it was an argument between a man and a woman. "I can't believe you did that," she said. "I think we need to take a break. Starting now."

"Please, Amy," he pleaded. "I didn't have a choice. He wouldn't quit harassing you. Someone had to do something."

"Hush," she said loudly. "Do you want the whole world to know? It's embarrassing." She must have noticed us, because she stopped abruptly and said under her breath, which carried perfectly, "Great. Someone heard us."

I half expected them to go in a different direction now, but they continued on, right for this entrance. As they came further into view, I could see she was short and small-boned, with a mass of dark wavy hair. He was tall and sturdily built, with brown skin and chiseled features.

"Amy, Josh," Oliver said as they got closer. "How are you tonight?"

The pair exchanged glances. "Dr. S., what are you doing here?" Josh asked. He feigned a laugh. "We barely escaped with our lives from the common. Joke. You hear about the burning tent? It was quite the scene." He reached for Amy's hand and she allowed him to take it. "We got separated in the stampede, which was scary."

"It wasn't one of the regular fireworks," Amy assured us. "Someone's personal one went wild. It hit that synthetic fabric and poof. Flames straight up into the sky."

"I can't believe they sell those," Josh said, shaking his head. "Talk about dangerous. Someone could have been killed."

When the couple moved forward as if to brush past Wesley and go inside, Oliver said, "Hold on a minute. I was just telling Wesley that Thad was attacked tonight. Outside the Master's Lodge Gate. He's in the hospital."

There went any element of surprise the police could use in questioning these students, but really, if they didn't hear about the stabbing from him, the rumor mill would inform everyone sooner or later.

Amy gasped, then, tellingly, glanced at Josh. "What do you mean, attacked? Someone beat him up?"

"Man, that's awful." Josh sounded upset. "Is he okay? Which hospital is he at?"

Oliver, thankfully, withheld a few details. "I'm not quite sure of his exact injuries. And I'm guessing they took him to Addenbrooke's. We'll follow up."

"It was probably a robbery," Wesley put in. "I heard about someone getting mugged on King Street a couple of nights ago."

"I bet they were after his phone," Josh said. "They're a hot commodity." He pulled his out and began working the screen. "Let's see if the little rat answers." He held it out, flat. "It's on speaker." The phone went right to voice mail. *Hey, this is Thad. Send me a text, 'k? Hate voice mail.*

Wesley shrugged. "Obviously it's shut off. Maybe the police can track it. If it's stolen, I mean."

"I didn't check his pockets," Kieran said. "So I can't answer that."

Amy and Josh focused on him, then me. "Hi," Amy said, clearly conveying *Who are you?*

"Kieran Scott," he said. "Oliver's cousin. And Molly Kimball."

"Josh Blake," he mumbled. "Amy O'Donnell." He gestured. "We live here."

Oliver stepped away from the entrance. "And we'll let you get inside and be on our way. I wanted to stop by and inform you about Thad."

A chorus of thank-yous and good-nights followed as we continued along the path. Soon all three vanished inside, more lights popping on upstairs soon after.

"Who were Amy and Josh talking about, do you know?" I asked. "Someone has been harassing her?"

"Yep." Oliver gave a heavy sigh. "Thad. He and Amy went out a few times last year. She broke up with him and started seeing Josh. Thad couldn't let it go."

"Ugh." Having been subject to unwanted attention myself, I could sympathize. "Too bad they both live in the same building." That had to make it worse since Amy couldn't get away from him.

"Those are our most coveted lodgings," Oliver said. "I'm sure neither wanted to budge."

"The college didn't do anything?" Kieran asked. "She shouldn't have to put up with that."

Oliver nodded. "Oh, I agree. I tried to get her to report him. But she refused, said she could handle it." After a pause, he said, "Thad doesn't handle opposition well, shall we say. He's been known to get back at people if they cross him."

Had Thad pushed someone to the breaking point? The crime might look like a random if vicious robbery, except for one thing—the weapon. That was no ordinary knife.

Seeming to read my mind, Oliver abruptly changed direction, saying, "Let's go this way. Something about the knife is bothering me."

I wanted to concur but kept quiet instead. The jury was still out whether I trusted Oliver, although I wanted to. If only I hadn't heard him threaten Thad. While letting off steam, sure, and not to his face, but still . . . Oliver was on the list of people who were upset with him. Amy, as well, and perhaps Josh, if Thad was still hitting on his girlfriend. Or tormenting her.

As we entered another court, I thought back to the conversation we overheard. *Someone had to do something.* Was that *something* stabbing Thad, to shut him up for good? Ugh. My stomach turned over.

"This is the main court," Oliver said. "Library, dining hall, classrooms, offices, chapel are all here in this section."

A glance told me this was the oldest section. The buildings had crenulated tops, like a castle, a couple of squat towers, and fancy chimneys. It must be wonderful to live and study in such a venerable and beautiful school. Here at St. Aelred, I could almost still hear the tread of monks as they strolled along the cloisters.

Oliver used an electronic key at one of the arched entrances, a jarringly modern feature when the double door was ancient, blackened wood set with hobnails. "Ah, here we go." He opened one side, holding it open for us to go ahead.

We were in a wide corridor with a flagstone floor and an aroma of polish and cold stone. Oliver opened another wide door and we were in the dining hall, which had a beamed barrel ceiling, wainscoting, and deep-set arched windows high in the walls. Long tables lined with benches provided seating. He crossed the floor to a display case, one of several near the fireplace.

"I was right," he said, his voice ringing out in the quiet room. "Come see."

Kieran and I scurried over to the case, which contained a variety of ancient weapons, medals, tiny prayer books, and other items.

"What are we looking at?" Kieran asked, the question that was on my mind.

"Right there." Oliver pointed to an empty space on the second shelf, next to an elaborate silver scabbard. "The dagger in that set is missing. Scandinavian, iron blade, with a silver cross handle and beaded ornamentation."

"Like the one Daisy found on the street?" I asked, a sinking feeling already supplying the answer. The missing dagger appeared to confirm that Thad's stabbing was connected to the school, committed by a student, faculty member, or staff.

"Exactly." Oliver squared his shoulders. "I'd better report this. To the police and to the master."

Kieran was examining the case. "Was this locked?" Then he answered his own question. "The lock is broken. See?"

Oliver took a close look at the lock, then snapped a picture with his phone, followed by one of the empty case. "I don't know about you, but I really need that drink now. Come on. I'll make calls from my office."

My thoughts were whirling as we trailed Oliver to another part of the college and up a flight of stairs to his office, located with the other faculty in his department. Who had attacked Thad? Had Oliver really been surprised to see the dagger lying in the street? Had he known all along where it had come from?

"You doing all right?" Kieran whispered as we walked down the upstairs corridor.

"I'm okay." I was relieved that he had asked. Maybe he wasn't upset with me about directing the police to Oliver's jacket.

"Home at last," Oliver said with a stilted laugh, switching on the wall light. Although not terribly large, the office was charming, with tall, mullioned windows, paneling, a small fireplace, and built-in bookshelves. He sat behind the massive desk and pulled open a drawer. "If I leave teaching, I'll miss this room."

"I can see why," I said. I felt the same way about the bookshop, which was equally atmospheric.

Oliver placed a bottle of Irish whiskey on the blotter, along with several small paper cups. He uncapped the bottle and held it over the first cup. "Who wants a snort?"

Whiskey wasn't my favorite choice but I said yes anyway, as did Kieran. Once he handed us our drinks, he lifted his cup in a toast. "'What's drinking? A mere pause from thinking.' Lord Byron." He tipped the cup to his mouth and swallowed. Then he set it on the desk and picked up the whiskey. "Hit me again." He held the bottle out to me with a questioning look.

Still enjoying my first smooth, peaty sip, I shook my head. Perhaps my problem with whiskey was quality, not the liquor itself.

"I'm good, thanks," Kieran said. He crumpled his empty cup and tossed it into the trash.

After downing his second shot, Oliver gave a gusty sigh and picked up the desk set receiver. "Master first. I'm not looking forward to this. At all."

Kieran turned to me. "Why don't we step out? Give Oliver some privacy?"

Although I wanted to hear Oliver report the dagger to the police, I nodded before swallowing the rest of the whiskey. His conversation with the master wasn't any of our business and was sure to be difficult. The whole college would soon be in an uproar over the attack.

Out in the hallway, we paced back and forth, pretending interest in the lackluster portraits and landscapes hung at intervals. Despite Kieran's earlier inquiry, he didn't speak or touch me, which wasn't like us. Usually we were drawn together like magnets whenever we were alone. The distance between us made me ache but now wasn't the time or place to bring it up. And I certainly would, as soon as possible. If Kieran had an issue with me, I wanted to address it head-on, get things out in the open, and clear the air. Three clichés in a row but they worked. I don't do well guessing what someone is thinking or feeling.

Light, quick footsteps sounded on the stairs. Kieran and I turned to watch as a young woman hurried toward us down the hall. She was tall and slim, dressed in jeans and running shoes, her long brown hair in a ponytail.

"Hello," she said. "Is Oliver around?" She had a lilting accent. Italian?

"He's in his office," Kieran said. "I'd wait, though. He's talking to the master."

"About Thad?" So she already knew. "No wonder he didn't respond." Who did she mean—Thad or Oliver? "Excuse me." The woman pushed past us, forcing us to step aside, and rapped loudly on Oliver's door three times. When he put his head out, annoyed, she said. "It's the police. They're asking for you at the porter's lodge."

CHAPTER 4

Oliver's brows knit together. "That doesn't make sense. I didn't call them yet." Then his eyes flared wide and he put a hand to his mouth. "Thad. Did he—"

Her shoulders went up. "I don't know. I was in the lodge when Detective Inspector something or other showed up. I distinctly heard him ask for you. Didn't you get my text?"

"Text?" He shook his head. "I was on the phone." Then, as if remembering, he glanced over his shoulder. "Crap. I've got the master on hold. Be right back."

The three of us left in the hall stared at each other. "I'm Kieran," he finally said. "Oliver's cousin."

"And I'm Molly," I put in, not wanting to wait for Kieran to continue. I didn't want to hear any evidence of our rift in his voice or how he introduced me.

"Sophie Verona," she said, putting a hand to her chest. "I teach in the department with Oliver. We manage the Gothic Literature Institute as well." She made a face. "Which is supposed to start tomorrow with Oliver's lecture about *The Fatal Folio* at Hazelhurst House."

"Will it be canceled?" I asked, knowing the topic was inane but wanting to say something rather than go back to staring at each other.

Thad must have died. Why else would a detective inspector show up? They handled major crimes like homicide. My heart skipped a beat. Had they assigned Detective Inspector Sean Ryan? Not only had he and I run into each other on past cases, he was dating my mother. Only occasionally so far, but she was pink-cheeked and happy for days after each of their encounters.

"I sure hope we don't have to cancel." Sophie sighed. "That might sound selfish but it's our signature event. Takes the committee all year to plan. And we have sponsors with expectations . . ."

"Say no more." One of the first things I'd done at the bookshop was develop a roster of author signings and book discussions. "Even though events are a ton of work, they're necessary to stay visible."

Sophie gave me a closed-lip smile. "Exactly. This year we have the best program ever. The sad part is, Thad was one of our main volunteers. We couldn't have done it without him."

That was probably the first nice thing I'd heard someone say about Thad. "How about honoring him at the conference? If you hold it. It would be a nice touch."

She nodded. "You're right, Molly, it would. We'll definitely do that."

Oliver appeared in the doorway. "The master will be here shortly. Emergency meetings to be convened, at least for our department."

The phone rang inside the office and he darted back to answer it. A moment later he was back. "I'm meeting the detective inspector in the dining hall."

"Why there?" Sophie asked.

Instead of answering, Oliver set off down the hall. I followed, wanting both to stay informed and to talk to the police. They'd get back to me eventually as a listed witness so I might as well shorten the process.

After a moment's hesitation, Kieran came along, as did Sophie. "What's going on?" she asked us as we clattered down the stairs. We didn't bother to answer her question either.

We encountered two officers and a porter in the area outside the dining hall. "Ah, there you are, Dr. Scott," the porter, an older man, said. "If you're all set, Detective Inspector, I'll get back to my post."

"Please do," Detective Inspector Sean Ryan said. "Thank you for your assistance." His keen eyes roamed over our faces. "Miss Kimball." A small, wry smile tugged at his lips. "Fancy meeting you here." It was always *Miss* on a job. Molly the rest of the time.

Naturally everyone—except Kieran—stared at me in surprise. Even the porter paused, a bemused expression on his face. I gave Ryan a little wave, including his usual sidekick, the lovely Sergeant Gita Adhikari, in the greeting. "I'm glad to see that you landed the assignment."

Ryan's brows rose for an instant, then he nodded. After brief introductions and the display of warrant cards, he said to Oliver, gesturing to the dining hall, "Show me." As Oliver unlocked the door, he said to us, "Miss Kimball, Mr. Scott, please wait. I'd like to talk to you. Dr. Verona, what is your connection here?"

Sophie bit her lip. "Thad worked for me. He was my office assistant at the Gothic Literature Institute. If there's any light I can shed, any way I can help . . ."

"I appreciate that. Give the sergeant your details and we'll talk. Right now—" He again gestured toward the dining hall.

Ryan and Oliver went into the hall and Adhikari started taking down Sophie's contact information. I found a bench and sat. Kieran joined me. "What a night," he said, slumping back and crossing his arms. He gave me a crooked smile. "You didn't even get to see the bonfire."

"No, but everything else is burning nicely." I was sure that Thad's death would have ripple effects on Oliver, Thad's family and friends, and St. Aelred. Not that we'd gotten verification that he had died. I found my phone and brought up the local news,

The headline struck me like a blow, making me gasp. "Cambridge Student Dies in Knife Attack." The story was at the top of the page, above others speculating about the crime, moaning about Bonfire Night violence, and discussing city crime statistics. *The identity of the student is being withheld for notification of next of kin.*

Kieran's head swung around. "What is it?"

Unable to speak past the clog in my throat, I showed Kieran the screen. *Thad's poor parents.* Tears were pooling in my eyes now, my nose running, and I searched fruitlessly in my pocket for a tissue. That's right, I'd given them to Tim. To wipe Thad's blood off his hands.

"Come here." Kieran put his arm around my shoulders and pulled me close. No distance between us now. His nose was in my hair and his voice a whisper in my ear. "My parents . . . they're close to his family. Everyone is going to be devastated."

"Did you know Thad well?" I asked, my heart swelling with sorrow.

He shook his head. "Not really. We never hung out. He was quite a bit younger."

That made sense. Kieran was twenty-nine, a year older than me. Thad had to be what—around twenty-three or -four? Enough of a gap as a child and teen to mean different social circles.

Sophie was leaving now and Sergeant Adhikari went

into the dining hall. Somewhere a clock chimed eleven. Being next to Kieran had drained all the tension from my body. I yawned and snuggled closer. "Mind if I take a nap?"

His chest rumbled with a laugh. "Molly," he began.

I put my hand up, feeling for his lips. "Shh. Not now. I'm sleeping." Any discussion could wait as far as I was concerned. We still needed to get through interviews with the police so who knew how late we'd finally get to bed. Tomorrow I planned to work at the Hazelhurst House library—thankfully, the start time was flexible—and attend Oliver's lecture there. If it was still on.

◆◆◆

Detective Inspector Ryan interviewed me in the empty dining hall, I'm sure after getting approval from someone. We sat across from each other, Ryan squinting at his tablet in the poor light. Despite the wall sconces and hanging chandeliers, the room was wreathed in gloom.

"Miss Kimball, you placed the call to nine-nine-nine. Can you tell me what preceded your call? Begin with why you were in St. Aelred's Way."

I took him through the evening, starting with our dinner at the Magpie and the change in plans requested by Oliver, to meet him at the Master's Lodge Gate. When I mentioned that Daisy and Tim were with us, he grunted and made a note, probably to circle back with them as well.

"Did you see or hear anything as you came down the lane?" Ryan asked.

"Yes. Footsteps. We were about halfway to the gate when someone came running toward us. Tall, dressed in black."

He leaned forward. "What did the person look like?"

"I don't know. They were wearing a Guy Fawkes mask. So was Thad." For the first time, this really hit me. Both he and the runner were wearing masks. Were they together? Or was it only a coincidence?

Ryan sagged back in disappointment. "Mask. Got it. Any identifying features? Hair? Hands? How about the clothing?"

The jacket. Which was very similar to Oliver's. I shifted in my seat, knowing that describing it to Ryan was going to open up a can of worms for Kieran's cousin—and probably affect us. However, if I didn't mention it and the details were in the original police report, Ryan would want to know why.

Pressure grew in my chest the longer I sat silent, my ears humming in the dense silence of the ancient hall with its thick stone walls. Finally, I let out my breath, knowing I didn't have a real choice. I didn't have to say the jacket was exactly like Oliver's, though. I wasn't positive, right?

"The jacket had reflective silver trim and logo," I said, pointing to areas on my person to illustrate. "The brand is a popular one used by cyclists and runners, I understand."

He nodded, making a note. "What happened next?"

The tightness in my chest was back as I took him through finding Thad on the ground, Kieran recognizing him and trying to help, and Daisy locating the weapon nearby. "As you know, I placed the call for help."

"Where was Dr. Scott during all this?" he asked.

"He came along right before the police arrived and we've been with him ever since." Grateful someone had provided a bottle of water, I took a drink. I still had a lot to cover. "After the ambulance and police left, we stopped by Thad's stair to inform the other students who live there about the attack."

"Do you know their names?"

After listing the three students, I paused, wondering if I should share the rather incriminating remarks Josh and Amy had exchanged.

"What is it, Molly?" he asked, his tone sharp. Then his features smoothed. "Sorry. Miss Kimball."

I waved his apology off and relayed what we'd heard. "I have no idea if it's relevant. I thought you should know anyway."

He gave a quick nod. "What happened next?"

"We came here, to this room, and Oliver realized a dagger was missing. I think he might have recognized it out in the street. Then we went up to his office." I omitted the drinking whiskey part. "He was on the phone with the master when Sophie Verona came along and told him you wanted to see him."

Why had Ryan asked specifically for Oliver? I didn't dare ask. He hadn't called the police about the knife yet. Had someone implicated Oliver in the attack?

Another missing piece of information—from me— was Oliver's threat toward Thad, accidently overheard at Hazelhurst House. My tender conscience was telling me I should mention it, as I had Josh and Amy's conversation. But who hadn't used hyperbole when angry with someone? Besides, he had been talking to himself, not directly to Thad.

In the end, I kept my mouth shut. It was hearsay, I reassured myself. Any case they built against a killer had to include physical evidence. If Oliver was innocent, there wouldn't be any.

By the time Ryan let me go, I was wrung out, exhausted, and ready to crawl home and into bed. Kieran and Oliver rose to their feet when I came out into the hall. I managed to muster a half-hearted laugh. "Well, that was fun. He said to send you in, Kieran."

"Are you going to wait?" Kieran asked.

"Have to, don't I? I'm not walking home alone." Vehicles were heavily restricted in the center, so I couldn't take an Uber all the way anyway.

"I'll try to make it quick," he said, ever thoughtful. "You look wiped out."

"Yeah, I am." Bottle of water still in hand, I shambled over and slumped onto the bench. "See you soon."

After the door closed behind him, Oliver asked, "How did it go?" He wasn't wearing the black jacket with silver trim now. It must be in his office.

"Okay, I guess. I always worry that I might forget an important detail." When I wasn't omitting one on purpose.

"They're searching Thad's room," he said. "And the forensics team is out in the alley."

"Sounds standard," I said, wondering if they'd turn up anything out there. Probably not with the way we'd all trampled the area. Hopefully they had or would find Thad's phone. That might give them an idea who he had talked to or met with tonight.

I was dying to ask Oliver questions about the other students—Wesley, Josh, and Amy—but didn't quite dare. Not here, right outside the interview room. Unless the attack was truly random, which I doubted, one of them might know something. Or even be guilty. Especially since it looked like the murder weapon came from St. Aelred. Someone off the street wouldn't have had access to the case or even known where to find the weapon.

No, my money was on someone from St. Aelred being the killer. From what I'd learned so far, Thad had been a difficult person. Who had he angered to the point of murder?

CHAPTER 5

The first part of our walk home passed in silence. I was practically staggering, I was so emotionally wiped out. It was after midnight, and the streets were fairly deserted now, with only the occasional pop of a firecracker in the distance. Except for glimpsing a few bursts of color above the rooftops, I'd missed most of the Bonfire Night celebrations.

And stumbled into another murder. If only Oliver had met us at the Magpie. We wouldn't have been anywhere near St. Aelred tonight and I would have read about Thad in the news. As Thad's tutor, though, Kieran's cousin would still have been affected. And he was the crux of the issue between us, I knew.

We'd had a moment of warmth on the bench but now Kieran was distant again, his eyes glassy with exhaustion. Grief as well, since he knew Thad. In light of that, bringing up any issues was probably a bad move, for now at least. Especially since he hadn't said anything to me, it was only something I *felt*. Like a cool breeze blowing through a cracked door.

Magpie Lane at last. Our steps slowed as we reached the bike shop. "Want to come up, Molly?" he asked. "We deserve a nightcap, don't you think?" Kieran had a flat above the shop, even though his family lived in an incredible manor only a few miles away. He liked both the independence and the ease of caring for such a small space, he'd told me.

"I could use one," I admitted, following him around back to the staircase door.

He unlocked the door and switched on the light, then stood back to let me enter first. At the top of the stairs, the flat was one large space, with a bedroom and bathroom to the far left. Kieran's building was much newer than the bookshop, but it had many nice features, including thick ceiling beams, wide-board floors, exposed brick, and a balcony. We'd spent many an evening in warmer weather sitting out there, eating dinner and drinking beer.

I kicked off my shoes and sat on the overstuffed sofa while Kieran went into the galley kitchen. "Beer or shot?" he asked. "I've got Irish and Scotch whiskey."

"I'll take a shot of Irish." Beer before bed was too much liquid.

"Not quite as good as Oliver's," he said while pouring into two small glasses. "He's more of a connoisseur."

The mention of Oliver gave me an opening but I waited until he joined me on the sofa and handed me my drink. We settled back in our corners, legs outstretched and feet almost touching. I lifted my glass in a toast and took a sip, welcoming the burn in my throat and chest.

"Kieran," I said at the same time he said, "I'm sorry."

We laughed. "You go first," I said, relieved.

His gaze went to the glass he held. "I'm worried about Oliver."

Braced for criticism, I wasn't expecting that. "What? What do you mean?"

"You heard him." Kieran pressed his lips together. "He

was really angry with Thad about messing up his promotion."

So he was concerned about the threat too. "I get that. But I'm gathering a lot of people were mad at Thad. Besides, Oliver was only blowing off steam."

Now he looked at me, his dark brown eyes gleaming. "You think?" Then he shook his head. "Oliver can be impulsive. And he has a bad temper. He was sent down from more than one boarding school, you know. His poor parents wondered if jail was next."

I contrasted the images his words evoked with what I knew of the adult Oliver. He was personable, energetic, and seemingly sanguine about a career switch to novelist. "I admit I don't know him very well," I said. "He kept it together pretty well tonight."

Kieran nodded. "He did, didn't he?" After considering that for a moment, he said, "I'm sorry I was annoyed with you. For pointing out his jacket, I mean. I thought . . . maybe he had done it." His nose wrinkled. "I can't believe I actually said that." He tossed back the rest of his whiskey as if to wash away his words.

"Well, say you're right." His chin whipped up, mouth hanging open. "Hold on. I have a point. You said he's impulsive and hot-tempered. Or was in the past. That doesn't line up with the Oliver we saw tonight. Was he upset or edgy when he arrived at the gate? No. If he were guilty, would he identify the murder weapon and lead the police to the case in the dining hall? Again, no."

He tapped his fingers on his knee, considering what I'd said. "You're right. The old Oliver would lose his temper and run off for a while, then creep back, ashamed and apologetic. He'd be more likely to confess rather than pretend he was innocent."

"You know him better than anyone," I said. "So hang on to that. If the police focus on him."

He put his glass on the coffee table and sidled closer. "I get it now. How you felt when Aunt Violet was a suspect." He put a hand to his midsection. "It makes you queasy. As if the world just got turned upside down."

"Yeah, it was really special," I said, sarcasm in my tone. "I'm sorry you're having to deal with it. Plus, you knew the victim." I set my glass down and put a hand on his knee. "How awful."

Our faces were close now and after a moment filled with sweet energy, he kissed me. To my enormous relief, the rift was mended and we were back to normal. Meaning, in love and very, very happy. Even with a murderer on the loose.

◆◆◆

Later, back at the bookshop, at who knows what hour, I checked the shelves for a copy of *The Fatal Folio,* hoping George hadn't bought our last one. I'd never read it—in fact, much of the early gothic canon was new to me—and I was looking forward to diving in. Discovering rich and untapped veins of literature never ceased to thrill me.

We had several editions, and I chose the most battered, least valuable one to read. Then, with Puck at my feet and a glass of water in hand, I headed up to my room. Once tucked among the down pillows and duvets, Puck purring next to me, I opened the book with anticipation. Besides enjoying a new story, I was hoping to discover clues to Selwyn Scott's identity. Every author left a trace of their personality, attitudes, and outlook on their work. It was inescapable and individual, like fingerprints.

The Fatal Folio

My name is Matthew Marlboro, and I am a humble bookseller by trade, with a modest establishment in the City of Cambridge near the gates of Trinity College. Despite the size of my shop, and the limited wares that I carry, through Providence and hard work, I have developed a reputation for obtaining the finest manuscripts and folios. Rare books, some printed by hand, on topics that span the esoteric, the religious, even the magical. My patrons have learned that I never ask questions nor do I reveal their requests or purchases—or their desire to sell extra books in their collection—to anyone.

It is this reputation for discretion, I believe, that brought me my most difficult, challenging, and dangerous quest to date. A quest that almost cost my life, not to mention my sanity.

Late in the winter, a gentleman named Dudley Coates, nephew of the Earl of Mercia, paid me a visit. Since said Earl is without issue after the loss of three wives, Mr. Coates is the heir presumptive. Although I didn't know it at the time, his inheritance was the motivation for his request—that I help him obtain the only existing copy of The Ramblings of a Monk, *written around the year one thousand in a monastery in the remote, mountainous region of Piemonte, in Italy.*

When I asked why the manuscript was available, Mr. Coates said that it had been sold several times already, when the monastery fell on hard times. This I already knew, but I prefer to pretend ignorance sometimes, to discern the depth of a patron's knowledge. *The present owner was a nobleman in the village of Malvagio, he said, which confirmed my understanding. Through his contacts, he'd heard that the book was for sale and wanted me to accompany him on a trip there, to represent his interests and negotiate the purchase.*

I'm not one to venture far from my little lair, with its stacks of books and aroma of ink and paper and leather, although I do make annual trips to London and I've been to Paris once or twice. However, I have finally taken on an assistant, so a prolonged absence would not hinder my regular trade.

Though I kept it to myself at this juncture, I was most curious to view The Ramblings of a Monk. *According to the rumors and speculations that often arise around rare manuscripts on decidedly arcane topics, it held a peculiar sort of power, giving rise to its informal title, whispered at every level of the book trade:* The Fatal Folio.

I admit to pressing one old bookseller, a veteran of the trade, about the rumors. How exactly did the book get its name? I asked. Was it so valuable that men had killed to possess it?

His answers were evasive. He claimed not to know exactly how the book exerted its power, only that many owners had died with it in their possession, often within an uncommonly short time after adding the book to their collection.

I raised this point with Mr. Coates. "Aren't you worried about the book's, er, possible effects?"

"It's not for me," he said. "It's a gift for the Earl. I know he will appreciate this rare and beautiful addition to his extensive library." He gave a hearty laugh. "Those superstitious rumors only add to

*its novelty value. How can a book kill someone?
Unless it falls on your head."*

    *Using hindsight, his remark should have been
the first clue that something was amiss. At the time,
however, I was so enamored with the opportunity
to see the storied tome, to examine such a gem of
literary genius, that I readily agreed to accompany
him in a fortnight hence.*

One thing immediately struck me about *The Fatal
Folio.* The main character was a bookseller in Cambridge.
Since authors often drew from real life, was it possible
that Selwyn Scott had been acquainted with whoever was
running Thomas Marlowe at the time?

Here was a possible point of connection to *The Fatal
Folio.* I thought of the library cupboard crammed with
papers. Did they include bills of sale for books? Tracking
down purchase information for valuable and important
titles would be an important step in appraising the collection.

I'd only been hired to catalogue, but perhaps Lady
Asha would let me poke around and see if any of the library's books had come from my bookshop and who in
the family had bought them. This wasn't only of personal
interest to me. If Selwyn Scott had a relationship with
the bookseller at the time, perhaps they had included my
ancestor as a character. With a different name, of course,
but Marlboro was pretty close to Marlowe.

Sitting up, I reached for a notebook and pen. At the
top of the page, I wrote *Who is Selwyn Scott?* Under that,
I listed Samuel, Frances, and Agatha Scott. First action
item: *check bills of sale for book purchases. Connection
to Thomas Marlowe relevant?* It was only a theory at this
point.

I checked my phone one last time before turning off the lamp. Nothing from Oliver about the research project, which wasn't surprising. He had other, more pressing things on his mind tonight.

∿

The tempting aroma of breakfast sausage teased me out of sleep. That and Puck's paw gently batting at my nose. It didn't matter to him that I'd only gotten six hours' sleep and my head was full of pea-soup fog. His dish was calling.

"Cut it out." I pried my eyes open to find his nose practically touching mine. "I'm getting up, okay?"

He jumped down with a thump disproportionate to his actual body weight and ran for the door. Moving much more slowly, I sat up, pushed the covers aside, and reached for my tartan robe. Sheepskin slippers went on my feet.

With Puck leading the way, I slowly clomped down the stairs and turned right to enter the kitchen. This long room, warmed by a vintage AGA stove, was where we hung out during off hours. In addition to a long wooden table that seated eight, a couple of armchairs and a squashy sofa formed a seating area. Aunt Violet's knitting basket marked her chair and both arms of the sofa held books in progress for me and Mum.

"Morning," Mum said, turning to smile at me. "Coffee is ready." One of the first items we'd added to the kitchen was a French press. We had to have our daily java.

"Awesome. Is there anything I can do to help?"

She waved that off and as I pulled out a chair, brought me a steaming mug. "How was last night?"

Last night. Scenes flashed through my mind. Thad,

lying on the ground. The bloody knife. The police interview. The terrible news that Thad had died.

"That's right," I said. "You don't know." It had been far too late to wake Mum and Aunt Violet up when I finally got home from Kieran's. I also have to admit to deliberately pushing the whole dire experience aside for a moment. I knew firsthand how consuming a murder case could be.

"I don't know what?" Mum sent me a look as she returned to the stove, where she flipped the sausages.

Stalling, I took a sip of coffee. To tell her would mean that my enjoyment of this—purring cats, hot coffee, and a delicious breakfast on the way—would be swamped by the grim murk of reality.

"Molly." Mum banged around at the stove a little louder than necessary.

I knew she was worried that I'd run into trouble. Which I had, although it hadn't resulted in harm to me. After a couple more swallows, I said, almost in a monotone, "There was an untimely death last night. Kieran and I came across the scene. We were with Daisy and Tim, on our way to the common. It was a student from St. Aelred, where Kieran's cousin teaches."

Mum whirled around, the spatula in her hand. "What? Oh, no." She put the tool down and turned the gas low before coming over to me. "I'm . . . I . . . I don't know what to say." She took the seat beside me and leaned close, concern etching her brow.

I spun the mug in circles, needing to do something with my hands. "Yeah. It was pretty awful." As briefly as possible, omitting my suspicions about Oliver, I took her through the night's events. "Hopefully Sean Ryan will get to the bottom of it fast," I concluded.

"I hope so too." Mum leaped up, unable to hide her

reaction to his name, and returned to the stove. "Kieran's family knows the young man? Does that change your plans for today?"

Good question. My phone was in my robe pocket, so I sent Lady Asha a text, expressing condolences and asking if she still wanted me to come out today to work on the library. Then I checked the Gothic Institute's website. *The conference is still on*, read a banner. *No changes to the agenda*.

That must mean Oliver was still giving his lecture about *The Fatal Folio*. Lady Asha wrote back immediately, saying it was up to me if I came out today. Although I was exhausted, I told her I'd be there. With Oliver's lecture and the possibility of others from the Gothic Institute and St. Aelred attending, Hazelhurst House was the place to be. If there was any progress in finding Thad's killer, I wanted to be there.

Aunt Violet wandered down to the kitchen as Mum was dishing up sausages and scrambled eggs. "My timing is spectacular as always," she said, her eyes twinkling. "Thanks for breakfast, Nina." As she sat down, I noticed she was wearing yoga pants and a stretchy long-sleeve top instead of her usual robe.

"What have you been up to, Aunt Violet?" I asked, scooping up a forkful of eggs. Puck and Clarence were both hovering at my feet, hoping for stray crumbs. I might have dropped a golden morsel or two, accidentally on purpose.

She poured milk into her mug. "I was doing senior yoga. They have videos online, you know. I like the instructor, although she's a bit chirpy for so early in the morning." She cocked an eyebrow. "After that, I checked out the news. There was a murder last night at St. Aelred.

Isn't that where Oliver Scott teaches? Such a handsome lad."

"Yes, it is." I inhaled a breath, filling my lungs to give my great-aunt the full story. "And I'm a witness. Again."

Aunt Violet was riveted as once again I went through the previous evening. "You've got quite a few suspects," she said. "Those three students and that other instructor. It wasn't Oliver. He's too dishy."

"Aunt Violet," I protested. "Good looks aren't a reason not to suspect someone." I hastily added, "Though I agree, it wasn't him. He helped the police figure out where the murder weapon came from."

"Which only a true criminal mastermind would do," Mum put in. "From what you've said, Oliver is too transparent for that kind of manipulation."

"Exactly." I glanced at another text, this one from George. "Oh good, George is going today." I wrote back, asking if he'd like a ride. The only drawback was that I would be staying at Hazelhurst House all day. He accepted, saying that he would take the bus back.

After a last bite of sausage and egg and a refill of coffee, I hurried off to get ready for my day at Hazelhurst House. Hopefully progress would be made on both mysteries—Selwyn Scott's identity and Thad Devine's murder.

CHAPTER 6

"Oh, this is something, innit?" George let out a long, low whistle as we approached Hazelhurst House. "It's like we're walking right into a book." Seated beside me in the Cortina, George was clutching his copy of *The Fatal Folio*. He had also brought a messenger bag containing notepad and pens, a metal water bottle, and a package of McVitie's biscuits, his favorite snack.

"You've got that right," I agreed, although in my case, the book was more Cinderella than a gothic tale. I still pinched myself now and then, thinking, *Am I really dating a member of the* nobility? So bizarre.

I slowed even more as we passed by the bridge over the moat. People were parking right up ahead in a small gravel area, and I scanned the lot for a space.

There was a spot. I slid into the space, thwarting the Mini Cooper behind me. Spitting gravel, the driver sped past toward the overflow area down the lane.

George shook his head at such reckless driving. "They better not have dinged the paint, throwing rocks that way."

"I hope not too." Every time I drove this precious relic, I prayed to return it unscathed. The car was older than me by more than a decade.

After we climbed out, George took a good look at the

Cortina before grunting in satisfaction. "Looks all right."
Seeing the Mini's driver coming along on foot, he sent a
glare in that direction.

It was Sophie Verona, who barely spared us a glance
before marching on toward the manor. Walking slowly to
give her time to get out of earshot, I said, "That's Dr. Verona from St. Aelred. She's in charge of the symposium
and Thad was her assistant." On the way out, I'd given
George the scoop on the murder and my inadvertent involvement. Third time today and I was getting the spiel
down.

George nodded sagely. "Oh, I see. Has a lot on her
mind, does she?"

"I'd say so." I picked up the pace. "On another topic,
how do you like the book?" I nodded at *The Fatal Folio*.
"I started reading it last night."

"Enjoying it so far," George said. We were crossing the
bridge now and as we reached the other side, he whispered, "Blimey."

The bridge was the former drawbridge and now we
passed under a massive arch and entered a courtyard. I'd
been to a party in the summer here, complete with tents
and tables, potted plants, and a string quartet. Now only
a couple of vehicles were parked near the main entrance
opposite the arch.

On the steps, a young man was holding open the door
for his female companion. After a second, I recognized
Josh Blake and Amy O'Donnell, both in jeans like everyone else. She wore a long lavender sweater that set off
her dark hair while he had donned a green fleece zipped
to his neck. Last night's events seemed to have made me
far more conscious of outerwear choices. Would I recognize the killer's jacket if I saw it?

"Hello," I called, putting on a burst of speed. When

they turned with identical puzzled expressions, I said, "Molly Kimball. We met at St. Aelred last night."

"Oh. Molly." Josh's face cleared. "You did look a little familiar . . ."

"Hey, it was dark." And we were all reeling from the attack on Thad. "This is George Flowers," I said. "Big gothic fan."

"The Brontë sisters are my main area of study," George said, his accent as lofty as any toffee-nosed academic's. "Now I'm broadening my scope to include Selwyn Scott and other early authors."

We were through the door and inside the Great Hall, which featured everything medieval fortress. Suits of armor. Paneled walnut wainscoting. Hanging tapestries and a fireplace large enough for the proverbial ox. Rows of folding chairs in the middle indicated this was where the lecture would be held.

"I love the Brontës," Amy said. "Have you been to Haworth?"

George had, last summer, and he and Amy began an excited conversation about the Brontës' home village as we all slowly moved toward the action.

Oliver was standing near the podium talking to Lady Asha and Sophie Verona, and a group of fifty or so attendees were choosing seats or browsing the refreshments to one side, Wesley Wright from St. Aelred among them. To my surprise, Daisy was behind the buffet table.

"Excuse me," I said to Josh. "I see someone I know."

Laughing, he stayed on my heels. "And I see a scone with my name on it."

"Tea and Crumpets in Magpie Lane," I said. "Everything is excellent."

Daisy glanced up from arranging a platter and saw me. "Molly, I didn't know you'd be here today."

"Right back at you," I said. In addition to scones, there were jam and lemon curd tarts, eccles cakes, and cinnamon buns. "Oh, yum." Despite my hearty breakfast, I had to have one of those buns dripping with brown sugar and cinnamon.

"The caterer canceled late yesterday," Daisy said. "Kieran suggested Lady Asha call me, and thankfully I was able to fill in. I doubled my batches this morning and here I am." Daisy had a small operation with only a couple of part-time employees. One of them must be holding down the fort.

"And we're glad you're here." I put a bun on a plate, thinking I'd mosey along and grab a cup of tea as well. The line was building up behind me. "Talk later?"

"You bet." Daisy smiled patiently as someone asked her a convoluted question about ingredients.

I flopped a teabag into a cup and added hot water, then carried my treats and a conference packet to an aisle seat in the back. The ability to make a quick getaway influenced my seating choices at events and lectures. Not that I thought Oliver would be boring. It was habit.

Kieran entered the room from the back, waving when he spotted me. Dressed in a mossy green sweater over a button-down, jeans, and polished boots, he looked great. Very casual lord of the manor. In front of me, two young women nudged each other and started whispering.

"That's Dr. Scott's cousin," the redhead said. "He lives here." They glanced around, eyes wide with amazed envy.

"Is he single?" the brunette asked with a laugh. She shrank back in her seat. "Don't look. He's coming this way."

Suddenly, I couldn't resist the urge to show off my boyfriend, just a bit. I leaned forward. "I'm sorry, he's not. Single, I mean."

Their heads swiveled around. The brunette frowned. "How do you know?"

In response, I lifted my hand and waved as Kieran got closer. "Hey, sweetie. Saved you a seat." I hadn't, but there was an empty chair next to me. I moved over.

"Sweetie?" he mouthed as he sat down. He gave me a quick kiss. "Good morning. How are you?"

The women's ears were practically standing straight out as they pretended not to listen, tempting me to say something naughty about last night. Instead I said, "Wonderful, thanks, despite the lack of sleep." There. Semi-naughty. "Catch up later, after this? I'll be in the library."

He rested an arm across the back of my chair. "Speaking of the library, we have a little surprise later."

I leaned close; luckily the lusty women seemed to have moved on, tittering between themselves. "Can you tell me?"

"We put the original manuscript on display," he said under his breath. "We'll let everyone walk through and view it after the lecture."

"Wonderful. They'll love it." I had been thrilled to see the pages penned by Selwyn Scott, and I was sure this group of gothic fans would be equally as enthralled.

Sophie Verona stepped up to the podium and adjusted the microphone. "Good morning," she said, her voice echoing in the high-ceilinged room. "Welcome to the first event in this year's Gothic Institute. We gather to learn, enjoy our favorite genre, and have a good time." A brief round of applause broke out. She cleared her throat. "Before I introduce Dr. Oliver Scott, who will be speaking to us about a novel penned right here at Hazelhurst House, I have some sad news to share."

The audience began to shift around and whisper, and I guessed most of them already knew about Thad.

"I'm sorry to report," Sophie went on, "that Thad Devine, my assistant, and a true student of the gothic, was attacked and killed last night." Gasps flew around the room. "The case is in the hands of the most capable Cambridge police." As people started to babble, she put up a hand. "I'd like to have a moment of silence for Thad before we begin." It was a nice touch, also a way to rein in the audience.

Silence settled over the hall, everyone's heads bowed. Then, after about fifty seconds or so, a startling rattle and crash broke the quiet.

A suit of armor near the wall collapsed, sending the helmet rolling across the floor. It ended up close to Oliver's feet. Not missing a beat, he picked up the helmet and holding it, said, "Did you arrange this, Lady Asha? I couldn't ask for a more perfect introduction to my talk, 'Cursed Objects in the Gothic.'" Everyone laughed and, as Oliver took his place at the podium, settled in to listen.

"How did you like the talk?" I asked George when he ambled up to me after the lecture. "I certainly learned a lot. I like the way he identified common themes."

Oliver had compared the coveted manuscript, *The Ramblings of a Monk*, to Wilkie Collins's moonstone and the monkey's paw in the short story by W. W. Jacobs. The objects were alluring—well, the monkey's paw for its purported power—appealed to humanity's worst instincts, and provided a comeuppance. He'd also touched on themes like gothic settings and weather, as well as eccentric characters and a mood of brooding danger.

"I did as well," George said, showing me the notes

scrawled on his notepad. "I'll be reading with a much more informed eye." He glanced around, noticing that people were lining up at the back of the hall. "Are you going to see the manuscript?"

"Not right now," I said. "Kieran showed it to me the other day so I don't need to clog up the queue."

"Lucky you," George said with envy in his voice. "You're cataloguing the library, Violet said?"

"I am. Oh, George, you'll love it. They have so many first editions, bought hot off the presses." I had an idea. "If you can hang around a while, I'll give you a private tour." I was sure the Scotts wouldn't mind. Kieran thought the world of George.

George beamed. "I'd love that, I would. Well, I'd better get in line. See you later." He strode off toward the group waiting to view *The Fatal Folio.*

I went over to the refreshments table. Daisy was letting people pick at the remains while packing up what she could. "Heading out soon?"

"I am." She placed extra paper plates and napkins in a tote. "See you back in town?"

"Why don't we grab a beer at the pub later?" I could use some time to decompress and a chat with my best friend. "I have a lot to tell you."

Daisy checked to be sure no one was listening. "About Thad? The police called me earlier. They want another interview."

I nodded. "Kieran and I were at the college talking to the police until almost midnight. And we met several of Thad's friends. All of whom are here today."

"Any theories?" Daisy asked. "I know it's early days . . ." She combined three stacks of paper cups and tossed them into the tote.

"Sort of." Thad's harassment of Amy was all I knew so far. This wasn't the place to discuss that, though. "Do you need some help?" I offered belatedly. Daisy hesitated. In response, I skirted the table and put my bags down. "What should I do?"

"Thanks, Molly," Daisy said. She handed me a plastic container. "Start with the baked goods. I'm going to leave the extras."

Between the two of us, we soon had the buffet table cleared and everything packed in totes stacked on two dollies. The hall was mostly deserted now, with only an occasional person passing through. Everyone must be in the library.

"I'll bring the van around," Daisy said, jingling keys. "Be right back."

Pulling out my phone, I sat on the closest chair and checked for messages. I also snapped a picture of the hall and posted on the bookshop social media page. *Where it all began. #TheFatalFolio #GothicLiteratureInstitute*

"Food all gone?" Wesley Wright stood in front of the empty table. His curly hair was a mess, one corner of his collar was turned up, and his eyes were red-rimmed. He looked like the poster child for a bad night, and I could guess the cause.

"I'm sorry, we just packed up," I said. He gave a tiny groan so, taking pity on him, I picked up the container of scones and peeled off the lid. "Here."

He took one, his fingers fumbling. "Thanks." He tossed his hair out of his eyes and took a bite. After swallowing, he said, "Do I know you from somewhere?"

"I was with Oliver last night." I left it at that.

"Oh yeah." He crammed the rest of the scone into his

mouth. "Thad." He grimaced, blinking rapidly. "I can't believe he's gone."

"You roomed near each other?" I asked, to confirm what I'd gleaned.

"Right next door." His Adam's apple bobbed. "He was my cousin."

I inhaled sharply. Thad had been his family member as well as a friend. "I'm so sorry."

"Wesley?" Amy was in the doorway at the back of the room. "You're going to miss the exhibit if you don't hurry."

He threw me a wry smile. "I'd better scoot. See ya." He shambled off to join Amy.

Daisy soon returned and I pushed one dolly while she did the other. Outside, we loaded the van and Daisy closed the double doors. "Well, Molly, I'd best be off. Send me a text when you're free later."

"Will do. Hopefully we can get together and catch up." I stood in the fresh—very fresh—air for a moment, watching as she drove across the former drawbridge and along the drive. A frosty winter sun touched the battlements and a small flag snapped in the wind. A sense of timelessness, of vast history stretching back centuries, settled around me. We all had our brief moment and this was mine. A librarian from Vermont privileged enough to curate and preserve great literary works while spending time in some incredible places, like the courtyard of Hazelhurst House.

Unlike Thad, whose life had been abruptly cut short. How tragic and unfair.

Behind me, the double doors opened and attendees began to emerge, chatting and laughing. The event was over, which meant I should go find Kieran. After we

ate, I'd settle down in the library and continue the cataloguing job.

Inside the Great Hall, Kieran and some helpers were
stacking chairs and carrying away the podium and
tables. "Mum said lunch in ten," he told me, pausing his
work.

I checked the time on a grandfather clock. Almost
noon. "I'd better go find George. I promised him a tour
of the library."

"Ask him to stay and do it after," Kieran suggested.
"George is a favorite of hers so she won't mind at all."

George sure did get around. "I'll do that." I set off
through the hall in search of my friend.

●∤●

After a delicious lunch of pea soup made with local ham,
Kieran accompanied George and me to the library. It had
been locked after the attendees viewed the manuscript and
Kieran had the keys.

We waited in silence while Kieran searched the bundle for the right one. "Ah, here we are." He turned the
brass key with a decisive click and then opened the door.
"I'll be heading back to town shortly, George, if you want
a ride."

"That would be lovely," George said. "I was planning
to take the bus."

"No need. Hang out with Molly here and I'll swing
round to get you." With a nod, Kieran withdrew, leaving
us alone.

"Where to begin?" I said as George and I crossed the
carpet. I put my laptop bag on the table. "As you can see,
the library is divided into sections by subject. The fiction

is right over here." That was his area of interest. "The books are more or less in order by author."

George padded along behind me, admiration shining on his good-natured face. "This library is like a time capsule. The history of a family's love of books."

"Good way to put it." No doubt the Scotts' collecting choices could serve as commentary on the reading tastes and interests of literate Brits through the centuries. I gestured. "Here are the Brontë sisters, if you want to take a look."

He moved closer to the shelf, the admiration replaced by awe, and carefully removed the oldest book, a copy of *Wuthering Heights*. "It's a first edition, all right. Published under the name Ellis Bell."

"Why don't I fire up my laptop? That can be the first entry." The catalogue could be sorted by author as well as classification, so entry order didn't matter.

As I went back to the table, I felt a cold breeze. Glancing around, I didn't see any source of cold air. A gust down the fireplace? That didn't seem likely.

"Someone leave a window open?" George asked. "I feel a draft."

"Maybe." I moved toward the closest set of windows, covered by long curtains to protect the books from sunlight. "Though I have no idea why anyone would open a window in this weather." When I pulled back the curtains, I discovered that the tall casement windows were open slightly. "How dumb was this?" I pulled them closed.

On the way back to the table, I noticed a glass cabinet sitting on another table. That must be where they'd displayed *The Fatal Folio*. "Kieran put the manuscript away, huh?" I commented.

George looked over his shoulder. "Did he?"

I took a closer look at the case. The glass at the back was broken, and the cabinet lock lay on the table.

The open window, the empty case, and the broken glass added up to a terrible conclusion: the *Fatal Folio* manuscript had been stolen.

CHAPTER 7

The loss of this rare and irreplaceable manuscript hit me like a blow to the stomach. "George, it's gone!" My shout was a rude intrusion in the hushed atmosphere.

"*The Fatal Folio*? *No*." Even under the shock of this revelation, George carefully shelved the book he was holding before trucking across the carpet to my side. Gnawing on his lip, he carefully examined the case. "I'm afraid you're right. Someone has gone and lifted the book."

"But who? How?" I found my phone, which was the quickest way to reach Kieran in this huge house. I pressed his name then put the phone on speaker.

"Molly. What's up?" By the clanging in the background, I guessed he was in the kitchen.

"We need you. Someone stole the *Fatal Folio* manuscript." Too bad the curse wouldn't extend to the thief, I thought darkly.

Leaning over my shoulder, George spoke toward the phone. "She's right, mate. Someone broke into the case."

A brief silence as Kieran absorbed this. "I'll be right there. Don't touch anything, okay?"

The window. "I think they went out the window. It was open. I shut it before I realized."

"Don't worry about that." He disconnected.

I sank into the closest chair. "This is horrible." Even though the manuscript wasn't mine, I felt both violated and outraged. These emotions weren't unfamiliar. When I was in college, someone had stripped my bicycle, leaving only the frame. I hadn't locked it up correctly. Of course, this was a much worse situation, but this room had been locked too . . . how had they done it?

George rubbed his chin. "It had to be one of the lecture attendees, don't you think?" He wandered over to the window and checked behind the floor-length curtains.

"I didn't go on the tour. How did it work?"

"We lined up and walked through, each person getting a moment or two to study the manuscript through the glass. Then we went out that door." He pointed to a door I hadn't paid attention to. Not the cupboard.

I went over and tested the handle. Locked. "Where does this take you?"

He shrugged. "A sitting room. We went through there and back into the hall."

"Was anyone watching as you all filed through the room?"

George frowned as he thought. "Not really. Lady Asha unlocked the doors but then she was called away. Dr. Scott stood by the case for a while but he too left after I went through. Or so I assume. I saw him in the Great Hall."

"Someone hid in here," I said. "They must have. By then both doors were locked, so they went out the window."

Kieran strode through the doorway and headed right for the empty case. We joined him there.

"They broke in," George said, pointing out the lock and the fractured glass. "Molly already solved the crime."

Kieran looked at me. "I have a theory that might work," I temporized. "Someone hid in here, behind the curtains, probably, and after the doors were locked, broke into the case." I went over to the window. "This window was open when George and I came in. Only a crack so it took a few minutes to notice."

Kieran inspected the window and peered outside. On this side of the building, there was a grassy strip edging the moat, with a footbridge leading to gardens a short distance away. "And off they went," he muttered.

The three of us stood in agitated silence for a moment. Kieran sighed and took out his phone. "We need to call the police."

After placing the call, Kieran went to find his mother and break the news. George and I sat in the library, at loose ends until the officers arrived.

"Can you bring me that copy of *Wuthering Heights*?" I finally said. "I need to get something done today." *Or at least try to.*

George hopped right up. "Sure thing." He carried the book over to the table where I'd set up my laptop.

With a few clicks, I brought up the program. "Here we go. Entry number one."

What a thrill to handle such a rare and beautiful book, to think of the history behind it, the quest of Emily and her sisters to get something published. It hadn't been easy—Charlotte's first book, *The Professor,* wasn't published until 1857—but their work had left a lasting legacy. A copy like this had sold more than a decade ago for over $100,000.

A sudden thought jolted through me. Had the thief taken anything else? I scanned the shelves, looking for gaps in the books. I couldn't see any. Perhaps Lady Asha should take a look. She must know where the most valu-

able books were located, even if they hadn't been cata-
logued yet.

My heart sank at having to make this suggestion. What
a frustrating and unfair situation. Lady Asha had kindly
opened her home to a group of scholars only to be ripped
off.

The officers and Lady Asha returned with Kieran. I
recognized them immediately as Constable Johnson, a
woman with curly red hair, and Constable Malago, a gorgeous young man with burnished skin.

Constable Johnson nodded when she saw me. "Miss
Kimball, isn't it?"

"That's right," I said. "I'm an owner of a bookshop in
Cambridge. This is George Flowers, my friend. We're the
ones who discovered the theft."

"You were here in the library why?" Constable Malago
asked.

I didn't take offense. It was his job to ask questions. "I
was hired to work on a catalogue of the library. George
and I both attended a lecture this morning and he was
hanging out with me for a while."

"They didn't steal the manuscript," Kieran said. "I can
personally vouch for them both."

"So can I," Lady Asha put in.

"What lecture?" Constable Johnson asked.

I let Kieran answer. "My cousin, Dr. Oliver Scott, from
St. Aelred, spoke on *The Fatal Folio*, among other gothic
books, as part of the Gothic Literature Institute symposium going on this week."

"So he spoke on the book that was stolen?" Constable
Malago clarified.

"Yes, which is why we had it on display," Kieran said.
"We figure it happened sometime between the viewing
and when I let Molly and George into the library, about

half an hour ago." He gave the officers details about the morning's events. "After everyone went through, both doors into the room were locked. My mother has the only set of keys."

"But how—" Constable Johnson started.

"We think they went out the window." I pointed. "That one was open a crack."

"We felt the draft when we came in here," George added.

The officers went over and peered outside, exactly the way we had earlier. Although they didn't say anything, their expressions seemed to confirm my theory.

Who had stolen the handwritten manuscript? "Is there a list of attendees from this morning? Or a sign-in sheet?" I hadn't signed in but that didn't mean others hadn't. "Did you sign in, George?" He shook his head.

Everyone looked at Kieran and Lady Asha. "Maybe?" Kieran took out his phone. "I'll send Oliver a text and ask."

The officers were examining the broken case. "Was the manuscript always kept in there?" Constable Johnson asked.

Lady Asha shook her head. "It was usually in storage. We only set this up for the event today." She grimaced. "What a mistake."

"You couldn't have known, Mum," Kieran said. "Whoever did this worked fast. The viewing wasn't announced until after Oliver's talk."

He had a good point. Without advance knowledge, the thief had come up with a strategy to steal with lightning speed. Maybe they'd gone through once and then circled back, at the tail end.

"No cameras in here, huh?" Officer Malago asked, his gaze on the ceiling.

Lady Asha gave a little laugh of disbelief. "Not hardly. We have them outside, at the entrances, yes. We're not open to the public so cameras inside aren't necessary." She crossed her arms, frowning. "Well, they weren't."

"They aren't now, either, Mum," Kieran said. "We have alarms on the ground floor entrances and windows."

"Which we turned off this morning," his mother said. "That's why they could go out the window without triggering the alarm."

The theft of *The Fatal Folio* was obviously a crime carried out during a very narrow window of opportunity.

Kieran's phone rang. "Oliver." He picked up and walked a short distance away. "I have bad news," he said. "The manuscript was stolen." A pause. "Yes, I'm serious. The police are here now. They want a copy of the attendee list, if you have one." After a little more conversation, he returned to us. "Oliver has an electronic sign-up sheet and a handwritten one from this morning."

"We'll be wanting to talk to Dr. Scott," Constable Johnson said. "We'll get those then."

Kieran passed along Oliver's contact information. The officers took pictures, dusted for prints—no luck there—and asked a few more questions. Then they were gone.

Sitting slumped in an armchair, Lady Asha put a hand to her forehead. "I can't believe this."

I couldn't either, and I still needed to raise another sore point. "As you know, I've just started the cataloguing." I picked up *Wuthering Heights*. "If this is a sample of what you've got here, then the collection is priceless. I hate to say this, but can you tell if anything is missing?"

"Oh, no, Molly," Kieran said, shock in his voice. "You think they took something else?" His gaze flew to the shelves.

"I hope not. But they were in here alone for a while, we think." My words painted a dismal picture, sending everyone's spirits plummeting even further.

Lady Asha leaped up from the chair, head craned as she stared at the shelves. "I don't see anything missing . . ."

"I don't either, Mum," Kieran said. He gave a helpless shrug. "Not that I have the shelves memorized."

There was one way we could find out, although it wasn't guaranteed to be thorough or complete. "Do you have any previous catalogues or records of what's here?"

Lady Asha brightened slightly. "We might. Remember the journal that Lord Llewellyn kept, Kieran? In the mid-1800s? He mentioned highlights of the collection and logged purchases."

"No," Kieran said. "But I'll take your word for it."

"That journal would be a huge help," I said. The older books might be mentioned and those were likely to be among the more valuable ones. "We can also check any invoices that were saved." I'd wanted to do that anyway, to see if the Scotts had bought books from my ancestors. That seemed such a minor and petty quest right now. Then I reminded myself that a relationship with the bookshop might shed light on Selwyn Scott's identity—it wasn't just idle curiosity.

Lady Asha strode toward the cupboard. "I'm going to look for that journal." Kieran handed her the key ring and she began flipping through the keys.

I was back at my laptop and George came over and sat beside me, a mournful expression on his face. "Bad business, innit?"

"It sure is, George." I went back to entering *Wuthering Heights* into the catalogue program. "I'm praying nothing else was taken. The loss of that one manuscript is bad enough. If it's sold to a private collector, we may never see it again." It wasn't only the piece's monetary value. It was also integral to Scott family and literary histories.

"People suck."

A laugh burst out of me at his pithy and far too accurate assessment. "Yes, they do." In my opinion, anyone who stole books—or defaced them or sliced out pictures—deserved their own circle of hell.

"You'll have to be on the lookout," George said. "They might try to sell the manuscript to Thomas Marlowe."

Still typing, I laughed. "Good luck with that one. We know where it came from." He was right in the sense that we bought and sold used books, specializing in the rare. However, as with works of art, we established provenance for the most valuable items. Books were portable and easily stolen.

"Maybe we should warn Violet," George said, his tone casual.

"Go ahead and call her," I said, knowing he was dying to fill her in. If I weren't so far behind, I would have done it already. "Fetch me another Brontë first, will you? Thanks."

Lady Asha bustled out of the storage room carrying a leather-covered journal. She set it down next to my computer with a flourish. "This is Lord Llewellyn's book inventory." She flipped it open to show me pages filled with dense handwriting.

At a glance, it looked like a rudimentary cataloguing system, with Lord Llewellyn noting titles, authors, editions, and supplemental notes.

"This is going to be very useful." Despite the situation, I couldn't keep the excitement out of my voice. "I'll add his notes to the catalogue. They'll really round it out." I glanced toward the cupboard. "Where's Kieran?"

Lady Asha followed my gaze, smiling fondly. "He's

sorting through the papers, looking for invoices for books. Never thought I'd see him take such an interest." Her significant glance at me revealed where she placed the credit for his new fascination with their library.

"Great," I said, trying to sound casual even though inside I was jumping up and down. This cataloguing job, besides being a plum project, was helping me build a relationship with Kieran's mum. "Any help is appreciated." Especially his.

Lady Asha tapped the table. "I'll let you get back to work. Break for tea in a couple of hours? I'll come get you."

"That sounds wonderful." Maybe I would get a solid start on the project today after all.

She left, and for the next hour or so, George ferried books to me while Kieran continued his work in the closet. Except for the tapping of keys and an occasional muttered exclamation from Kieran, the library was peaceful. I could almost forget the broken case sitting just out of my line of sight. Almost forget Thad Devine's murder.

We had worked our way through the Brontë family and I was logging an early edition of *Frankenstein,* shelved near the works of Mary Shelley's friend Lord Byron, when Lady Asha returned.

I pushed back in my chair, stretching. "Is it teatime already?" As always, the time had flown while I was immersed in books.

Lady Asha glanced at a wall clock. "I suppose it is. That's not why I came in, though." She glanced around. "Is Kieran still here?" He emerged from the cupboard. "I wanted to let you know that Sir Jon is on his way."

Sir Jonathon Yeats was a former MI6 agent, bookseller, and special investigator. I knew he wasn't here in the first capacity—or I hoped not—so which of the latter was it?

Or was it purely a social call? Sir Jon seemed to know everyone. In fact, he'd gone to college with Aunt Violet and I was convinced something was brewing there.

"Coming to tea?" Kieran asked, miming the act of drinking with pinky extended.

"Not exactly," Lady Asha said. "He's investigating the stolen manuscript. Something about a special task force."

Although relieved to hear that Sir Jon, with his experience and expertise, was going to help us, I couldn't help but be curious. While valuable and rare, the *Fatal Folio* manuscript wasn't reason enough to launch a full-fledged task force.

Something bigger must be going on.

CHAPTER 8

Thankfully it didn't take long to satisfy my curiosity about Sir Jon's visit. He joined us in a pretty little sitting room and, after a brief exchange of pleasantries and polite personal inquiries, said, "You must be wondering why I'm here today." He inclined his head toward Lady Asha. "Besides the opportunity to enjoy your company." Silver-haired, dapper, and trim, Sir Jon had the bearing and charm one might expect of a gentleman spy.

"You're always welcome here, Sir Jon," Lady Asha murmured. She sat regally over a huge tray holding a silver tea set and tiers with tiny pastries and sandwiches.

Sir Jon set his cup and saucer aside before reaching into his breast pocket for a small tablet and a stylus. "As happens now and then, I've been called in as a consultant to Scotland Yard. This time it's really up my alley." He gave us a closed-lip smile. "Rare books." In his retirement, Sir Jon had opened a bookshop specializing in military history and spy novels. He was also an antiquities expert and had helped apprehend smuggling rings.

"Have there been other thefts?" I asked. At Thomas Marlowe, we tried to keep abreast of these crimes, including details about what was stolen. If someone tried to sell us a stolen book, we would immediately alert the authorities.

"Here and there," he said. "Nothing that forms a pattern yet." His lips twisted. "Not like the London warehouse case."

We all glanced up involuntarily. Several years ago, a daring gang of thieves had entered a shipping warehouse through the ceiling and stolen dozens of rare books belonging to three dealers. These had eventually been retrieved after being buried underground in Romania. Some of the books were damaged, a situation that made a bookseller's blood run cold. While the criminals had gone to trial, questions remained regarding how they had known exactly when the books were there, since they were in transit, on their way to a book show in Las Vegas.

"We think some of the players are local," Sir Jon went on. "Hence the interest in your loss. With any luck, your manuscript will help us break the case."

"Let us know what we can do to help," Lady Asha said. We all nodded.

Sir Jon touched his table screen. "Thank you. Why don't we start with a few questions?" He paused. "Who knew the manuscript would be on display today?"

"No one," Lady Asha said. "It was a last-minute decision, right, Kieran?"

Kieran leaned forward, hands clasped between his knees. "This morning, before the lecture started, my cousin, Dr. Oliver Scott, who was speaking, said it was too bad people couldn't view the original manuscript. He was speaking on the same book, you see. So we went to Mum to ask if we could display it."

First a murder and now a theft, with Kieran's cousin right in the middle. I didn't like the fact that Oliver had suggested the display.

Lady Asha put a hand to her mouth. "I really thought it would be all right. I mean, we locked it in a case and the room was secured before and after the viewing."

"I'll have more questions about those specifics later," Sir Jon said. "Was the case monitored?"

Kieran and his mother exchanged looks. "If you mean, did we post a guard, no," Kieran admitted. "Everyone filed through, in one door and out the other. Most of the audience was students, so we thought . . ."

"Students steal too," Sir Jon said. "Unfortunately."

I thought of a high-profile case at Transylvania University, in Lexington, Kentucky. Four students had overpowered a librarian and made off with more than five million in rare books.

"Who went through the viewing?" Sir Jon asked. "Molly? George?"

"I didn't," I said. Since I'd already seen the manuscript and could access it anytime, I hadn't bothered. Now I wished I had.

George raised his hand. "Like Kieran said, we lined up and filed through the library. Each person got a minute, tops, to look at the manuscript."

Sir Jon nodded. "I'll take a look at the library after tea. Did you observe any odd behavior, George? Anyone who lingered? Made a strange comment?"

"Hmm." George gazed into his teacup. "To be honest, I wasn't really paying attention to anyone except to Amy and Josh, who were ahead of me." He made a shooing motion. "Hoping they'd get a move on. I was very eager to see the manuscript."

Amusement brightened George's eyes. "Josh said something funny. When Amy asked if he'd want to look inside the real fatal folio, he said, 'If I did, I'd be sending myself down from school. Mum and Dad wouldn't be pleased.'"

I laughed. "Good one, Josh." To Sir Jon, I said, "Amy and Josh are students at St. Aelred. Dr. Scott is one of their instructors."

"St. Aelred." Sir Jon's tone was contemplative. "A student was killed there on Bonfire Night. Stabbed outside the gate."

My insides twisted as images flashed through my mind. Thad sprawled on the ground. The antique knife. Blood.

I wasn't the only one who didn't want to veer into that territory. "Such a tragedy," Lady Asha said. "Thad was the son of dear friends." She set her teacup down with a clink. "Shall we go see the library?"

"So sorry for your loss," Sir Jon murmured. He tucked away his tablet and stood. "Lead on, milady."

◆◆◆

By the time I returned to Cambridge, dozens of books entered into the catalogue, I was more than ready for a beer and a chat with my best friend. After parking the Cortina, I swung by the bookshop to drop my laptop and wash up, then headed over to the pub. Mum and Aunt Violet were out, so updating them would have to wait.

Daisy waved me over to a two-top, where a pint of beer awaited. The benefits of text updates. I slumped into my chair and grabbed the glass for a healthy swallow of my favorite bitter. She watched with amusement, her glass already half empty.

"Ah. This really hit the spot." I lifted the glass in a salute. "Thank you."

"Tough day in the library?" Daisy smiled.

I glanced around to be sure no one was listening. "You could say that. The original *Fatal Folio* manuscript was stolen. Right under everyone's noses."

Daisy looked taken aback. "Today? During the event?"

"Yep." Anger churned and I gritted my teeth. "After the walk-through. We think the thief hid in the library. After lunch, George and I discovered that the case was broken and a window left open."

Daisy absently spun her glass, around and around. "So someone who attended the event . . . Was the exhibition publicized?"

"Exactly what the police wanted to know," I said. "No, it was a last-minute thing this morning. Oliver suggested it."

Something flashed in Daisy's eyes. "Oliver suggested it?" She shook her head.

"I know," I admitted. "He's the obvious candidate. In planning the theft, anyway. He wasn't in the library when it happened." If our theory about timing was correct.

"Would he actually steal from his own family?" Daisy asked, her brow furrowed.

"Hard to believe, isn't it?" There was another possibility, although it pained me to say it. "The theft *will* bring attention to the book, though. He's writing his own gothic . . . hoping for a big publishing deal . . . Gah. I hate to even say it." My lips twisted. "Sir Jon is on the case. If it was an inside job, it could get ugly."

Daisy laughed. "Oh, yeah. I wouldn't want him tracking me." She reconsidered. "Well, maybe I would, if I weren't in love with Tim."

"He's a hottie, isn't he? Even at age seventy-something." It wasn't only his well-preserved looks, accomplishments, and money. Sir Jon had a very attractive air of competence that gave the sense one was in good hands. Kieran had that quality too.

"For sure." Daisy picked up the menu card. "Let's eat. I want the steak-and-ale pie." She passed the card to me.

"Sounds good." I scanned the list. "Wild boar sausage? Wow. I didn't know they had that." Sausages with mash would be a good comfort food choice.

Daisy got up. "I'll go order." She circled her finger over our glasses. "Plus get two more."

"Thanks, friend." I sat back with my glass, savoring the thought of a delicious hot meal to come.

Daisy returned with two pints of beer and slid one across the table to me. "So tell me. Why is Sir Jon involved?"

I wasn't surprised that my smart friend was delving further into this point. Not much got past her. "Scotland Yard brought him in. There have been a few thefts recently and they're trying to figure out if they're connected."

"Hmm." Daisy sipped beer. "The one today seems more like a theft of opportunity."

"Or it's meant to look that way." Again, my heart sank at the realization that Oliver might have masterminded the situation. Maybe the exhibit was last minute but the lecture wasn't. It had to have been planned for months. "Having it stolen during the event spreads the suspicion around quite effectively."

The local police would have their hands full following up with the fifty people or so who had attended. They were probably relieved if Scotland Yard was taking over.

I thought of another possible mastermind. "There is someone else who could have planned it," I said. "Dr. Sophie Verona knew about the lecture. And she might have been aware of the manuscript." Maybe she'd quietly nudged Oliver to set up the exhibition.

"I know who you mean," Daisy said. "She did the introductions."

I hadn't mentioned Sophie to Sir Jon and I made a mental note to do so. With her involvement in the Gothic Institute, she had the expertise to realize the manuscript's value and place in literary history.

Thad had worked for the Gothic Institute, I recalled. Had he been aware of a plot to steal the manuscript and that was why he was killed?

I didn't like this idea, since it firmly pointed the finger at Oliver.

As if reading my mind, Daisy said, "I wonder if they've made any progress on the murder." In the pub's muted light, her face was pale. "I had so much trouble sleeping last night, I tell you. Then the interview with the police . . ." She shivered.

"That's right, you mentioned they called," I said. "How did it go?"

A server holding two plates aloft approached and she didn't answer until we had our meals and assured the server we were all set for now.

Daisy picked up her fork and pierced the top of her pie, letting the steam escape. "They came to the shop after I got back from Hazelhurst House. I didn't have time to go to the station and they respected that, thankfully."

"Was it Inspector Ryan?" I cut into a wild boar sausage, eager to taste this exotic blend.

"No, some underling." Daisy took a bite. "She wanted to confirm what I'd seen in St. Aelred's Way. Especially how I'd discovered the knife. Also if I knew Thad." She paused. "Or Oliver Scott."

My heart jumped. Were they focusing on Oliver?

Tamping down my fears, I asked, "*Do* you know Oliver?"
Daisy had known Kieran since he'd opened his shop.

Daisy's nose wrinkled. "I don't know him, know him.
He's come into the tea shop. And I've seen him with
Kieran, cycling or just hanging out."

"The knife came from the college," I said. "So the
killer wasn't random."

"That's what you said in your text."

Late last night, I'd texted Daisy with an update of what
had occurred after she and Tim left. "Remember the students I mentioned? They were all at the lecture today." I
hadn't given many details, not wanting to write a book on
my phone.

"Which ones were they?"

Between bites, I described Amy, Josh, and Wesley.
"Wesley is Thad's cousin. He told me that today."

"Aww, that's so sad." Daisy picked up her phone and
stared searching. "Last name?"

I thought for a moment. "Wright, I think." I gave her
Amy's and Josh's surnames too. "Thad was harassing
Amy."

Daisy lowered her voice. "So her boyfriend might have
killed him?"

"All four students lived on the same stair," I said. "Fa-
miliarity breeds contempt, right?"

"It can." Daisy absently nibbled at her meal while she
searched. "Here we go." She pushed the phone over to me.

The screen displayed an article in a tabloid, the kind
of publication Kieran and I appeared in all too fre-
quently for my taste. Then I read the article date: October
this year. "Wait, what? 'Close Call at Scottish Hunting
Lodge'?

"'The Honorable Thad Devine narrowly escaped death
during a family hunting trip in Scotland,'" I read aloud.

"'A shot went wild,' the divine Devine said, 'and I had to duck for cover.' The handsome lad laughs as he recalls the incident. 'We think it was poachers. They're becoming a real problem.'"

A photo with the article showed Thad and Wesley dressed in hunting tweeds, bird guns over their shoulders, the gray, forbidding lodge rising behind them and the rest of the party standing around in the background.

Naturally my suspicious mind went *there* immediately. "I wonder if this was a first murder attempt?" I scanned the rest of the article, which said the shooter had not been identified.

"Me too," Daisy said. "Hmm. Wesley was on the spot both times."

"Does look sus." I handed her the phone and turned to mine. After finding the article, I sent it to Inspector Ryan. I'd helped in past cases and I didn't think he minded too much.

After digging around, I learned that Wesley's and Thad's mothers were sisters. One had married into nobility, the other was a widowed schoolteacher in King's Lynn. Did Wesley resent his richer, entitled (literally) cousin—or did he enjoy going along for the ride? I shared my thoughts with Daisy.

"I can see him being resentful," Daisy said. "Especially if Thad rubbed it in. You said he wasn't the nicest."

"That's what I gathered." Having devoured every bite of the sausages and potato, I sat back with a sigh. "Did you find anything interesting?"

"Amy's and Josh's social media pages." Daisy again passed her phone over. "They look like a fun couple."

The photos on Josh's page showed two happy young people living it up in Cambridge. Clinking glasses at a pub. Dancing. Punting on the river. Amy lying with her head in Josh's lap under a weeping willow, both reading textbooks.

I scrolled down, scanning the posts. "No mention of his conflict with Thad about his treatment of Amy."

"Very mature," Daisy said with approval. "I hate it when people fight and trash-post on social media."

"St. Aelred wouldn't like it either, I'm sure." I couldn't help but wonder if the college preferred to sweep problems like harassment under the rug. That could be a big reason why Amy was reluctant to report Thad. If they weren't going to do anything about it, then it would only impact her negatively. I also wondered idly how much money Thad's family gave to the school. It shouldn't have a bearing on discipline but let's not be naive.

"So," Daisy mused. "We have Wesley, Amy, and Josh as possible suspects. Amy and Josh definitely had problems with him. Wesley might have. They all had knowledge of and access to the weapon. All were at college that night."

I remembered a throwaway remark Josh had made. "Josh and Amy got separated at the bonfire after the tent caught fire. So either one of them could have done it, potentially without the other knowing."

"Whoever stole the knife waited for a good opportunity?" Daisy guessed.

"Unless they arranged to meet him outside the gate . . ." I was thinking out loud. "His phone is missing so no way to check."

"The runner in the mask." Daisy shivered. "That was probably the killer." She held up forefinger and thumb a short distance apart. "We were that close to them."

"It's a strong possibility." I thought about the options. "Unless they went the other way. Or into the school."

"My mind is spinning." Daisy rested her head on her hand. "So many possibilities. So confusing."

"Oh, yeah," I agreed. "All we can do is pull the threads and see which one unravels." For everyone's sake, especially Thad's family's, I hoped the unraveling would happen quickly.

◦|◦

Replete after my large meal and time with my best friend, I lumbered across the street to the bookshop, grateful I didn't have far to go. After hashing over the murder and book theft, we'd turned to more pleasant topics. Tomorrow afternoon we were going to attend a showing of classic gothic films at St. Aelred. Not only were we both interested in the movies, it would give us a chance to snoop around. Er, I mean, learn more.

Upstairs with my cat, I crawled into bed and opened *The Fatal Folio*. Would the original ever be returned to Hazelhurst House? I wondered with a pang. It was a terrible loss—and an infuriating crime.

The Fatal Folio, cont.

Our trip to Italy was plagued with ill omens from the start. As we set sail on a packet out of Dover to Calais, we were immediately met with tumultuous seas that almost swamped our ship, making Mr. Coates grievously ill.

To my surprise, I wasn't affected by the swells that rocked our craft in a most sickening manner, back and forth, back and forth like a demented cradle. In contrast, Mr. Coates clung to the rail, afraid that the ship would sink and he would be trapped below. Despite his valid fears, I knew deep within that we would live to continue our journey.

Our quest for The Ramblings of a Monk *had a certain dreadful inevitability about it, as if fated by a Hand greater than us. Wheels had been set in motion, I sensed, and nothing could stop them now.*

Despite spending many of my waking hours engrossed in the written word, I've never had trouble discerning the difference between fiction and fact. I am quite able to close the covers of a novel and consign the contents to the realm of dreams, enjoyed but soon forgotten. This sense of forces beyond our control, of destiny guiding our steps, was foreign to me.

As an ever-growing landmass on the horizon marked the next stage of the journey, I wondered, Will I ever see Cambridge again? I pictured my shop, friendly lights glowing in a purple dusk, the rows of dear, dusty tomes and the aroma of ancient paper and ink.

No answer floated on the cold wind. I heard only the caw of gulls, shouts of "Land ho," and the fervent, thankful prayers of my suffering companion.

CHAPTER 9

Fated by a Hand greater than us. The phrase kept coming to mind the next morning, as I sat in the bookshop waiting for customers. I couldn't help but wonder if the same was true of me, that fate was behind my involvement in all these murders. Three times now I'd been going innocently about my business only to discover a dead body.

Rather disconcerting, as George would say, followed by a fervent, "Bloody hell."

The weather wasn't helping my mood. It was a dismal day—heavy gray clouds lowering, rain hitting the diamond-pane windows with a splat, a fierce wind howling around the eaves. The gusts were strong enough at times to make the building creak.

Then the lights flickered. "Seriously?" I said. "We'll be breaking out the oil lamps next." Actually, the battery lanterns. No open flames allowed in a bookshop.

Mum came across the floor from the back, two mugs in hand. "Still slow?"

"Absolutely, positively yes." I took the cup of tea. "Thanks. You're a godsend."

Carrying her mug, Mum went to stand at the front window. Both cats turned over and looked up at her expectantly and she gave them equal time with pats and chin rubs.

"Not many people out in this deluge," she said as two umbrellas bobbed past on their way to the tea shop.

"Who can blame them?" I hoped the rain slowed by this afternoon, when Daisy and I planned to attend the film festival at St. Aelred. Cycling would be faster, but we couldn't carry umbrellas on our bikes. We'd have to walk and risk getting soaked.

Mum came over and joined me behind the counter, taking "the squeaky chair," as we called it. Every time the sitter moved, it let out a horrendous squawk.

"We really should get rid of this thing," she said, moving gingerly.

"We say that every time then forget about it." I uploaded another gargoyle photo from a local church, Our Lady and the English Martyrs, for our gothic-novel promotion.

"I'll make a note." Mum picked up her phone and typed. Then she frowned.

"What is it?" We were already getting likes on the gargoyle photos. What was it about those ugly things? They fascinated people.

"Sean sent me a text." That would be Detective Inspector Sean Ryan to most of us.

"And?" The Institute was holding a Gothic tour later this week and maybe I'd find other inspiration for posts. Sometimes I photographed books in relevant settings and that went over well.

"He canceled our dinner date. Two major investigations." Mum set the phone down with a sigh. "I understand but . . ."

"It's a drag. I get it." For a moment, I wondered what the second investigation was. Then it clicked in. "I bet he's working with Sir Jon on the book thefts." In between all the busyness of the past day, I'd managed to update Mum and Aunt Violet about the incident at Hazelhurst House. As fellow booklovers, they had been appalled.

"Probably. If Scotland Yard is involved." Mum sipped her tea. "He's Cambridge's lead investigator," she added, pride in her voice.

"I'm sure." With a little help from his friends, I thought cheekily. "With any luck, the cases will be solved quickly and you can go on your date."

Mum sighed again. "I hope so." She was staring toward the windows, at the storm. "This time of year gets to me. So gloomy. Months of cold and bad weather ahead."

"It's better than where we used to live," I said. "Six months of winter there." Although I hadn't experienced a full year in England, I had heard that spring comes earlier than in Vermont, with roses blooming in March instead of June.

"True." Mum put down her mug and stretched. "Maybe we should plan a holiday in Spain. Or the French Riviera."

Beaches, sun, good food, and fruity drinks. "I'm in." I'd finished the social media updates. The store inventory was up to date. I wasn't returning to Hazelhurst House until tomorrow. So, what should I do next?

Researching Selwyn Scott came to mind. It was possible one of the Cambridge libraries had documents related to the author in their collection. From the publisher or personal correspondence. Probably not a letter saying, "Guess what? I'm Selwyn," though we could hope.

Fortunately, the University of Cambridge had a site that searched all one hundred libraries at once. We also had an account that allowed full results to be shown, a University courtesy for a local bookstore that we really appreciated.

I typed in the publisher's name, Lackington, Hughes,

Harding, Mavor, & Jones, the house that had also published *Frankenstein*, and Selwyn Scott, to get results that referenced both.

"Hurray!" I cried, startling Mum and the cats. A letter from Selwyn Scott to the publisher, dated 1841, was available at St. Aelred's library. I turned the laptop screen so Mum could see. "I can stop by there today. Daisy and I are going to the film fest."

"What do you think the letter will tell you?" Mum asked.

"Well, I doubt it will reveal Selwyn's identity, because then it wouldn't still be a mystery. Even Charlotte Brontë kept hers a secret until she met her publisher in person." I'd read Charlotte's letter to a friend describing meeting Mr. Smith in London, after years of correspondence as Currer Bell. "There might be some clue, though. I won't know until I see it. No stone unturned and all that." Plus, as a fan of Scott's work, I was thrilled to find an actual letter written by the author. Two hundred years was a long time and very little survived.

I snapped a picture of the record for use later, then sent a text to Daisy to see when she could leave. The screening was scheduled for three and maybe we could go by the library first.

Anytime, came the reply back. *It's dead and my assistant can handle closing.* The tea shop closed at two.

We had a plan. The front door opened, the bells chiming. At first all I could see was a big black umbrella. Then it snapped shut to reveal a young man. He stomped his wet feet on the rug and said, "Do you have a copy of *The Fatal Folio*? I just read a story about it online. Someone stole the original?"

"We sure do." I pushed back my chair and stood. Nothing like a crime to increase interest in a title.

Although the rain and wind had eased by the time Daisy and I set off for St. Aelred, we still held umbrellas aloft, rain slickers covering our clothing. The storm was forecast to circle back around later.

An early twilight made the ancient city look even more lovely and mysterious. Bells rang out, causing a flock of crows to rise up, cawing, from a bare, twisted tree in a churchyard. Lights glistened on wet cobblestones and fog floated past the spires.

This time we went to the main gate at St. Aelred, where we gave our names and purpose of our visit to the elderly porter. He asked to see identification with apologies. "It's just that we must be extra careful right now, you understand."

"We get it," I said, digging out my wallet. If there was another murder, they would know who was inside the walls at the time. The problem with Thad's murder was that it occurred outside the gate, thereby widening the pool of possible suspects.

Except for the knife. That was a mistake that would haunt the killer. Its use spoke to premeditation, which begged the question: Why not use something commonplace and anonymous? Such quandaries plagued me.

"Here you are, miss." The porter slid my card across the ledge. "Have a nice afternoon."

"Thank you," we called, released to enter the inner sanctum.

I'd downloaded a map and now I studied it to locate the library. "This way."

The library was across the first court, its entrance marked by slim marble columns and a decorative lintel. Inside, the library was a mix of old and new like many college buildings. There were computer stations, card catalogues, and rolling stacks. In contrast, another room featured carved wood bookcases and hanging chandeliers.

At the desk, I made my request to a librarian, who directed us to wait at a table. Soon she approached holding an archival folder. "You're in luck," she said. "There are several letters from Selwyn Scott to the publisher." She twinkled at us. "I feel like I'm hearing that name everywhere lately."

She probably was. "I'm working for Lady Asha Scott," I said, wanting to establish my credentials. I'd already mentioned I was here on behalf of Thomas Marlowe, which gave me an open door all over town. "At the family's request, I'm researching the author to see what I can learn."

The librarian pointed a finger at me. "I bet Selwyn was a pen name. I've looked at the family tree from that period and there isn't a Selwyn."

"That's what we think too." I reached for the folder, eager to look at the letters. "If we figure it out, we'll let you know."

She clasped her hands. "I'd love that. When you're done, please leave the folder here." She tapped the table with her nails before trundling off toward the desk.

I unwound the string to open the folder. "If I didn't own a bookshop, I'd love to work in one of the college libraries." Talk about a dream job.

"You used to be a librarian, right?" Daisy scooted her chair closer.

"Yes, in Vermont. It was a very small-town library, which was fun in its own way." No rare manuscripts but lots of community engagement. My job had been slated to be cut in the next round of town funding, one reason

I hadn't been averse to moving to Cambridge. I'm not sure what I would be doing if I'd stayed.

Inside the folder were three document protectors, each holding a sheet of paper.

The top one read, in a slanting handwriting:

> *My dear Mr. Lackington:*
>   *Thank you for your kind review of The Fatal Folio and your judicious notes regarding its improvement. I have taken your suggestions under advisement and you will find the amended manuscript contained within. Assuming all meets with your approval, I look forward with great anticipation to the publishing of The Fatal Folio next year.*
>   *Allow me in conclusion to express my sense of the promptness, frankness, and intelligence which have marked your dealings with me.*
>   *Yours Respectfully, S. Scott.*

"None of my writer friends like editing either," Daisy said wryly. She had a number of regulars who worked on books and papers at the tea shop.

I took a picture of the letter, wishing I could compare it to the manuscript. I didn't want to assume that the same hand had written both.

One of the other two letters expressed pleasure at how well *The Fatal Folio* was selling. The third held a surprise. Selwyn Scott was writing another book, tentatively titled *Among the Ruins*.

"Ooh, that sounds good," Daisy exclaimed. "Have you read it?"

"I didn't even know it existed until now." Had Selwyn finished the book? If so, why hadn't it been published?

Here was another literary mystery to solve. I took a picture of this letter too and sent it to Kieran with a text.

Been holding out on me? Wink.

He shot a response right back. *What? Never heard of it.* A pause. *Want to look?*

You bet. I followed that affirmation with an update about where I was and my plans for the evening. *Catch up tomorrow?*

"Ready?" I replaced the sleeves in the folder and tied it before leaving the library, calling a soft thank-you to the librarian.

"I'm so excited," I said once we were outside and could speak more freely. "I wonder if the other manuscript still exists." I pictured us tracking it down, then having it published to great fanfare and acclaim. There would be tons of interest, I was pretty sure.

"I hope so," Daisy said. "I want to read it." We shared a grin. "Where to now?"

I consulted the symposium program. "The theater is in the same building as the dining hall. Follow me."

We entered through the main door, then paused to get our bearings. A directory hung on the wall and we headed toward it.

"Here for the films?" Josh, Thad's friend, had come in right behind us.

"We are," I said. "Is that where you're going?" I crossed my fingers mentally. This was an opportunity to talk to one of Thad's friends—well, his enemy, at least as far as Amy was concerned. Josh had also been at Hazelhurst House when the manuscript was stolen. Had Thad clued Josh in that the rare text might be displayed? That would presuppose that Oliver or Sophie had discussed the possibility.

"I am," Josh said, scanning the crowd. "I'm supposed to meet Amy. Maybe she's already in the theater."

After I introduced Daisy, we ambled down a corridor, joined by others on their way to the event. Josh didn't move away so I stayed on his heels, thinking we might be able to sit together.

Amy was seated in an empty row in the screening room, watching for Josh, whom she waved over. "Hi," she said when she noticed we were with him. "You were at Hazelhurst House, right? And with Dr. Oliver the other night?"

I took the seat next to Josh. "Correct on both counts. I'm Molly. And this is Daisy. She catered the lecture at Hazelhurst House yesterday. Tea and Crumpets."

Amy nodded, recognition in her eyes. "So nice to meet you. I adore your scones."

Daisy looked pleased. "Thank you. Come by the tea shop anytime."

"Definitely," Amy said.

The lights flickered, signaling that the show was about to begin. People found seats or shuffled around in the ones they had, getting comfortable.

Sophie Verona rose from a seat in the front row and moved to the middle aisle to address the room. "Good afternoon, everyone. One of my favorite activities on a cold, rainy day is to curl up and watch movies. How about you?" The audience called out in agreement. "The first film today is almost exactly one hundred years old and it also has the distinction of being the second film to be adapted from Bram Stoker's book, as you will see in the credits."

She flipped through some notes. "Since *Nosferatu* was such an early, groundbreaking film, see if you can pick out elements and tropes that have become standard for the horror film genre. After this film, there will be a refreshments break and then we'll watch *Dracula*, the 1931 classic staring Bela Lugosi, who became synonymous with the character. He *was* Dracula, many feel. Note the differences and similarities between the two films and we'll discuss at the Headless Monk later."

"Where's that?" I whispered to Josh.

"Our local," he whispered back. "At the end of St. Aelred's Way."

"So sit back, relax, and prepare to be creeped out," Sophie concluded before returning to her seat.

The audience clapped and the house lights went down.

"Boo." Someone wearing a Guy Fawkes mask thrust their face into our row, from behind Josh and Amy. Amy gave a little scream.

The joker pushed up the mask. Wesley Wright, Thad's cousin and fellow student. "Heh-heh. Got you."

Amy slapped at Wesley's shoulder. "Cut it out."

Besides being startled by the sudden intrusion, I was shaken. Did Wesley not know that his cousin was killed by someone wearing one of those? Then my suspicious mind replied—perhaps he did know. Maybe he—

Flickering black-and-white images filled the screen, followed by a swell of music. I set my uneasy speculations aside to concentrate on the movie.

Here was genre element number one, the dramatically eerie sound of a pipe organ. The story of *Nosferatu* opened with a happy couple, Thomas and Ellen Hutter—replacements for Jonathan Harker and Mina Murray in Stoker's *Dracula*—but soon he was sent on a journey to a mysterious faraway land, Transylvania, to Count Dracula's—or in this case, Count Orlok's—castle.

Although the movie was silent, the actors and music conveyed the storyline with ease, occasional text filling in details.

The count's scary shadow, with his long fingers, was a classic, as were the tropes of the slavish henchman and beautiful woman in peril.

All of these weren't new to literature, of course. *The Fatal Folio* had many of these elements, including the ship on stormy seas and torturous journeys, as did other early gothic novels. Writing in the late 1800s, Bram Stoker had built on earlier works, as all authors did, consciously or not.

At the end, everyone clapped, then started shifting around in their seats.

"Want to stay for the next?" Daisy asked.

"Maybe." I stretched. "Not sure I'm up for a marathon."

People were getting up and sidling out of the seats, eager to take a break. "Why don't we decide after refreshments?" she suggested.

"Sounds good." I followed Josh and Amy out of the row, Daisy behind me.

In a group, we trooped up the aisle. Josh made his fingers into claws. "'Blood. Your precious blood,'" he quoted from the movie, swiping at Amy.

She laughed and ducked, then picked up the pace. "I'll be hearing that for a while, I'm guessing."

Behind us, Wesley put out both arms and got in on the act. "'The Master is here.'"

"Another classic line," I said. Every time I saw one of these movies, I wondered how and why grotesque "masters" attracted followers.

The refreshments were set out in another room and students were milling around inside there and in the hall. We got in line for the mulled cider and cinnamon donuts on offer. Wesley kept putting on his mask and tapping people on the shoulder, cracking up when he startled them.

"Looks like he's taking over for Thad," Josh murmured to Amy.

Amy frowned. "I sure hope not." She shuddered. "What a nightmare."

Josh shook his head. "You're telling me."

A few minutes later, donuts and hot cider finally in hand, we were chatting about the movie when a familiar figure came striding down the hall.

Detective Inspector Sean Ryan, with his sidekick Sergeant Adhikari right behind him. *Uh-oh.* Were they here to make an arrest?

They paused to confer, then Ryan came directly toward us, warrant card displayed. "Mr. Joshua Blake? Please come with us."

CHAPTER 10

"What's going on?" Josh asked, glancing around. "Am I under arrest?"

Amy's face had gone pale and she was shrinking back, almost hiding behind her boyfriend. "He didn't do it. He was with me." *Except when they were separated.*

A patient expression I recognized settled over Ryan's face. "We'd like to talk to you, Mr. Blake. Down at the station. We also have a warrant to search your room."

The other students around us had stopped talking and were listening. If I didn't understand that the police needed to use the element of surprise, I would resent Sean Ryan right now. This must be incredibly humiliating for Josh and Amy. One student in the corner even had his phone out and was recording the encounter.

Unless Josh had killed Thad, I reminded myself. Then he deserved much more than embarrassment.

"All right. Let's do this." Josh set his drink and donut on the closest table.

Detective Inspector Ryan didn't say we couldn't, so Amy, Daisy, and I trailed behind as they left the building and headed across the grounds to Josh's lodgings.

By the time we were halfway across the court, Amy

had begun to cry. "I can't believe this is happening. Josh isn't a killer."

"They must have some evidence," I said in a low voice. When she bristled, I added quickly, "I mean that Ryan gets his ducks in a row before he acts. He might be wrong at times, but he doesn't bully people. And he's fair."

Her lip curled. "Do you *know* him?"

I shrugged. "Sort of. We've run into each other before." I left out the part about him dating my mother. We'd stopped walking for a moment, watching as the officers escorted Josh along the path, one on each side of him. "Josh needs to get a good attorney. Right away."

Amy's eyes were wide. "Have you been in trouble, Molly?"

"No," Daisy snapped. "She's solved cases. Put the police right back on their heels, she did."

"Really?" The young woman tilted her head, regarding me speculatively. "Can you help Josh?"

Unless he's guilty. "I can try," I said. "After we see what's what."

We continued on, moving faster through the drizzle to catch up to Josh and the officers. Two other constables were waiting at the lodging entrance. Ryan showed Josh the search warrant and he nodded before handing over his key and then entering the code on the building entrance. The officers disappeared inside.

"Josh." Amy threw herself into his arms. "We need to get you an attorney."

He put his arms around her. "On it. I'll call my dad." He kissed the top of her head. "See you later, babe."

After he walked off toward the main gate, Amy began crying again. "This is unbelievable," she said, swiping at her eyes. She shuffled toward the building entrance. "Want to come in? I've got wine."

I glanced at Daisy, who nodded. "Sure. I could use a glass myself."

Amy keyed in the code and then held the door for us. Other than this sign of the modern age, the building was historic, everything Cambridge college lodgings should be. Mullioned windows. Carved woodwork. Wide sills to sit upon and read a book.

Each level had two rooms on the landing and Amy lived on the second floor. "Josh is across from me," she said, digging for her key. She pointed with her thumb. "Thad and Wesley are upstairs."

The door to Josh's room was open and we could hear the police walking around inside. She took a step in that direction. "I wonder what they're looking for."

I was dying to know as well but when she kept moving, I whispered, "Don't." They wouldn't appreciate her intrusion.

Of course she didn't listen. Pushing the door open a little more, she stood in the doorway. Naturally Daisy and I moved over so we could see inside as well.

Josh's room was quite spacious, consisting of a living area with sofa, chairs, and desk as well as a bedroom nook. One officer was looking under his bed while the other was rummaging through the closet. They didn't seem to notice us, they were so absorbed.

The officer at the closet pulled a jacket out, holding it by the collar with a gloved hand. "What do we have here?" It was black, with silver thread designs. "Come take a look."

Getting to his feet, the other officer crossed the carpet. When the first officer pointed something out on the front, he grunted. "Yep. That's blood, all right."

Blood? A thrill of shock raced up the back of my skull. Was that the jacket the killer had been wearing? Was Josh the killer?

"That's not his," Amy blurted. "Someone put that there."

The two officers spun around, comical expressions of surprise on their faces. "What are you doing here, miss?" one said.

Amy pivoted and ran for her room, pushing past us. "Quick, quick. Get inside." She thrust the key in the lock and pushed the door open. After we hurried inside, she darted around the door and slammed it, then turned the locks.

"I can't believe what we just saw." Amy stood leaning against the door, arms splayed out and shock on her face. "Josh did not kill Thad." She shook her head. "He doesn't even own a coat like that."

Was she in denial or had someone planted the evidence in Josh's room?

"Are you sure?" Daisy asked.

Amy's glance at her was full of contempt. "Positive. I spend more time in his room than mine. I know every item of clothing he owns."

Daisy put up her hands. "Sorry. Just asking."

Amy tossed her keys into a bowl. "I know. Don't mind me. This is all extremely upsetting." She gestured. "Have a seat and I'll get the wine."

As Daisy and I took seats on the brocade sofa, I glanced around in curiosity. Amy's room was laid out almost exactly like Josh's, decorated in a style that I called literary bohemian—antique furniture, silk shawls draped over chairbacks, peacock feathers, stacks of books, and posters from films like *Jane Eyre* and *Rebecca*. A moody painting of a castle hung over the tiny fireplace, which appeared unused.

"Can you tell I'm obsessed with the gothic?" Amy asked as she uncorked the wine. Her burst of anger seemed to have dissipated. "I'm especially interested in the concept of female agency in gothic novels."

"There isn't much, is there?" I ventured, thinking of the woman-in-peril trope that characterized most books in the genre.

"More than you might think." Amy filled three glasses with red wine. "Jane Eyre is the perfect example, with her determination to rise and her refusal to submit to bullies." She carefully carried two glasses over and handed them to us, then brought over her own, sitting across from us in an armchair.

"She saves Mr. Rochester," Daisy pointed out. "That was brave."

"Exactly." Amy took a swig of wine and grimaced. "What a rotten turn of events. I'm really worried about Josh." Her gaze fell on me. "Can you actually help?"

I shifted on the cushion, feeling put on the spot. Did I want to wade into this situation? "I can try," I finally said, swallowing my doubts with a slug of a pretty fair Merlot.

Amy edged forward in her chair. "Please do. I know he's innocent. Oh, I admit he hated Thad—well, we all did." She winced. "I know. Don't speak ill of the dead. He was horrible, though." A haunted expression flitted across her pretty features. "There was that time in the laundry room . . ."

I could imagine. "We don't need to go *there*, Amy. Why don't we focus on the facts of what happened the night Thad died. That's what the police will do." Although motives were fascinating and could point to possible guilt, the police had to build a case with hard evidence.

"What facts? Josh and I went to Bonfire Night together." She pressed her lips together. "I'll swear to it."

"But you were separated for a while," I reminded her gently. "I heard you and Josh mention that."

Amy scowled. "So?" She leaned forward. "We were apart maybe half an hour. In that time, Josh came back here, changed clothes, grabbed a knife, met up with Thad, and stabbed him? Then changed back and came to find me, cool as a cucumber?"

Put like that it did seem far-fetched. Perhaps Josh would be acquitted even with the bloodstained jacket working against him.

Or Amy was lying and the pair of them had worked together to kill their nemesis? This unpleasant thought reminded me to stay neutral. It wasn't wise to take a theory and run with it, to put blinders on when confronted with conflicting information.

I recalled what Josh had said to Amy right after Thad was killed, while they were walking across the green to their building. *I didn't have a choice. He wouldn't quit harassing you. Someone had to do something.*

"Maybe the jacket was planted in Josh's room," Daisy said. "To frame him."

"That's what I think," Amy said, her eyes lighting up.

When they both looked at me, I said, "It's possible. Who can get in the building? You have a code at the door, right?"

Amy shrugged. "They don't change it that often. Plus Josh has a hidden key. We all do. We all trust each other on this stair." She paused. "Well, we did."

I had a feeling that particular halcyon period was over. "It was the four of you in this section, right? You, Josh, Thad, and Wesley." She nodded. "I understand Thad was Wesley's cousin. Were they close?"

"Ha." Amy's expression was mocking. "No. More of a love-hate relationship."

This was interesting. "What do you mean?"

Amy kicked off her shoes before curling up in her chair. "Thad bullied Wesley all his life." She shrugged. "Thad had all the advantages, including a wealthy and titled family background. He was a year older and bigger and stronger. Wesley was his little servant, did whatever he wanted, whenever." She moved two fingers like legs running. "I'd hear Wesley going up and down the stairs day and night, fetching Thad food. Running errands. Et cetera and so on."

That sounded awful, abusive in fact. "Why did Wesley put up with it? Surely he could have gone to a different college, at least."

Amy's smile was knowing. "The Devine family has a long tradition at St. Aelred. They've been attending here since the place was founded, practically. Plus given tons of money. Thad's parents are helping pay for Wesley's tuition. How could he and his schoolteacher mum say no to an offer like that?"

How indeed? Had Wesley's cousinly affection turned to hatred? Maybe he'd wanted to get out from under Thad's thumb once and for all. Wesley was in his room when Thad was attacked—or so he said. With Josh and Amy out for the evening, he could have easily killed Thad without anyone noticing his movements. Thad wouldn't have been wary about meeting his cousin.

The mask. He'd worn one identical to the killer's tonight. Talk about a bold, in-your-face move. Maybe Wesley wasn't the malleable mouse everyone thought he was.

"What?" Daisy mouthed while Amy was turned the

other way. She knew me well enough to tell when the wheels were turning.

I gave her a tiny headshake as I mouthed back, "Later." I didn't want to theorize about Wesley in front of Amy.

"What do you think will happen now?" I asked. "With Wesley's tuition, I mean?"

Amy drank some wine, considering the question. "I predict"—she held up a finger—"Thad's parents will take Wesley even more closely under their wing and will lavish all their displaced parental affection upon him." She made a face. "Or what passes for such."

"They're not the best parents?" Daisy guessed.

"You could say that." Amy pursed her lips. "They sent Thad off to boarding school at age eight. That's where I think he learned to be a bully. Survival of the fittest, you know. Barbaric, isn't it?" She sniffed in disdain.

"The hunting lodge incident," Daisy said suddenly. "Was that the first attempt?"

Amy's expression sharpened. "You heard about that?"

"It made the newspapers," I said, not wanting to admit we had been cyber-sleuthing.

Amy finished her wine then uncoiled. "Want a refill? I do." She picked up the bottle and filled her glass, the liquid glugging. When she raised the bottle to us, we both shook our heads.

Drinking as she walked to lower the liquid level, she returned to her chair. "Where was I? Oh, yes, the hunting lodge incident. I was there."

Daisy and I exchanged glances. "Really?" I said. "Were you hunting?"

Amy shuddered. "Me, shooting birds? No way. I was in the lodge, sitting by the fire with the old aunties. Knitting.

Well, they were. I was drinking hot toddies. It was frigid in that place, I tell you. One sweetie told me I should have worn my woolies. Imagine that? Long woolen underwear."

I certainly could, having been raised in Vermont. "Was Josh at the lodge?"

Amy nodded. "He and I hadn't gotten together yet, so at that time, he and Thad were mates. I was there with Thad. Our final date." She gnawed at her lower lip. "Not that he agreed we should stop seeing each other." Her laugh was bitter and broken. "I was probably the first person to ever say no to him."

And his response had been that of a spoiled adult brat. Mindful of her pain, I didn't want to probe into his actions after the breakup. Then my pulse thumped with a realization. *She* also had motive and opportunity to kill Thad. And, even if she claimed to have been sitting inside during the shoot, she might have easily "gone for a walk" and taken a shot at Thad. Would she go so far as to implicate her boyfriend, though? That was the rub.

I glanced into my glass. We had seen her pour the wine. It had been a fresh bottle. *Paranoid, much?* A chronic uneasy suspicion was another unpleasant side effect of investigating murders. Which I didn't set out to do, ever. No, my involvement was the *hand of fate*. I snorted and my swallow of wine almost went up my nose.

"Are you okay?" Daisy asked.

"Fine. Just thinking about something I read."

Amy set her glass on a side table. "Hold on. I have an idea." She went over to the basket that held her keys and fished through the contents. Holding up a key, she said, "Want to go upstairs with me? To Thad's room?"

I wasn't going to say no. I did have to ask a question first, though. "Are the police finished with it?" Not a good idea to intrude upon a marked crime scene.

Amy unlocked her door and peered out. "Think so. The crime scene tape is down." She stepped into the hall for a moment. "The officers that were in Josh's room are gone, so the coast is clear."

Daisy pushed herself up out of the soft sofa. "What are you looking for up there?"

Amy tossed the key and caught it. "Thad had some things of mine. I want to get them back before his family comes and packs up." She made a face. "I don't fancy running into his parents."

I took a final sip of wine and stood as well. "That might be awkward, judging by what you've said."

"Definitely." Amy sighed as she led the way. "I suppose I'll have to go to the funeral. And I'll send flowers. Need to do the right thing."

As we approached the staircase, music with an eerie, hollow sound and monotone vocals began to blast from upstairs.

Daisy paused to listen. "'Promised Land.' Cold Cave."

Interesting choice, with its dark, post-punk mood. Being forced to listen to loud music at random times wasn't something I missed from dorm life, that was for sure.

"Thad loved that band," Amy said.

As we trudged up the stairs, the music was like a soundtrack for three women approaching the room of a slain man. Were we making a huge mistake?

Maybe so. Amy halted on the landing, hugging herself. Coming up behind her, I saw she was staring at an open doorway, the music pouring out in a crescendo of sound.

A quick glance to my left confirmed that the music wasn't coming from the room with a huge *W* hung on the door.

Who was inside a dead man's room?

CHAPTER 11

For a wild moment, I wondered if we'd been wrong. Maybe Thad wasn't dead after all. It had all been a huge mistake.

Amy clearly had the same thought. "Thad?" she asked, her voice rising. Then she shook her head and frowned. Squaring her shoulders, she marched forward and pushed the door open.

Daisy and I crowded through behind her.

The room was empty, a tablet on a desk and a speaker stack the source of the music. Amy stomped across the carpet and hit a couple of commands.

Blessed silence. She set the tablet down and looked over at us. "That was strange." She rolled her eyes. "The kind of thing Thad would do. He loved practical jokes."

Now that the music mystery was solved, sort of, I took a good look around. Thad's room was very similar to the others in layout and size but it was a royal mess. Clothing tossed everywhere, leaning stacks of books, a dozen mugs—clean—lined up on the windowsill.

"All the cleaner can do in here is tidy up and take care of garbage," Amy said. "Thad was a slob." She opened a bureau drawer. "Also a pack rat. So my cards are probably still here." She retrieved several greeting cards out of the drawer.

Thad's desk was heaped high, except for a space in the middle where a laptop probably sat. The police must have that. I wandered over to poke around while Daisy studied a bulletin board covered in clippings, photographs, and other bits and pieces.

On the floor near the waste can sat a stapled set of pages. I bent to pick it up. Above the title, "Retribution as Theme in the Victorian Gothic," someone had written in red pen: *You can do better.*

Amy was beside me, several envelopes in her hand. "Let me see that." After a moment, she said, "Huh. This is the same topic where he got an A, I'm pretty sure."

"They let you revise your work?" I was surprised since we didn't get many do-overs where I went to college.

"Not usually. I guess Dr. Verona had a soft spot for Thad." She tossed the paper on the desk. It hit another stack of papers, which then fell to the carpet in a cascade. "Great."

"I'll help you." I had to reach behind the desk for one elusive piece of paper, which turned out to be a spread-sheet. *Gothic Institute* and the year were typed in the heading. Below were rows of expenditures and numbers, some circled with question marks.

Amy took the page. "Oh yeah. Thad was the admin for the Institute. They might want this."

She started sorting through his desk, so I went over to stand beside Daisy at the bulletin board. "Busy guy," she greeted me.

I understood immediately. Half of the flyers on the board were for events at the college and around town—concerts, lectures, sporting events. The rest were pictures, tickets, and business cards, including one for Reginald

Dubold, Fine Books, which naturally jumped out at me. I wasn't familiar with Reginald, although Aunt Violet had relationships with many bookstores and dealers in the area. All over England, actually. Amy was sitting on the rug, looking through a stack of books. Every now and then she put one aside.

"Find my money yet?" a voice said in the doorway.

We all jumped. Amy dropped a book. "Wesley." She put a hand to her chest. "You scared me."

He sauntered into the room, hands in pockets, eyeing each of us in turn. "What are you doing in here?"

At the note of accusation in his voice, Amy flushed. I cringed, huddling closer to Daisy. As Thad's cousin, Wesley certainly had more rights here than we did.

Amy held up a book. "Retrieving my things. You know how Thad was—always borrowing, never returning." She glanced through the stack. "I think some of my most important titles are missing, which is a real pain. They're hard to find."

Sold to a bookstore? I snapped a picture of Dubold's business card for a possible follow-up.

Wesley sat at the desk and opened a drawer. "Yep. I should have warned you. Anything you gave him, you might as well consider gone."

"What was that about money?" I boldly asked. "Did he owe you?"

A wry smile twisted his lips. "I should have taken my own advice before I lent him over a thousand pounds. Never saw a dime of it, even after his allowance came in from Mummy." His tone was pure vinegar.

"Oh, Wesley," Amy said. "A thousand pounds? That's a lot."

"Most of my spending money for the term." Wesley opened then slammed a drawer, making the contents rattle.

"I suppose I'll have to hit up Aunt and Uncle for it. They probably won't believe me."

"Nothing in writing?" Amy asked sadly.

"Nothing in writing," Wesley confirmed. He leaned on the desktop, resting his head on his hand. I wanted to ask him if he'd set up the music but he looked too depressed. Maybe the intent had been to relive times with his cousin, play his favorite tunes.

He sat up abruptly. "Where's Josh?"

Amy set a fine edition of *Jane Eyre* on her stack. "You don't know? He's down at police headquarters being questioned. They also searched his room."

Wesley leaned back in the chair. "How did I miss all that?"

"I have no idea," Amy said. "They arrived while we were having refreshments after *Nosferatu* and dragged him away." For a moment, it looked like she would say more, probably a mention of the bloodstained jacket. Then she clamped her mouth shut.

"Really? They think Josh killed Thad?" Wesley's face was alight with some kind of emotion. It looked like relief to me.

"He couldn't have done it." Another book thumped. "We were together all night."

"That's not—" Now Wesley was the one clamping his mouth shut. He'd been with us when Josh and Amy admitted to being separated by the chaos after the firework went wild. For some reason, he'd thought twice about confronting her. Because we were here—or for another reason?

He began to swivel back and forth in the chair, drumming his palms on the desk. "How long are you going to be?"

Amy looked up. "A while. Why?"

Wesley shrugged. "I'm thinking about heading over to the Headless Monk to drown my sorrows. Maybe play a game of billiards. You probably want to wait here for Josh, though."

Amy picked up her phone and checked it. "I really should. I wonder how long he'll be there." She looked at me. "Any idea?"

"How would she know?" Wesley laughed.

"Molly solves mysteries," Amy said. "She's well acquainted with police procedure."

He regarded me from under his mop of curls, fingers tapping on the desk. "Seriously? Never would have guessed."

"My identity as a mild-mannered bookseller is a cover," I said, deadpan. "I'm really working on Her Majesty's service."

"No kidding," he squawked. Then he realized I was joking. "Very funny. So how long does an interrogation take?"

"Depends how much ground they need to cover," I said. And how strong a suspect someone was. "Hours sometimes." If Josh had a history with Thad, he could be there all night while they prodded and probed. The bloodstained jacket found in his room had only strengthened the case against him—at least for now. I hoped Josh had managed to retain an attorney. Not that Inspector Ryan wasn't scrupulous in his dealings. It was the smart thing to do, especially with that jacket showing up.

Amy pushed herself off the floor with a sigh. "Maybe we should go to the pub. I could use some distraction."

Daisy looked at me. I could go either way, although this was a good opportunity to get to know Amy and Wesley and perhaps pick up clues. That said, I was also ready to go home and enjoy another chapter of *The Fatal Folio*.

Before I'd decided, Amy said, "Coming, you two? I'll buy you a drink. The least I can do after you were so kind tonight."

"We didn't do anything special," Daisy protested.

Amy put a hand on her shoulder. "You were there for me. Believe me, I needed the support." After handing Wesley her stack of books, the cards tucked inside one, she ushered us out and locked the door.

⁕

With a claim of being the third-oldest pub in Cambridge, the Headless Monk was suitably picturesque. Tumble-down Tudor on the exterior, inside the front rooms were snug and wood paneled with wall sconces. As we walked in, a solitary man in a red leather booth lifted his head. Oliver.

He waved and we all veered in that direction. "Dr. Scott," Wesley said. "Fancy meeting you here." He smirked as he shrugged out of his jacket and hung it on a peg.

"Home away from home," Oliver said. He lifted his mug. "'Eat, drink, and love. The rest is not worth a nickel.'"

"Lord Byron," Wesley said. He pointed his forefingers like guns. "What can I get you, ladies?"

At Amy's urging, we decided on gin and tonics, then settled in the booth. Wesley could bring over a chair when he returned with the drinks. Amy went to help him.

"What have you been up to?" Oliver asked me. "Any progress on the Selwyn Scott mystery?" In contrast to his usual energetic and magnetic personality, Oliver seemed tired, almost depressed. He nodded at Daisy. "Nice to see you again."

"A little," I said. "I found several letters to his publisher in St. Aelred's collection. That's not the big news tonight, though." Amy and Wesley were busy at the bar so I hurriedly said, "The police took Josh down to the station for questioning. They also searched his room." I stopped there, again not wanting to talk about the jacket, which was surely a key piece of evidence.

Oliver reared back. "What? No."

"I'm afraid so," I said. "After that, we hung out with Amy for a while—she was quite upset—and then Wesley invited us out for a drink. So here we are."

He stared down into his mug, frowning. "I can't quite believe that Josh . . . Oh, he's got a temper when riled . . . but still."

"Did you hear about the shooting incident at the hunting lodge a couple of months ago?" I asked. "Thad was almost hit by a stray bullet."

Oliver looked incredulous. "No. What hunting lodge?"

"His family's. It made the papers," I said, bringing up the article on my phone and showing it to him.

He scanned the article, and I thought I saw his eyes flare when he read something. I didn't know quite how to ask about his reaction. Finally, I plunged in anyway. "Did something strike you about the incident?" I asked.

Handing me the phone, he shook his head. "It's nothing."

"What?" If I knew him better, I'd grab his sweater and shake him until he spilled.

He ran a hand through his hair, a gesture that reminded me of Kieran. "The hunting lodge is pretty close to Edinburgh. I was up there at a conference the same weekend, presenting on 'Setting in the English Novel.' The coincidence surprised me, that's all."

Amy and Wesley were still at the bar so I brought up the theft at Hazelhurst House. "Have you heard any news about the stolen manuscript?"

Oliver winced. "No. I feel so awful about it. A case of the best intentions paving the road to you know where. Sophie feels terrible too."

"Sophie? Why is that?"

"It was her idea originally. When we were discussing the event agenda the night before." Oliver shrugged. "Of course it's not *her* fault. I blame myself for talking Kieran and Aunt Asha into it." He looked even gloomier now and I regretted bringing up the subject.

His revelation opened up new possibilities. Maybe Sophie Verona *was* behind the theft. The timing would seem to eliminate Thad's involvement, but she might have discussed the manuscript with him before his death.

"Whose idea was it to hold your lecture at Hazelhurst?" I asked, knowing I was edging onto the thin ice of suggesting that the crime was premeditated.

Oliver immediately caught on, his eyes narrowing in suspicion. "I'm not sure." Still staring at me, he took a drink. "It was one of those brainstorms that seem to pop out of nowhere."

"On a happier note," I said, quickly changing the subject, "I found a mention of another Selwyn Scott manuscript in a letter from Selwyn to the publisher. What was it called, Daisy?"

"*Among the Ruins*," Daisy said, investing the title with drama. "Sounds like another gothic to me."

Oliver's eyes lit up. "I never knew there was a second book. How marvelous." He chuckled. "Rather remiss of me not to have read Selwyn's letters. I guess we Scotts took him for granted."

I sought out and cherished every scrap of information about my ancestors. Not everyone was like that, though.

"Here we are." Amy and Wesley arrived at the table, drink glasses in hand. She plopped one in front of me. Wesley gave Daisy hers and they sat, Amy next to Oliver, Wesley in a spare chair.

"To better days," Amy said, holding her glass aloft. We all clinked. A buzzing sound erupted from her pocket and she pulled out her phone. "And here we are already. Josh has been released, he's back at the college. No arrest and he's got a smashing attorney."

"That *is* good news," I said, relieved to have more time before an arrest was made. I wasn't convinced that Josh was guilty, despite the jacket. It appeared the police weren't either.

"I've got to go." Amy downed her drink in three gulps. "So much for savoring a quality G and T."

"Me too," Wesley said between slugs of beer. "I want to hear the update."

I did as well but there wasn't a graceful way to invite myself along. "Pass along our best wishes," I said. "Hope to see you again soon."

"I will." Amy slid out of the booth. "Are you going on the Gothic tour tomorrow night? I'm one of the docents."

"My friend George mentioned that," I said. "I'd love to tag along."

"Me too," Daisy said. "It sounds like fun."

They exited in a flurry. As the door shut behind them, Oliver said, "*Among the Ruins*, hmm? I hope we can find it. It would be quite the coup."

CHAPTER 12

After a chilly walk home to the bookshop, I was glad to see lights on. I'd sit with whoever was up for a while and unwind, I decided. Maybe make a sandwich, since I hadn't had dinner.

In the kitchen, Aunt Violet was in her armchair, knitting away on something soft and moss green. The two cats lay curled near the AGA, which released comforting warmth. "Hello, dear. How was your night out?"

As I unwound my scarf and unbuttoned my coat, I wondered where to begin. "Do you have a while? A lot's been going on." While I'd kept my aunt and mother updated, we hadn't had an opportunity to really hash things out.

"All the time you need." Aunt Violet paused her knitting to push up her eyeglasses. "I understand Sir Jon is now involved." She smiled. "That rascal is always up to his neck in something."

I turned the flame on under the kettle. "He sure is. Sean Ryan too."

Mum appeared in the doorway, dressed in her robe and slippers. "I thought I heard voices."

"Tell the truth, Mum," I joked. "It was Sean Ryan's name that lured you."

"Oh, go on with you." Mum bustled over to the cupboard and pulled out a tin. "Shortbread?" She opened the tin and held it out to me.

I bit into the crumbly, buttery biscuit. "Who wants cocoa?"

Soon we all held mugs, the shortbread tin going around a couple of times. I took Aunt Violet and Mum through the events of the evening, then recapped all that had happened so far, including the murder, the hunting accident in Scotland, and the theft of *The Fatal Folio*.

"My goodness, that's a lot to happen in a few days," Aunt Violet said, blue eyes round behind her glasses. "Well, except for the hunting accident, of course. I think it's related, though, don't you?"

"It's a strong possibility." Picking up my phone, I brought up the picture of Reginald Dubold's business card. "Do you know this dealer? Thad Devine had his card."

"He's a bit dodgy." Aunt Violet's expression went sour. "I was almost stung once, after your uncle Tom died. He handled many of our more valuable sales. Reginald tried to sell me something with a dubious provenance. Thankfully Sir Jon, who was my mentor at the time, stopped me from making a serious mistake."

"So he's on Sir Jon's radar, then." I wondered if Reginald would be a stop on the investigation into the stolen manuscript. "I wonder why Thad had his card. There are certainly plenty of reputable bookdealers in Cambridge, including us."

"He talks a good game," Aunt Violet said. "Besides, Thad's transaction might have totally been aboveboard. Not everything Reginald does is crooked. He'd be in jail."

Despite the shortbread, my belly was really rumbling

now. I got up and made a ham-and-cheese sandwich on homemade bread with mayonnaise and mustard, pickles on the side.

"How's the cataloguing job going?" Aunt Violet asked.

"Really well," I said between bites. "Now that I've gotten started. Oh, by the way, here's something else new and exciting. Selwyn Scott wrote another book." I told them how we'd found the reference to *Among the Ruins* and that Kieran and I were going to search for it. I'd notified him by text and he was very excited.

"Wouldn't that be a find," Mum said, her eyes glowing. "I can't wait to read it."

"Me either." I hoped that we would have the opportunity. "Speaking of Selwyn Scott, would you like me to read you a bedtime story?"

They both wanted to listen, so, after running upstairs to retrieve the book and catching them up on the story so far, I began.

The Fatal Folio, cont.

Traveling through the mountains above Turin soon proved to be the most arduous part of our journey to buy The Ramblings of a Monk. *The road was narrow, rocky, and in some places, almost nonexistent. On one side precipitous slopes rose, on the other, a sheer drop to the valley below.*

In contrast, a carriage ride across France into Italy seemed a dream of comfort despite the long days and uncomfortable nights. We had only one day in Paris to my disappointment, and I extracted a promise from Mr. Coates that we would linger there on the return trip. I encouraged his greed by suggesting that we might purchase other books from the nobleman's library and sell them in Paris to recoup the expense of our travels.

As one might guess, our forced closeness as traveling companions had not improved my impression of Mr. Coates. He was rude and demanding, treating innkeepers, carriage drivers, and serving maids and lads with utter disdain, as if he were the Earl of Mercia already. Though it must be noted, in my experience those of truly noble demeanor are considerate to all. I was forced to tip from my own meager resources to help mitigate his deplorable behavior. He was not savvy enough to realize that we are dependent upon these so-called inferiors, our very lives held in their hands.

Now, for instance, as the horses strained to pull our carriage over the pass. Only the skill of the driver kept us steady and safe on this treacherous route.

Finally we achieved the height of land and the driver paused. "There is your destination," he said, pointing his whip. "Malvagio. We will reach the village before dark."

Malvagio was merely a cluster of houses with one church tower and a larger villa on a rise outside the town. Tumbled ruins near the villa must be that of the monastery once home to the cloistered religious who had penned The Ramblings of a Monk. *We had seen many such towns in our travels. Although remote and out of the mainstream of human commerce, they were picturesque in their own way.*

Perhaps it was only my fancy, suffering as I was from exhaustion and frayed nerves, but a deep foreboding struck me at the sight of our destination.

There was nothing obvious to arouse such uneasiness. As I said, Malvagio was exactly like dozens of other small Italian villages.

Why then, as the driver clucked at the horses and the carriage began to descend, was I blanketed with an overwhelming sense of dread? It was as though something dark and monstrous lurked behind the sunshine and blue skies, the red-tiled roofs set among green foothills.

By the time we rolled into the center of the village, where a fountain burbled and old men sat and gossiped, I had convinced myself that my imagination was overwrought. Here, in the square, all appeared docile and domestic, with women carrying baskets of produce and bread or hanging out laundry. Children shouted and ran, their high-pitched voices echoing among the narrow streets.

The coach rumbled to a stop in front of an inn. Mr. Coates hoped the Duke would offer us rooms but, hating to presume, we had booked here, in this pleasant-looking building with windows that opened to the square.

The coachman unloaded our luggage as a tall, ungainly man came out to assist us. He picked up our bags under both arms and carried them off without a word.

"I hope we see them again," Coates jested. He turned to the coachman. "Thank you for your service. Can we stand you a meal and a night's lodging?" Coates spoke a rough sort of Italian, as did I. Enough to get along.

The man shook his head. "I'd better be off," he said, peering up at the sky. "Dark will soon be upon us and I want to get over the pass." With a tip of his hat and a bow, he was up in the seat again and soon the horses were clattering away over the cobblestones. There goes our link to the wider world, I couldn't help but think.

Weary, we trudged up the hotel steps and entered the lobby. Here a squint-eyed gentleman sat behind a large reception desk. "Good afternoon. Signore Coates and Signore . . . Marlboro?"

"That's us," Mr. Coates said. He bellied up to the desk and got us signed in. After the business was concluded, he said, "We'd like to freshen up and then pay the Duke a visit. How do you recommend we travel to the villa?"

The innkeeper almost dropped his pen. "The Duke? What business do you have with him?"

Mr. Coates scowled. "That is of no concern to you, my good sir." He tapped on the counter. "Please do answer my question."

The man's eyes darted back and forth. "You must approach on foot," he finally said. "You won't find a carriage or a cart to take you. Not from this village."

My companion's mouth dropped open and I must confess that I was equally flabbergasted by the innkeeper's assertion. What reason could the villagers possibly have for refusing transport to the villa? Surely, as a feudal lord of sorts, the Duke would expect the villagers to take care of his visitors.

"It wasn't always that way," the innkeeper said as though guessing my thoughts. His eyes shifted about again. "Only of late, after recent events."

"This is an odd turn of affairs," Mr. Coates said, turning to me. "Perhaps we can hire horses." He

addressed the innkeeper again. "There is a stable with horses for hire?"

The man nodded. "There is. I will direct you when you are ready to go."

Despite being weary and travel-stained, we were soon upon our way again after a quick washing up and change of attire. The stable was easily found, and two able steeds were supplied. Mr. Coates, who had a more subtle mind than I gave him credit for, told the livery that we were taking a ride in the countryside. There was no mention of the villa or our purpose there.

"It's odd, is it not," I said as the horses ambled up the dusty road into the countryside, "for the villagers to have such an aversion to their better?"

Mr. Coates shrugged. "Perhaps he is a harsh master. That's not of any importance to us. I plan to purchase the book and be on our way tomorrow. There is no point in lingering." After a moment, he amended that. "Unless he does have other interesting volumes to peruse, as you suggested."

"We won't know until we ask." My heart lifted at the thought that the Duke might have taken ownership of additional gems from the monastery library. Such religious orders often housed marvelous collections, including ancient illustrated manuscripts and rare and arcane tomes. In light of this possibility, I had come prepared to make purchases. Such opportunities did not come along very often.

The road wound up the mountainside, providing vistas of the valley and the peaks beyond. Flowering shrubs and scented herbs lined our way, the *fragrances familiar but unidentifiable to my un-trained senses.*

Mr. Coates appeared blind to the beauty sur-rounding us, keeping his gaze fixed on the road ahead and urging his mount along whenever the poor beast faltered.

"What a place," he said, scoffing. "Talk about primitive." He gestured toward the village huddled below. "Did you see how they all stared at us?" He puffed out his chest. "They aren't used to people of refinement, that much is obvious."

I held my tongue, not wanting to admit that I found the place charming if rustic. The people were kind although reserved, and I was eager to see if Italian cuisine lived up to its reputation. There was much to be said for a simple meal beautifully pre-pared.

The road finally leveled out, and we approached the villa through an allée of pointed cypress trees. Walls surrounded the grounds with a tall ironwork gate providing access. This stood open.

Inside the gate, we dismounted, staring up at the elegant house. Several stories high, it had arched windows, a tower at one end, and a set of hobnailed double doors. The walls were the pale plaster so common in this land and the roof was tiled in red.

Our footsteps crunched as we crossed a gravel forecourt. Nothing else stirred, the only sound the whisper of a fountain nearby.

Neither Coates nor I spoke as we ascended the broad, shallow steps to the front door. A bell rope hung to one side and he pulled hard. The bell sounded faintly.

Again he tugged on the rope, making the bell peal.

Both of us were becoming perturbed at this lack of response when finally the door creaked open. A young woman, her long black hair unbound, dressed in a white flowing gown, stood in the doorway. "Can I help you?" she asked in the local dialect. In contrast to the inelegant tongue, something about her spoke of fine breeding. This was no servant.

Mr. Coates took off his hat and bowed low. "We are here to see the Duke. We have an appointment. Mr. Coates and Mr. Marlboro."

She put a hand to her mouth, her gleaming eyes wide. "I am so sorry to have to tell you this. The Duke—my father—is dead."

CHAPTER 13

Sunshine glinted on the windows of Hazelhurst House as I approached via the winding drive. The storms of yesterday had been swept away by a strong wind and bare tree limbs danced and swayed.

What a gig. Working in the manor library was a position right out of a novel. I even had the brooding—yet kind—hero, Kieran. I pictured him dressed like Lord Byron, all tumbling curls, cravat, and fitted suit jacket. *Yum.*

Lady Asha had said I could park in the courtyard, so I drove across the former drawbridge and took a spot next to the estate Land Rover.

Imagining myself wearing an empire-waist Regency gown, I gathered my laptop and messenger bag and did my best to sweep up the steps. I'd also been told to let myself in, so I did, juggling my belongings and trying to feel like I wasn't intruding.

The entrance hall was deserted, the silence broken by the sound of distant vacuuming. What a job it must be to keep this place clean and in good repair. Although Lady Asha had cleaners, gardeners, and a cook, she did quite a lot herself.

In the library, I dropped my things on my usual table and flicked on the lights. All seemed as I had last seen it, except the broken cabinet was gone. I wondered if the police were examining it for clues, although I hadn't seen so much as a fingerprint on it. Whoever stole the manuscript was clearly smart enough to wear gloves.

Once my laptop was booted up and ready to go, I went over to the bookshelves to pull books for the next set of entries. I was working my way methodically from left to right, top to bottom, also using a numbering system to identify the shelves. My orderly librarian brain ached at this state of affairs, but we needed to be practical. Reorganizing by classification and alphabetically would be a huge job. With my system, imperfect as it was, they could quickly find a book without searching.

I worked for the next hour or two, developing an efficient rhythm despite the temptation to stop and savor. I promised myself that once the cataloguing was done, I would revisit my favorites and really enjoy them. I would also give Kieran and his family a tour of the highlights, I decided. They probably didn't even know what they had.

"Knock, knock." Lady Asha stood in the doorway. "I hope I'm not interrupting."

I finished an entry. "At a good stopping place, actually."

"Want tea? I've made a pot."

"Sure. I'd love a cup." I got up from my seat and stretched. As always, I felt a little nervous around Lady Asha. Not only was she stunning, brilliant, and titled, she was Kieran's mother. I wanted to make a good impression and, at the same time, not humiliate myself somehow.

We took tea in the small sitting room. Beside the brew, there was a plate of mini scones—cinnamon, blueberry, and apple.

"You can't eat just one," Lady Asha quipped, choosing a cinnamon scone. "This size is guilt-free."

"They're delicious." I took a nibble of an apple scone, not wanting to appear greedy.

"Graham likes the apple ones too," Lady Asha said, referring to her husband.

"How is he?" I asked tentatively. I hadn't seen him lately.

She made a face. "Good days and bad days." She sighed. "Struggles with the new medication."

"I'm sorry to hear that." Although my own father had died of cancer, I didn't want to delve into the topic too deeply. I didn't know if she'd welcome it.

"We'll get there," she said briskly. "Now tell me, how's it going in the library?"

"Very well, so far." I briefly went over my cataloguing rationale and gave an update on how many titles were now in the system. "You've got some incredible editions. It's a real pleasure to do this job for you."

"It's a pleasure to have you here." Lady Asha refilled our cups with hot tea.

A brief silence fell and I racked my brain for something to say. "Did Kieran tell you? I found a reference to a second Selwyn Scott book."

"No." Lady Asha's mouth opened. "He didn't. Not yet."

I found the image of Selwyn's letter on my phone and showed it to her. "See the reference to *Among the Ruins*? It was never published. That I can find, anyway. Perhaps the manuscript is still here somewhere."

"This is exciting," Lady Asha said. "Shall we start looking?"

"Right now, you mean?" I said. "I'd love to, of course, except I should continue work on the catalogue."

She waved her hand. "There's no deadline. Besides, if we find it, I'd like Thomas Marlowe to help us get it printed. You can be our publisher."

Now there was a carrot. Established publishers had advantages, namely existing distribution channels and relationships. But with a title this high profile, we'd have no problem getting publicity or selling books.

"We'll produce a beautiful limited edition and then more of a mass-market printing so everyone can afford a copy. Plus ebooks," she went on.

"It sounds like you've given this a lot of thought," I said.

Lady Asha took another scone. "I've already been thinking about a reprint of *The Fatal Folio*. It's in the public domain so anyone can publish it. Our edition would be special, though, with illustrations and family history." She smiled. "Which is why we want to find out who Selwyn Scott is."

"What a fantastic idea," I said. "I'm sure the media outlets will be all over it."

"I think so too." She made a face. "We'll give them something besides our personal lives to talk about." She took a bite of scone. "I'm earmarking the money for maintenance of this place. It's a real money pit."

I could imagine. "Another great idea, finding a new source of income to support your ancestral home." Discovering a copy of *Among the Ruins* would not only further boost interest in *The Fatal Folio*, it could double the revenue potential.

The ice broken, we chatted about this and that the rest of teatime. Then we returned to the library, where Lady Asha unlocked the big closet.

"I'm always finding something new in here," she said. "It's far from organized."

Since Kieran had first shown me the closet, I'd been dying to poke around. For me, old documents were like messages from the past, clues to former lives. In this case, we were looking for information about a specific person—Selwyn Scott.

"I'm glad they kept so much," I said as Lady Asha turned on the light. "Most people throw things away as they go."

She laughed. "You should see the attic. It's enormous and packed to the rafters."

I would love to. Had I said that out loud? Hopefully not. I didn't know Lady Asha well enough yet to say such a thing. "Where do we begin?" I asked instead.

"With that." Lady Asha pointed to a large, arched trunk in the far corner of the room. "I've always been reluctant to look inside." She gave a dramatic shudder. "It's the exact right size for a body, don't you think?"

Seriously? Then I saw the smile behind her hand. "That's my department," I said, stepping boldly forward. "I'm the one who stumbles upon murders."

I caught a glimpse of her startled expression and hid my own smile as I bent to fling open the lid, which wasn't locked.

To my relief, instead of gleaming bones, the trunk contained a heap of old dusty magazines and newspapers. Lady Asha joined me as I peered inside, reaching for the one on top. "It's a penny dreadful," I said with delight. These lurid illustrated publications were a forerunner of comic books. Then, as now, readers were entertained with wild tales of adventure, mystery, and horror.

The date was 1839 and the color cover showed a woman holding a candle creeping down a stone staircase, looming shadows illustrating the horrors waiting below. "*Terror in the Crypt,*" I read aloud. "By . . . no, yes it is. *Selwyn Scott.*"

Lady Asha looked stunned and I was pretty sure I did too, the way my mouth was hanging open. "I had no idea," she murmured, reaching for the magazine.

I gently handed it over, mindful of the crumbling paper. "A lot of authors wrote for these," I said, dredging my memory banks. "Mary Elizabeth Braddon, who wrote *Lady Audley's Secret*, for one." That juicy novel had been a bestseller in its day.

Lady Asha was already engrossed in the tale. Rather than interrupt, I sat on the floor beside the trunk and began to sort the contents. Plenty of penny dreadfuls and other publications of the day, many of which would be of interest to academics. Maybe the Scotts would consider donating these to a library or having them digitized at least.

I arranged them by title and then by date, with the oldest on top. My plan was to look through the magazines for other Selwyn Scott stories. We could have them reprinted, perhaps, either with the novels or in a separate edition.

"We should hire someone else to help you," Lady Asha said, still reading *Terror in the Crypt*. "The cataloguing job keeps growing."

"Not only cataloguing but maybe digitizing some of these." I patted the pile. "It would be a great student project. Then you could either donate or store the hard copies."

"Donate," Lady Asha said. "Except for copies with Selwyn's stories. Excuse me for a few." She wandered out of the closet, penny dreadful in hand.

I couldn't blame her. Selwyn's writing was engrossing. I continued to sort, forcing myself not to start glancing through the publications. My favorite features in vintage magazines included the advertising, which revealed social attitudes, and the fashion plates, and I knew if I started to look through them I'd be caught up for hours.

Once finished, I carried the half dozen penny dreadfuls containing a Selwyn Scott story out to the library, leaving the others in their neat stacks. They'd be all right there for now. I placed the magazines on the table next to my laptop.

Lady Asha was still reading. "Sorry, Molly," she mumbled. "I'm almost done."

"No problem. I have a request." Once she looked up, I said, "I'd like to look through the receipts and ledgers for any transactions involving Thomas Marlowe. I'm trying to see if there is a connection between Selwyn and the bookshop. The main character is a bookseller in *The Fatal Folio*. Marlboro is very similar to Marlowe."

"It is." She nodded. "Go ahead. Look through anything you like." Her smile was rueful. "Sorry to bail on you."

"No problem. I adore poking around in old papers."

"I'll make lunch," she called as I went back into my cave. "Text if you need anything."

I patted my pocket to confirm I had my phone. "Will do," I called back.

The ledger books were in their own section, along with boxes containing receipts. If some of the slips were for books, they would give us the ability to reconstruct when acquisitions were added to the Hazelhurst House library.

A small desk and chair had been placed in the closet, which maybe at one time had functioned as an office. After finding ledgers with the right span of years, I sat down with those and the boxes of receipts. My plan was to make a quick scan of the entries and then cross-reference the paperwork if I could find it. The receipts were very faded with the elaborate penmanship of the day. Hard to read, in other words.

The ledgers contained entries regarding the estate, including money in and money out. Sales of livestock. Payment of wages. These were fascinating in their own right, a snapshot of daily life in that time.

My heart leaped. Here it was, Thomas Marlowe, with a sum. Someone had bought a book from my ancestors. Rather than stop and search after every entry, I took a picture. Once I had a few, I'd make a stab at finding the receipts. There might be a "sold to" noted.

The door to the library shut with a sudden slam, making me jump in my chair. A draft? These old houses were full of them.

Not liking the door shut, I got up to open it.

I twisted the knob back and forth. The door wouldn't move. I turned hard and pulled with all my strength. Still nothing.

Was I locked in?

How could that happen? The lock required a key.

Annoyed and puzzled, I went over to the desk and picked up my phone.

I blinked. No bars. *Figures.* Holding the phone high, I paced around the closet room, trying to get a signal.

Still nothing. I sent a text anyway. *Locked in closet. Send help.*

Sending . . . sending. With a growl of frustration, I exited my messages. Sooner or later, Lady Asha would come looking for me. Right? Hopefully before I starved to death.

I was in the far corner of the room now, and behind a set of shelves set slightly away from the wall, I spotted another door.

Here we go. I could exit that way. No rescue needed.

Squeezing behind the shelf, I examined the door to

see which way it opened. Outward, which meant I didn't have to try to move the shelves first.

The next test. Was it also locked?

I turned the knob and was rewarded when the door readily opened, releasing a gust of cool, stale air. Taking a cautious step forward into the darkness, I switched on the phone flashlight.

A flight of winding stairs rose ahead of me.

My heart skipped a beat. Having read many a book featuring a mysterious old mansion full of secrets, I adored exploring. What would I find up those stairs?

Normally I wouldn't poke around on my own, of course, without permission from the family. But right now I had no choice. Well, besides waiting in the closet for someone to unlock the door.

Nah. I nudged through the door and checked out the steps. Chiseled from stone, they were in fairly good condition. Reviewing my mental map of the manor, I realized they must lead to one of the towers, part of the original manor. Like many buildings of the era, the house had started as a stone keep and then was expanded with wings here and there.

Holding the phone in front of me, I slowly ascended the staircase. After an interval, I noticed an arched bricked-up section. There used to be a window there, I guessed.

On I went, my little light beaming through the darkness. The steps ended at a tall but narrow wooden door, arched like the window casing. My pulse leaped. What was behind that door?

If I were in a gothic novel, it would be something horrific. Or a curse would strike me once I entered.

Fortunately, I was Molly Kimball, bookseller living in the twenty-first century.

I twisted the knob.

Light from two windows flooded a small, circular room furnished with a desk with carved legs and matching chair and a green velvet chaise longue. An ornate gold inkstand sat on the desk and a single piece of paper covered with handwriting was sitting on the leather blotter.

Who had used this room, with its beautiful sweeping views of the countryside, as their writing garret? I couldn't help but think it was a perfect place to pen novels.

Holding my breath, I moved to the desk and picked up the page. *Among the Ruins, Chapter Twelve.* Text followed, scratched out in places, other additions on the side.

I was almost certain that Selwyn Scott had worked in this room. Did it hold clues to the author's identity?

CHAPTER 14

My phone bleeped with a text, a very modern intrusion into this atmospheric nook. I sat on the chaise longue to read, immediately raising a huge cloud of dust. Ugh. I hopped back up.

Where are you? Kieran.

I'm in a tower room off the library.

???

He didn't know about this room? I started to write back before realizing it was ridiculous and called him instead.

"Molly. Where did you go? I'm in the closet and you're not there."

"Someone locked me in. I didn't have service so I tried to find another way out."

"I know. Mum got the text."

"Go to the back right-hand corner and look behind the shelf." Footsteps and shuffling noises informed me that he was following my instructions.

"Up these stairs?" His voice echoed.

"Yes. Haven't you been in there before?"

"No." Footsteps. "We weren't allowed to mess around in the closet, in case we destroyed anything important. Not that we wanted to, anyway. Old papers didn't interest us."

The footsteps grew louder as he continued upward. I went to the landing to wait, grinning as I shut the door partway behind me. I wanted him to experience the same wonder and surprise that I had earlier.

He appeared around the last bend, his face turned up toward me. "There you are."

"Here I am." I couldn't hold back a giggle of glee. "I didn't know you were coming out here today."

"I wasn't. I ended up delivering bicycles in the village so decided to pop by and see you."

"I'm glad you did." I was still blocking the door and he gestured in confusion. "Hold on. You're going to love it." I stepped back as I opened the door. "Ta-da."

Kieran walked inside, head swiveling as he took in the room. "Wow. Talk about untouched by time."

"Sure looks that way." I darted over to the desk. "And guess what?" I held up the page. "Selwyn Scott wrote this. It isn't too much of a stretch to think that this was his or her writing room."

He came to stand beside me. "This is from the new book." He glanced around. "Where's the rest of it?"

"Not here." The desk didn't have any drawers and I didn't see anywhere else a manuscript could be concealed.

Still holding the page, he said, "I hope someone didn't discard it." He nodded toward the fireplace. "Or burn it."

"I pray they didn't," I said, groaning. Where could the book be? Hazelhurst House was huge and we might never find it.

Kieran carefully set the paper on the desk, in the approximate position it had rested. "We should document everything. In case we're right about Selwyn using this room."

"Good idea." I started snapping photos of the room. "By the way, I wonder who locked me in the closet?"

"About that," Kieran said. "When I tried the door, it wasn't locked."

I lowered my phone. "You're kidding. It certainly was when I tried it. In fact, it shut by itself first. I thought it was a draft." A thought occurred to me. "Was the key in the lock?"

Kieran's eyes widened. "Actually, yes. I thought Mum had left it there."

She might have. I hadn't noticed. "Could it have been the cleaner?" Maybe they had closed the door and locked it, then thought better of it afterward, once they realized that I was inside.

He shrugged. "Possibly. They already left or I'd ask."

On second thought, the cleaner doing it by accident didn't sit quite right with me. For one thing, the light inside was on, which anyone would have noticed. Had I panicked and imagined that the door was locked? Maybe it had a tendency to stick.

"It was probably all in my head," I mumbled. "I've been reading too many gothic novels. What must your mother think of me?"

Kieran patted me on the shoulder. "Don't worry about it." He gestured around, grinning. "Besides, something good came out of it. We found Selwyn Scott's lair. We think."

"True." Excitement renewed, I started toward the door. "I can't wait to show her these pictures. Oh, and guess what? Your mother and I discovered some Selwyn Scott stories in the penny dreadfuls we dug out of a trunk."

"Awesome. You'll have to show me." He switched on his phone flashlight and led the way down the stairs.

As I followed, I did resolve one thing. Next time I worked alone in the closet, the door would be propped open with a chair. Imaginary situation or not, I didn't want to experience that trapped, helpless feeling again.

After a long and productive afternoon of cataloguing, I arrived at the bookshop in time for tea. Once I'd shared my updates, including Lady Asha's exciting idea to reprint Selwyn Scott's fiction, the three of us read another chapter of *The Fatal Folio*. This time Mum did the honors. I sipped tea and listened, transported to nineteenth-century Italy, where the death of the Duke of Malvagio had just been announced to the main characters.

The Fatal Folio, cont.

"Dead? What do you mean he's dead?" Mr. Coates practically shouted, his fists clenched in frustration. "I've come all this way . . . he can't be dead." To my alarm, I noticed that his complexion was turning an ugly crimson, as if he were about to have a fit.

"Sir," I said, putting a restraining hand on his sleeve. "Control yourself. This young woman is grieving her father." I bowed to her and said, "I am most sorry to hear of your loss, signorina. Please accept our condolences. We have come a great distance to see your esteemed father on a matter of business. Perhaps we may discuss that with you?"

She nodded and, with a cautious glance at Mr. Coates, said, "Would you like to come in? You must be fatigued after your journey."

As we followed her into the villa, I whispered, "Flies with honey, old man." He sent me a glare but refrained from arguing.

We had entered a magnificent entrance hall with marble floors, a sweeping staircase, and arched doorways. Paintings in gilded frames and ancient tapestries hung on the walls along with a display of medieval weapons.

Our hostess showed us to a salon located through an archway. Here elegant groupings of furniture stood around, placed on priceless carpets from the Orient. "I will fetch refreshments," she said in her musical voice. "Please have a seat."

She swept from the room and we perched on a sofa near the fireplace to wait.

Mr. Coates took inventory of the room. "What a fine place," he said. "Such rare and exquisite furnishings."

"Indeed." I cleared my throat. "After we stay long enough to be polite, I think we should take our leave. The situation is an incredible disappointment to be sure, but perhaps we can make up for it with a sojourn in Paris. We will find a suitable gift for your uncle there."

Mr. Coates scowled. "Nay. Who is to say we cannot still purchase the book?" A crafty look came into his eyes. "Perhaps we can bargain a better price with the lass."

That offended me, since I prided myself on fair dealings. Not that I ever turned down a bargain, no, that would be foolish. However, I refused to enter into deceptive transactions. "We must pay the price agreed. Taking advantage of a young woman in her grief would be despicable." He didn't look convinced so I added, "It would also dishonor your uncle. Would he be happy if he knew you had counted the cost of his gift?"

The frown still lingered but I could tell he was coming around to my way of thinking. "Perhaps a generous offer will conclude the business swiftly."

"That's my man," I said with hearty approval. "I for one am eager to see home again." I thought of my little shop with longing, my days puttering around the shelves filled with the utmost contentment and joy. The wanderlust that had sometimes plagued me had been well and truly quenched by this ordeal abroad.

The young woman swept into the room again, followed by a manservant carrying a tray. She directed him to place it on a low table near us.

Two pitchers sat on the tray, one of water, the other of wine. When she looked at me, I said, "Water first, please, and then wine." The dusty ride had made me thirsty.

Mr. Coates requested the same, and we chatted about inconsequential pleasantries while we sipped a very fine vintage from the villa vineyard. The young woman's name was Estella Vitucci, we learned, and she was the only child of Octavius Vitucci, the Duke of Malvagio.

It must be a lonely life for such a young, vital person, I guessed, especially now. Mr. Coates, in his bumbling way, inquired about her marriage prospects and the disposition of the property. She was betrothed, she said, to a young man from Milan. He had been detained on business but would soon arrive. The slight frown that creased her forehead indicated to me that perhaps this betrothal wasn't to her liking.

Mr. Coates noticed her expression too, and I could see the greed in his eyes. Not only was Estella comely and intelligent, she was an heiress. I hid a sigh behind my wineglass, hoping I wouldn't have to rein him in from committing a grave social faux pas. First he wanted to cheat the heiress and then, the next moment, snatch her up for himself.

Before I accepted another such commission, I resolved, I would investigate the character of my buyer more carefully. No amount of money was worth the aggravation of spending much time with an unpleasant man like Mr. Coates.

Even the opportunity to view a rare book like The Ramblings of a Monk wasn't enough compensation. So far, the book hadn't come up in our conversation and I decided to go ahead and broach it. The sooner we knew if it was available to us, the sooner we could depart this remote outpost.

"Signorina?" I said gently. "As we mentioned, we had arranged to see your dear, departed papa on business. We hoped to purchase a book from him."

Her brows rose. "A book? Papa had a very fine collection. It was his passion, you see, to locate and obtain rare volumes."

This sounded promising. Rather than hone in on one book, I said, "Would it be possible to view the library? I'm a bookseller by trade, you see, and my patrons have empowered me to make purchases on their behalf." I laughed, hoping to lighten the mood.

"We are all book lovers, you see, and cherish the opportunity to care for rare editions."

"Papa would have enjoyed your visit," she declared, her face lighting up. "He liked nothing better than discussing the books in his collection, not only their history and condition but the contents as well." She drew herself up with pride. "He was a very learned man, often sought for his opinions and judgments."

"I regret we did not have a chance to meet," I said with sincerity. "He sounds like a wonderful man."

Impatient, Mr. Coates shifted beside me. When he opened his mouth to speak, to no doubt urge Estella to show us the library, I quickly said, "This vintage is excellent, is it not? What do you think, Mr. Coates?" I couldn't allow him to trample upon my delicate negotiations with ill-considered remarks. He had the subtlety of a wild boar.

He stared at his glass as if he had forgotten he was holding it. "Er, yes, Mr. Marlboro, it is excellent. Haven't had such fine wine in ages."

I inquired about the vineyard operation and other aspects of the estate, all questions designed to put our hostess at ease. Then, once my glass was empty, I placed it on the table. "Is this a good time to view the library?"

She immediately stood, smoothing her skirts. "Absolutely. This way, gentlemen."

We crossed the entrance hall and went down another corridor to reach the library. This room was also large and finely proportioned, with arched windows overlooking a formal garden. Despite these attractions, our attention went immediately to the bookshelves. Set in arched alcoves trimmed with wooden columns, they filled the other three walls of the room, save for the interruption of a fireplace.

My senses immediately sharpened, nostrils flaring at the familiar and beloved aroma of ink, aged paper, and calfskin. A quick scan of the spines informed me that this was indeed a well curated and spectacular collection.

"I could spend months in here," I said, quickly adding, "Not that I'm proposing any such thing."

Estella laughed. "As I said, my father would have enjoyed meeting you." She gestured toward the shelves. "In your communication with him, was there a particular title that you were seeking? I have not attempted to sift through his correspondence yet."

"All in good time," I said in a soothing voice. "It hasn't been long, I assume."

She shook her head. "Only a week." A look of distress twisted her fine features. "He was here, in the library, when he was stricken. It was so sudden, he barely had time to cry out."

"What a terrible thing. Again, I'm so sorry." An ailment of the heart, perhaps? That is not so unusual in a man of middle years.

Estella moved forward, toward a large desk set to one side of the fireplace. "He was sitting there." She pointed to the chair, which sat askew. "And he was reading that book. I haven't been able to force myself to touch a thing."

Trailing behind her, we also approached the scene of the Duke's passing. Mr. Coates, who was slightly ahead of me, gave a strangled cry.

"Mr. Coates," I murmured in reproof. Then my gaze fell upon the book the Duke had been reading. The Ramblings of a Monk, *also known as* The Fatal Folio.

The rumors I'd dismissed so readily immediately came to mind. Many an owner of the book died after it came into their possession. Now it appeared that the Duke of Malvagio had been added to that unfortunate company.

CHAPTER 15

George and Daisy showed up around six and we set off to St. Aelred for the Gothic tour. As we strolled through the streets, I told them about my day at Hazelhurst House.

"I wish I'd been there," Daisy said wistfully. "I'd love to find a secret room."

George chuckled. "Where Molly goes, adventure follows."

"It does seem that way," I said ruefully. "Believe me, I'm not looking for it."

"Have you figured out Selwyn Scott's identity yet?" Daisy asked.

I made a scoffing sound. "Not even close. All we have is bits and pieces that don't quite fit together."

"Who are the possible authors?" George asked.

"Agatha Scott and her children, Samuel and Frances Scott," I said. "They lived at Hazelhurst House when the book was written."

"Can you use the handwriting in the letter to the publisher to identify the author?" Daisy asked.

The obvious struck me. "Yes, I can. We found a page of *Among the Ruins*. I'll compare that." I wanted to stop right then and make the comparison, using the images in my phone. "How much time do we have?"

"Not much," Daisy said. "We might be late as it is."

I groaned. "Okay, I'll wait." If we hadn't been hoping to learn more about Thad's murder, I would have canceled. As we continued on, I said, "That library is a real trove. I'm hoping to find some bills of sale from Thomas Marlowe, to find out which books came from our store. That's another pet project of mine."

"They have paperwork from two hundred years ago?" George sounded amazed. "Bloody unbelievable. I keep mine long as the taxman says then out it goes, shredded."

"I know," I said with a laugh. "The Scotts never threw anything out, apparently. Lady Asha said the attic is stuffed to the gills."

"Ah, the attic," Daisy said. "I'd love to poke around in there."

"Me too," I said. "But I'd better stick to the library until that task is finished. Otherwise I'll be there all winter." Not that it would be a hardship, but I didn't want to strain my budding relationship with Lady Asha by being underfoot too long.

The tour group had gathered inside the main gate at St. Aelred. We joined the clusters of twos and threes waiting for the event to begin.

Daisy nudged me and I turned to see Amy approaching, dressed in a long black dress, shawl, and mob cap. Josh was beside her, wearing a Victorian men's suit and carrying a lantern on a pole.

"Love the costumes," someone called out.

Amy sketched a curtsey. "Good evening, my fine ladies and gents. On behalf of the Gothic Literature Institute, let me welcome you to St. Aelred College, where our tour begins." She pulled her skirt up a few inches to display laced boots. "I hope you're wearing appropriate footwear, because we're going to hoof it around town."

"We're ready," someone else said. "Lead on."

"Come with me," Amy said, whirling around. "Our first stop is here, in the main court."

She led us along the path to the center, where a slender campanile stood. As we approached, the bell gonged, three sonorous tones that made goose bumps rise. Once the echoes died away, Amy said, "We are very lucky tonight to hear the monk's bell ring. Or are we? It is said that the bell foretells a death."

A shiver went down my spine. Right before we'd found Thad lying wounded in the lane, I'd heard the bell. Daisy nudged me, her brows raised. She remembered it too.

"Take a step back with me to the sixteenth century, to the Priory of St. Aelred, founded in 1291. King Henry VIII is on the throne and he's made it his mission to dissolve every single monastery, order, and convent throughout England. Anyone who refused to take the Oath of Supremacy was killed, hence the Headless Monk we all know and love." People chuckled, getting the reference to the local pub. "A beloved monk named Brother Selwyn was one of the rebels, and he too met his death despite the many good works he did in the community. It is said that the bell rang three times at the moment of his death. That is the origin of this legend."

I wondered if the pen name Selwyn Scott was inspired by the brave monk. It was a possibility, especially given the family's connection to the college.

Amy allowed the audience a moment to absorb the story and stare at the bell tower before herding us toward the gate. "Our next stop is the fine chapel at King's College, built in the Perpendicular Gothic style. Along the way, we'll look for gargoyles."

Chatting quietly, the group exited through the gate, Josh's bobbing lantern leading the way. We paused at

St. John's to peer up at stone gargoyles perched high above.

"The word *gargoyle* comes from the French word gargouille, which means *throat*," Amy said. "An obvious reference to their function of diverting water away from buildings through their mouths. There's more to the story, however. The legend of Gargouille, the dragon." Now that she had had our attention, she went on. "This fierce creature was terrorizing people along the Seine, stealing their cattle and dining on livestock and humans alike. Then Saint Romain got on the case. He used his cross to subdue the dragon and led it back to Rouen, where it was killed and its head mounted on the church wall as a warning. So gargoyles have more than one function: diverting both rainwater and evil spirits."

"This is fascinating so far," Daisy said as we walked on.

"Totally. Amy is doing a good job." I was impressed with her confidence and style as well as her depth of knowledge.

George had his head tilted, searching out more gargoyles. "So many people don't bother to look up. Miss a lot that way."

With its two towers, multiple spires, and vast stained glass windows, King's College Chapel was one of the most magnificent buildings in historic Cambridge. Amy had arranged for us to go inside and as we trooped through the doors, an awed hush fell over the group. One of the finest fan-vault ceilings in the world arched eighty feet overhead, and twelve huge stained glass windows lined each wall, with even larger windows at the ends.

Amy pointed out a few key Gothic features and then allowed us to wander around and take everything in. Josh was standing by himself so I went over to say hello.

"How are you doing?" I asked, curious about his interview with the police. He hadn't been arrested, which was telling, especially in light of the jacket being found in his room. I also wondered if Amy had told him about requesting my help.

"Hanging in there," Josh said with a sigh. "Going downtown was quite the trip, I tell you." He rolled his eyes.

Amy came over, sliding her arm through his. "Why don't we have a drink at the Headless after the tour? Josh can fill you in on everything." She gave me a meaningful look. "Molly thinks you were framed too."

Not exactly. Yes, it was a possibility, but I had to keep an open mind. Rather than go into all that here, I said, "I'd love to. I'm with friends, so let me see what they're up to first."

"They're cool, right?" Josh inquired. "Bring them along."

"I'll ask them, thanks." For someone under suspicion of murder, Josh was surprisingly open. A sign of a clear conscience, or someone who didn't understand the ways of the world? Either way, I wasn't going to turn down the invitation.

Amy glanced at the cell phone tucked in her skirt pocket. "Time to move on." She strode away, clapping her hands to get everyone's attention.

We filed out of the chapel, back into the street. "Next stop, Little St. Mary's Lane," Amy said. "The most haunted spot in Cambridge."

"Ooh, that sounds interesting," I said.

As it turned out, the stories Amy told about the area were the interesting part, including the legend of a demon dog, Black Shuck, that was the inspiration for Sir Conan Doyle's *The Hound of the Baskervilles*. The lane itself was a tiny passageway lined with buildings and then with a fenced open space filled with tall trees and overgrown ivy. Wind rustled the branches, sending stray dead leaves blowing across the alley.

Daisy gave a little yelp, gripping my arm and pointing. "Someone's out there."

A hooded figure stood under a tree, barely discernable in the shadows. Something about the way they were watching us so intently was unnerving.

"It's the headless monk," George, not so easily spooked, cracked. "Look everyone, we have a visitor."

The person burst into action, pumping their arms as they ran through the garden toward a bordering street.

"Good job, George," I said, laughing.

Up ahead, Amy waved her arm for attention. "I have a special treat for us. We're going to punt back to the beginning of the tour."

People began chattering, exclaiming with relief at not having to walk all that distance. Amy herded us a block or so, where we all clambered aboard the flat boats. Daisy, George, and I were in the last punt, along with Josh and his lantern.

"I've got it easy," our punt chauffeur said as he poled us away from the dock. The other punts were carrying twelve passengers.

Something about him looked familiar. "Fergus?" I inquired.

"That's me." He gave a start. "Molly? How have you been? Staying out of trouble?"

"Not exactly," I said. I'd met Fergus during my first case here in Cambridge.

After he guided us out into the main current, he said, "I see you've been dating Kieran Scott." Humor in his

voice as he added, "Vermont lovely." That was one of
the tabloids' pet names for me. It was better than "rustic
beauty."

I groaned. Who didn't know, thanks to those intrusive
photographers? "Yes, we're quite happy."

"Glad to hear it." Fergus fell silent, concentrating on
poling us along the river.

At night, the Backs were lovely, glowing windows in
the buildings we passed, a waxing moon and stars above.
Aged trees leaned toward the water like courtiers waving us on. Water lapped against the banks and at times,
footsteps tapped on the walking paths. Except for the
distant hum of traffic and the glow of a phone screen in a
punt ahead, this could be any time in the past five hundred
years.

I sighed and leaned back against my seat, allowing all
that had troubled me to drift away for a few minutes.

"This is so peaceful," Daisy said, slumped beside me.
"I must get Tim to come out with me sometime." A cool
breeze gusted across the water, raising ripples and goose
bumps. "In the spring."

"Give me a shout whenever," Fergus said. "I'll give you
my card."

Daisy shared a smile with me at the chauffeur's slightly
forward offer. I still had Fergus's card somewhere, from
our first encounter. I supposed he was like a taxi driver,
with loyal clientele.

"Ah, young love," George said. At first I thought he was
referring to Daisy and Tim, but then I realized what he
was talking about.

A couple stood entwined under a streetlamp, kissing.
Both tall, dressed in wool jackets and jeans but bare-
headed, one fair, one dark.

As they pulled apart, I recognized them with a start of surprise. Oliver Scott and Sophie Verona. Colleagues, rivals, and, apparently, involved romantically.

I glanced at Josh, who knew them both quite well. He was watching with raised brows, his lips pursed as though to whistle. "Is that news to you?" I asked quietly.

"Uh-huh," he said. "Thought they couldn't stand each other."

It wouldn't be the first time that dislike had disguised feelings of attraction. Then another thought struck suspicious old me. Maybe their disdain was an act, to hide more than their involvement, which as professional peers shouldn't be a problem. Or was it, at a traditional college like St. Aelred? Although, if there was a policy against staff relationships, kissing in public certainly wasn't very discreet. Anyone could have seen them together tonight.

The punt moved on, leaving the couple behind in the dusk. Seeing the city from this vantage point really was enjoyable. We passed King's College, viewing the chapel from a different angle. Maybe it was an obvious choice, but the chapel was one of my favorite buildings, I decided.

Soon after, Fergus docked to let us out. Between the four of us, we put together a generous tip. "Text me anytime," he called cheerfully as we walked away.

The rest of the group dispersed and Amy came over to us. "I'm ready to hit the pub, that's for sure."

I turned to Daisy and George. "Want to get a nightcap at the Headless with Josh and Amy?"

"I'm in," George said. "Bit of a thirst on me."

"If you two are going, count me in," Daisy said.

We set off, walking abreast while Amy and Josh led the way, chatting about various details of the tour to each other.

"What was your favorite part?" Daisy asked.

"Well, the chapel," I said. "I was also fascinated by the story about Brother Selwyn."

"It's nice to know who your headless monks are," George said. "Poor chap. We'll have to have a drink for him."

Daisy and I laughed. "I never thought of it quite like that," she said.

We soon reached the pub, Josh holding the door open for us to enter. Inside, it was another quiet night, a fire crackling cheerfully in the hearth. We sat in the same booth and George offered to buy the first round.

"I really enjoyed the tour, Amy," I said. "I learned so much." Daisy chimed in with agreement.

Amy looked pleased. "I suggested a tour to the planning committee. Then of course I got assigned to put it on. You know how that goes."

"Oliver and Sophie run the Institute?" I asked, wanting to learn more about the organization. Thad had done the books, I remembered Amy saying.

"It's their baby," she said. "This is the third year. They're hoping we can hold it in Paris next year. Make it international. Draw speakers and attendees from all over Europe."

"Paris?" Daisy exclaimed. "That sounds awesome."

Amy nodded. "It would be. Sophie has been working on sponsors. This year she got some sizable donations, Thad said."

George returned from the bar, tray in hand. He deftly dispensed the pints and half-pints of Monk's Bitter, a signature house beer.

"I'd be bitter too," Josh said, raising his glass, "if someone cut off my head."

The rest of us followed suit, clinking glasses before taking the first swallow of the hoppy brew.

"So, Josh," I said, wiping foam off my upper lip. "If you still feel like it, fill me in."

He took another long swig before lifting his mug again. "Here's to an experience I never want to repeat." He tapped the table. "As you know, they took me down to the station for questioning. I was like, what are you talking about? I had nothing to do with Thad's death. I wasn't anywhere near him that night."

Amy moved closer to Josh, until her shoulder touched his. "Sure, we were separated after the tent caught on fire. There wasn't time to run back here and kill Thad, then go find me at the common."

"That's what I told them." Josh shook his head. "But . . . they found out about the knife."

I gasped, as did Daisy. George, who was somewhat out of the loop, took it all in as he sipped beer. "What about the knife?" I asked.

Josh's shoulders rose almost to his ears and he definitely looked sheepish. "I took a dare to steal the knife without getting caught."

"The knife from the dining hall?" I was mentally rearranging all I knew.

"That's the one." Josh traced a wet ring on the table with his finger. "We were always giving each other ridiculous dares. Loser had to buy the other one drinks."

"So . . . you took the knife. Where did it go after that?"

Josh's gaze met mine and though I searched for any sign of deceit in his gaze, I found only sincerity. "I gave it to Thad. The other half of the dare was putting it back."

"The *other* half?" I echoed. "Who came up with the dare?"

"Wesley," Josh and Amy said at the same time. "While we were eating dinner the other night," Josh said. "I made the mistake of saying how much I liked the knife. It really is a nice specimen of silverwork. Next thing I know, he's suggesting I steal it. And that Thad put it back."

"That was really risky, lad," George said. "Wouldn't you be in big trouble if you were caught?"

"Probably," Josh said. "Not Thad. He got away with everything. Yeah, it was really stupid of me. I would have had to convince the head that it was a prank, which it was."

I returned to the crucial point. "Thad had the knife. Was he in the habit of carrying it around?" Maybe it had been on his person and the killer had found it.

Josh snorted. "I don't think so. If he was taking it back to the dining hall, what was he doing outside the gate?"

That was the question. Had the killer stolen it from Thad's room? As Amy told us, they all had keys to each other's rooms.

"Who else knew about it?" I asked. I doubted that someone had rummaged through Thad's room looking for a murder weapon. That was about the only detail I felt pretty confident about.

Josh and Amy looked at each other. "We both did. Wesley. Oh, maybe Dr. Scott. Remember he was sitting close to us in the library, Amy, when we were talking about the dare? We didn't notice him at first."

Amy leaned away. "Yeah, I do. You don't think *he* did it? Seriously?"

Josh's expression was troubled. "I hate to even think it. I really like Dr. Scott. Remember what Thad told us? That he was filing a complaint against him?" To us, he said, "We tried to get him not to do it. But Thad was determined. He said he deserved an A and he was angry about getting a C."

I didn't reveal that I'd overheard Oliver's thoughts about Thad and that he'd shared the situation with me and

Kieran. Although I could defuse their suspicions by revealing that Oliver hoped to create a second career as an author, it wouldn't be a good idea to spill those beans. The last thing he needed was for the news to get back to the head of school before he was prepared to resign.

"Did he actually file it?" Daisy asked. "Or was it just a threat to get his grade raised?" I was curious about that myself.

Josh and Amy shrugged. "Haven't heard anything," Josh said. His brow creased with a scowl. "There's one person who's in the middle of all this." He paused and we all looked at him. "Wesley. He must have ratted me out to the police. I bet he left that jacket in my room to really seal my fate."

"You think *Wesley* killed Thad?" Amy asked. Her gaze grew thoughtful. "It does add up. He roped you two into stealing the knife, and he has access to your room, to slip the jacket in there."

Josh's fists clenched as he half rose out of his seat. "I have half a mind to go find the little weasel and beat the truth out of him. What a rotten thing to do."

"Whoa, whoa," George said, hands up. "Hold on, lad. Don't go making things worse. You don't need an assault charge."

Amy put a hand on Josh's shoulder and pushed him down. "He's right, Josh. They didn't arrest you, which means to me they're not satisfied that you did it. Putting the jacket in your room didn't work."

Wesley had now moved into first place as a suspect in my mind. However, wary of glib theories that later fell apart, I asked, "Who else has been in your rooms? Other friends? Staff?" Thad's murder seemed personal so I really didn't think one of the porters or room attendants had done it. We needed to be thorough, though.

"A few friends," Amy said. "No one that important." She thought for a moment longer. "Dr. Scott. He came to talk to Thad once. Oh, and so did Dr. Verona."

"Is that unusual?" I asked. "For professors to visit students?"

Josh grinned. "Depends." Amy elbowed him. "Ouch. I didn't mean anything by that. Just kidding."

Amy glared. "Well, it's not funny. Don't forget, Thad worked for the Institute. They probably had meetings related to that."

Or not. What a cozy little group they all were.

Josh sipped his ale, a contemplative expression on his face. "Would Dr. Verona and Thad have been meeting early in the a.m.?" He winced away from the vicinity of Amy's elbow. "Just asking for a friend."

"How early?" Amy asked, her tone suspicious.

He rolled his lips together. "Um, six a.m., maybe? I was getting ready to go for a run when I saw her go down the stairs. Saw her when I opened my door."

"What did she say?" Amy sounded aghast.

Josh shrugged. "Nothing. I waited until she was gone before leaving my room. Wanted to give her a little space, you know what I mean."

We knew what he meant. The possibility of Sophie Verona being involved romantically with Thad, a postgrad student, certainly added another layer to the situation. In my mind, Sophie moved to stand beside Wesley as the prime suspect.

CHAPTER 16

The Fatal Folio, cont.

"Isn't this book beautiful?" To my horror, Estella had picked up the fatal tome and was now smoothing the leather cover. As she touched the calfskin, it seemed to grow lighter, less stained and scuffed. Embossed motifs I hadn't noticed caught the light, a design of flowering vines twining along the edges.

I blinked away this illusion, horror growing as she began to open the cover. "Stop. Don't do that." I rushed to her side, prepared to wrest the book from her hands.

"What are you doing, Mr. Marlboro?" Mr. Coates asked. "I'm sure the signorina knows how to handle a fine book without your intervention."

"It's not that—" I broke off, unable to articulate my sudden panic, the certainty that the book itself was dangerous to any who touched it. What madness was this? Surely a result of the long, fraught journey and the shock of the Duke's death.

Estella was now seated in the Duke's chair, the

book open in front of her. She gave a delightful little gurgling laugh. "This book is wonderful. I can see why Papa was so enamored of it. He had to travel quite a distance to buy it, you know, even though it was written in the monastery here. Before all the monks died that year."

She said this so blithely, as if the demise of holy men all at once was not a matter of curiosity if not concern. "What happened to the monks?" I asked.

Her shrug was pretty, as were all her gestures. "Some sort of pox? All I know is that it went through the monastery with great speed. Ever since I was a child, we've been warned not to poke around the ruins. The air is said to be contaminated."

I exchanged a glance with Mr. Coates. This tale had to be a fable, to keep the children away from where they might fall or otherwise get hurt. If I had the opportunity, I would like to visit the ruins. Such exploration was a hobby of mine, especially sites of ancient origin and historic interest.

Estella began leafing through the book, the pages rustling and the gilded edges catching the light. I hadn't noticed the gilding before.

Stopping to read, she smiled, her eyes glowing. Now I doubted that she would even want to sell this book. Mr. Coates would have to find another gift for his esteemed uncle.

Mr. Coates moved to stand beside her. "Can I look on? I've been curious about this book for years."

Like a child might, she frowned up at him and hid the book against her bosom. "No, you may not. Papa said this book speaks to each reader. Sharing it with someone will only dilute the experience."

Although I was also curious to see what the book contained, I said, "Let her be, Mr. Coates. We are strangers, after all." To reassure Estella, I added, "But gentlemen. And as such, we must withdraw. Please let us know by tomorrow if you wish to sell the book or any other in the collection. We cannot linger in your country long, lovely as it may be."

To my surprise, she appeared disappointed. "You must leave me already? I have planned a delicious dinner for you. We rarely have guests, you see, especially since Papa died." She closed the book and placed it on the blotter before hopping up. "Please, look through the shelves. I am sure you will find something to your liking." She set her face in resolute lines. "I cannot promise to sell everything but I will entertain offers. Papa fortunately left a ledger with notes about each book and its value."

My guess, after dealing with many clients, was that she needed the money. It was a crafty move on her part to let us know her father had a good grasp of what the books were worth. Other dealers without as much integrity would probably try to take advantage of the young woman. I refused to behave in such an underhanded way, which is why my reputation was sterling and above reproach.

"We would be most happy to join you for dinner," Mr. Coates said with a bow. "I know that Mr. Marlboro is always looking for special editions for his patrons. I myself have other interests too. Thank you for your kind offer to browse the shelves." He sent me a greedy look of glee, barely refraining from rubbing his hands together. I *would need to disabuse him of the notions he obviously held about our hostess and her naiveté.*

⁕

The notion of a book that tailored itself to each reader stayed with me all morning while I updated the inventory for Thomas Marlowe. I was taking a day off from the cataloguing to catch up on tasks in the shop. Kieran and I were meeting for lunch in his apartment, which I was looking forward to. It felt like ages since we'd spent time together alone.

Tim was behind the counter in the bike shop when I arrived. "He's already gone up," he said, pointing to the ceiling.

"Thanks." I moved closer to the counter to ask, "How are you?" I hadn't seen much of Tim lately either.

"Fine, thanks." He continued to sort through slips as we talked. "Daisy told me about the tour you went on. I'll have to catch that next time."

"I think she has plans for you and her in a punt," I said, teasing. A nearby rack of jackets caught my eye and I began leafing through them. As I thought, they were the same brand the presumed killer had been wearing—the person we saw running down St. Aelred's Way.

"Those are very popular," Tim said. "We just got that shipment in. Second order this fall."

"Do you know who bought the last bunch?" I asked. "Their names, I mean."

His head came up. "What do you mean?"

"Remember the runner we saw that night?" I didn't have to elaborate. I held up one of the coats. "They were wearing this brand." My finger traced the silver design. "I noticed this. It's very distinctive."

Tim shook his head. "I see where you're going, but those jackets are sold all over the city. Not to mention online. There must be dozens, if not hundreds, around."

I backed up slightly. "*Can* you get a list of who bought them? Is it possible, I mean?"

He held up a slip. "I suppose so. We note the date, customer name, and what they bought on these slips. Kind of redundant because the point of sale also records the inventory number, which is what we use to reorder. The customer isn't logged in the computer, though, hence why they get a slip." Now he grabbed a fistful of the yellow pages. "It would be quite a task, looking through all these. Or cross-referencing them to the system entries, which we could do."

"I get that." I hung the jacket up again. "Did Daisy tell you the police confiscated a jacket like this from a student's room?"

"Uh-huh. I heard all about it." Tim's brow creased. "I hope you two are being careful. They haven't made an arrest yet so the killer is still out there."

"Of course we are." Kieran was waiting for me, so I probably should get going. I started toward the door.

Tim's words halted me. "I've been giving that night a lot of thought," he said. "The trainers the runner was wearing? I think I know the brand."

"Really? I was focused on that creepy mask and the jacket." I hadn't even looked at the runner's feet.

"I always notice shoes. Before coming here, I worked in a sporting goods store that sold a lot of high-end trainers." Tim picked up his phone and began searching. "I'm pretty sure they were wearing these."

I went over the counter to get a better look at the image. The shoes were bright orange and very pricey. "Men's or women's?"

"Both," he said. "Unfortunately. That *would* narrow it down some."

"You should tell Inspector Ryan," I said. "I'm sure they're grasping for any clue to narrow down the suspects."

He set the phone on the counter. "What if I'm wrong?"

"Let them figure it out. I know they'll be grateful to hear from you." I took out my own phone and sent him a text. "There. You've got his number now, so no excuse."

"Yes, ma'am," he said, eyes twinkling.

"Did that sound bossy? Sorry." I waved as I headed toward the exit. "Talk to you later."

Up in his flat, Kieran was at the stove, stirring something in a pot when I let myself in. "Molly. Good to see you."

I crossed the room for a kiss. "Good to see you too." I peered into the pan. "What is that? It smells great."

"Potato leek soup." He beamed with pride. "First time making my nana's recipe."

"Yum. Potato anything is a hit with me." I took a seat at the table, which was already set, and poured myself a glass of water. "How's your day going?"

"Very well, thanks." He threw me a look. "Even better now."

For a moment our eyes locked and then he gave a start. "Oops." He checked the flame. "I don't want this to burn." He tested the soup with a spoon. "It's definitely hot enough."

"Yes, it is," I murmured before laughing at my corny joke, as did he. I liked the fact that we could be lovey-dovey and joke about it too.

He ladled soup into bowls, pointed to fresh slices of bread and a dish of butter on a board, and we dove in.

"Delicious," I said as I scooped up the last morsel,

wishing I could lick my bowl like a child. Leeks made potato soup taste even better.

"There's more," he said. "Let me get it for you." He served us both second helpings. After we finished the soup, he put out a plate of bite-size brownies and made coffee in a French press. Mugs in hand, we settled on the sofa.

"What's new?" he asked. "Anything with the case?"

"Where to begin?" Sipping coffee, I organized my thoughts. Then I remembered the publisher's letter and the manuscript page. Despite the incredible temptation to compare them, I'd forced myself to wait until Kieran and I were together.

"Hang on," I said, getting out my phone. "Let's look at handwriting samples." He leaned close, watching as I lined up the two images.

One glance was all we needed. "They're not the same," I said, depressed. "See how these letters are rolling and round while the manuscript page is more spiky and cramped?"

"I sure do," he said, sounding equally disappointed. "What does this mean? Any ideas?"

"Um . . . maybe Selwyn had an assistant. That person might have handled correspondence."

"Even if they were the same, we still wouldn't know who Selwyn was," Kieran pointed out. "We need something with his or her real name to compare."

"Good point." With a sigh, I put my phone aside. "Back to our present-day mystery." I told him about the tour the previous evening, including chatting with Josh and Amy at the Headless Monk pub, and, finally, Tim's shoe clue.

"Do you think Oliver did it?" he asked, his voice pained.

I hastily thought over what I'd shared. Had something I said implicated Oliver? Not in particular, I decided, although, to be honest, he was still on the list of suspects. He had motive and opportunity and perhaps access to the weapon. He'd visited Thad, according to Josh and Amy.

"Why do you say that?" Like a coward, I dodged the question. "Does he have orange shoes?"

"I have no idea." He stared into his mug. "Don't get me wrong. I really can't imagine Oliver being violent. He has trouble killing houseflies. That night, though . . . it was dodgy the way he didn't show up for dinner. Not like him to stand me up. Then yesterday, he . . ." His voice trailed off.

"He what?" I prodded when he didn't continue.

Kieran looked miserable. "He told me that Thad did file a complaint with Dr. Cutler, requesting a review of how Oliver is grading papers."

"Does that matter now? Thad is—" I heard myself and stopped.

"Dead. I know." Kieran's smile was wan. "He's still being asked to explain why he graded Thad the way he did. In the interests of being thorough, Dr. Cutler said."

That sounded horribly unfair. I thought of something else. "Oliver isn't the only professor Thad was difficult with. I saw some scathing notes from Dr. Verona on a paper he wrote. According to Amy, he rewrote the paper and got a higher grade."

"I bet Oliver refused to let him do a rewrite," Kieran said. "You should pass that along to Oliver. It might help his defense."

"Secondhand information? Maybe. Besides, he probably knows all about it, since he's seeing Sophie. I saw them together on the banks of the river. Last night, while we were in the punt."

"What?" Kieran gave a little yelp. "He hasn't said

anything to me. And in fact, I gave him plenty of opportunity, when we were talking about—"

"What?" I teased, although I could guess. I leaned over, landing against his shoulder. "About me, by chance?"

Kieran blushed, which was adorable. "I want to assure you that I don't gossip about us or share anything too personal."

I hooted with laughter. "I didn't think you do. It's perfectly normal to talk about your relationship with a close friend or relative." I snuggled closer. "I talk to Daisy all the time about us."

"Really?" He kissed my nose, smiling. "What do you say?"

I put my coffee down before it could spill. "That you're totally fabulous and I"—*Oops. Don't go there*—"really like you."

His mug joined mine on the table. "I really like you too."

The next hour or so was a wonderful interlude on a cold November afternoon. Kieran and I should meet for lunch more often, I decided.

"Molly." Aunt Violet's tone was brisk as she paused while shelving a book.

My shoulders lifted in a cringe as I anticipated her questioning me about my late return from lunch. Aunt Violet was due to leave for an appointment, I remembered.

"I'm sorry—Kieran and I, well . . . we got hung up."

She flapped her hand. "No matter. I wanted to tell you that you have a visitor." She nodded toward the red upholstered chair tucked between two bookshelves, my favorite seat in the shop.

Amy waved. "Hey, Molly." She sat with her laptop open, and, to my amusement, I saw that Puck was lying along the chairback and Clarence was sprawled across her shoes.

"I see you've met the welcoming committee," I said.

"They're adorable. Such fun to have shop cats." She struggled to rise, trapped by Clarence's heft. Puck reached out a paw and tangled it in her curly hair. "Ouch."

"Come on, boys. Let her up."

With a glare in my direction, Clarence rolled off her shoes and slunk off. Once Amy was up, Puck slid down to the seat. He began to wash, as if that had been his plan all along. They truly were incorrigible.

Amy closed her slim laptop and slid it into a case. "I'm looking for particular editions. Novels, mostly. I thought you might be able to help."

"That's right up our alley," I said, walking toward the desk. "We'll check the inventory first to see if we have copies." Amy could have asked Aunt Violet or Mum to help. The fact she'd waited for me was flattering, as if we were becoming friends.

I opened the point of sale system, which let me search. "Go ahead, shoot. Title and author."

Amy put her bag on the ledge then leaned forward on her elbows. "Remember when we were in Thad's room? I couldn't find all of my books?"

"I do." I waited, fingers poised to type. "I don't recall offhand which titles." Come to think of it, she hadn't mentioned specific books.

Licking her lips, she hesitated. "Um, I'm not quite sure how to say this."

"When you're ready." I had an inkling where this was going and found myself bristling in anticipation, which I did my best to hide.

She began fiddling with a rack of business cards. "I might as well come right out with it." She paused. "Did he sell you anything lately?"

"I can find out." I knew he hadn't because I'd never heard of Thad Devine until the day I met Oliver, but it didn't hurt to be thorough. "I'll search the system." We paid vendors by check, so if he had sold us books, he should be in there. A few keystrokes later, I shook my head. "We did not buy any books from Thad."

"You're sure?" She looked both relieved and disappointed.

"Positive. We don't pay cash. Well, unless we're at a flea market, maybe." We kept a small fund around for those impulsive purchases, which often paid off.

"Want me to look for copies?" I asked. "Hopefully you can replace those titles."

She groaned. "I guess so. Hopefully I'll be able to afford to buy them. They weren't cheap the first time."

That really was a drag, especially if she'd lent books to a friend. That's why I rarely ever did. Never got them back, most of the time.

"How's this? Give me the titles and all the details you can remember. I'll search around and see what I can turn up. Then, if you want to buy, I can handle that."

"Sounds like a plan." Amy pulled out her laptop. "I'm going to check the bibliography on one of my papers."

I found a lined pad and a pen, ready to take notes. If the books weren't in Thad's room, where were they? "Excuse me for saying this, but have you checked with Thad's parents? Maybe he took your books home."

"I doubt it. He didn't go home all term. Only up to Scotland for the shooting party. I was with him that weekend and he didn't have the books."

"That's pretty clear, then. I'll be happy to scout around for you." She began reading out edition information for me to jot down. Three books, classics by Charlotte and Emily Brontë and Daphne du Maurier. I also took her number, so I could text with any updates.

"Thanks, Molly," Amy said. She glanced at the old schoolhouse clock on the wall. "I'd better scoot."

"You have a lecture?" I asked, more to say something than because I cared.

"No, not this afternoon. I'm meeting with Dr. Verona so we can go over the Institute books. That's my new part-time job. Thad used to do it."

"Good luck," I said. "Thanks for coming in."

She slid her laptop back into her bag and slung the strap over her shoulder. "Are you coming to the dance later this week?"

"I might." I hadn't given the event much thought, although I'd noticed it was to be held in the cellars at St. Aelred. Great setting for a gothic dance.

"If you do, wear a costume. See you later." On the way out the door, she stopped to pat the cats, a gesture I—and they—appreciated. They were the real bosses around here, after all.

CHAPTER 17

After Amy left, I searched various bookdealer sites for the titles she wanted. Many were available overseas, which meant huge shipping fees, so I narrowed my results to the UK.

Reginald Dubold had one of the books and it looked to be a perfect match for Amy's. He was the dealer Aunt Violet had said was sketchy. Thad had his card.

Of course I put two and two together and jumped to conclusions. Thad had sold Amy's book to Reginald. I reached for the shop phone to call the dealer, then thought better of it. I would go in person, introduce myself, and scope out Mr. Dubold.

I glanced at the time. Aunt Violet was still out so Mum and I were the only ones here. It might be better to wait until tomorrow. His shop was within walking distance, on the other side of the Marketplace.

"Cup of tea, Molly?" Mum asked. "I'm going to put the kettle on."

"Love one, thanks," I said, needing the lift to get through the rest of the afternoon.

After we closed tonight, Kieran and I were going to grab pizza and ride out to Hazelhurst, where we planned to look at gravestones from the time of Selwyn Scott.

One entry in the family Bible had been obscured and we wanted to see if we could learn more in the family cemetery.

Was it strange that I was looking forward to an excursion to a graveyard? Of course, if Kieran was involved, I'd go anywhere. He made everything fun.

Mum soon reappeared, tray in hand. Along with mugs of tea, she had thoughtfully provided a plate of biscuits. A few of those would tide me over until pizza time.

◦•◦

Trade was slow, so around four, I settled in my favorite chair with my copy of *The Fatal Folio*. Both cats tried to sit on my lap, which was a first for Clarence. In the end, they squashed in, one on each side of me. I was basically wedged into the chair.

"You're going to have to pull me out of here," I told Mum, who was seated behind the desk working on the bookkeeping.

She laughed. "I see that."

I opened the book and began to read aloud, Mum and the cats as my audience.

The Fatal Folio, cont.

After a long afternoon in the library, where I found more than two-dozen other editions I wanted to purchase, Estella came to tell us dinner would soon be ready.

"You have both been so busy," she said, beginning to look through my stack. "All of these are of interest to you?"

I hurried to join her, noticing as I did so that she

had changed into a different dress for dinner. Still black, this one had a low, scooped neckline and puffed sleeves, and it rustled when she moved. Her perfume was light yet sweet, like a rose garden in full bloom.

Forcing my attention to the book she held, I said, "These are the volumes I am interested in. If you wish to keep any of them, I will not be offended."

She shook her head and set the book down, then picked up the next and studied it. "These subjects have no special meaning to me. I am happy for you to take them." She glanced around the library. "I may even find a new owner for this house and move. It is so lonely here."

I could well imagine, with only a small village nearby. Normally a woman of this age and beauty would be dwelling in a city, attending dances and soirees and fending off suitors. "Where do you think you will go?" I asked.

She waved her hand. "To my aunt's, in Milan, no doubt. She's been pressing me to set a date for the wedding." Her cheeks flushed. "With the death of my father so recent, I am in no hurry to be wed."

Not a surprise, yet a disappointment, as if I, a lowly bookseller from Cambridge, England, could offer this exquisite creature anything she would want. "Not an unreasonable aim on her part," I murmured. "After all, most people wish to engage in holy matrimony."

"Are you married, Mr. Marlboro?" she asked.

I shook my head. "Unfortunately not. My fiancée died of a fever before we reached that happy day." The result of my grief had been to drive me *further into the world of books. They at least lived on, forever if cared for correctly.*

"I am so sorry to hear that." She placed a gentle hand on my sleeve.

Mr. Coates of course could not accept that our conversation did not include him. "I am not married, either," he said. "In my case it is because I have not found a woman suitable, one who will be a perfect helpmeet at my country estate." He stood so as to puff out his chest. "I have great expectations, you know. A title, and a great deal of land."

Estella smiled politely. "How nice for you—and the future Mrs. Coates." The clock on the mantel struck. "Come. We will have a glass of wine before dinner."

After we washed our hands and faces, the silent manservant showed us to the drawing room. There Estella waited with the promised wine. As we sipped, waiting for the announcement of dinner, rain began to lash against the tall windows.

Estella went to the closest window to peer out. "The storm is here." As she said that, lightning flashed, followed by a boom of thunder that shook even this thick-walled dwelling.

I joined her at the window, which provided a vista of the monastery ruins and the valley beyond. Lightning illuminated the tumbled walls and the remaining bell tower in a most disturbing manner. To my fevered imagination, these ruins foretold the eventual demise that all men face, the crumbling of the external shell into dust.

"You will not be able to return to the village tonight," Estella said. "The road often washes out during these storms. Rocks sometimes wash down

and strike people, even causing them to tumble over the cliffs."

I exchanged a glance with Mr. Coates. This was an eventuality I hadn't foreseen. Our luggage was at the hotel and our horses were rented. "They'll think we ran off with our mounts," I said, only half-jesting.

"They will understand that you are stranded," Estella said. "It often happened to Papa's visitors. Any excess fees you need to pay, I will be glad to cover. Since you are my guests, after all."

"How considerate," Mr. Coates demurred. "But entirely unnecessary. We will accept your hospitality with gladness." There was more in his expression, I discerned, than relief at not getting drenched or worse during a possibly treacherous ride down the mountainside. He was gloating at the prospect of additional time here, either to continue looking through the library or to woo Estella. I hadn't missed the acquisitive glint in his eye when he gazed upon her.

Another reason could be that he hoped for another look at The Ramblings of a Monk. *During our time prowling the shelves, he told me he still hoped to persuade her to sell. Despite the fineness of the rest of the collection, that piece alone was almost worth all the rest. The storied volume would indeed be a suitable gift for a duke, and undoubtedly would become the centerpiece of his collection, which I had heard was quite fine.*

In any event, despite the machinations and plots of my companion, it appeared that we would be spending the night here, at the villa. And as Estella

*offered her arm for me to escort her into dinner, I
couldn't help but be glad.*

•|•

On the way out to Hazelhurst in Kieran's Land Rover, we
stopped to pick up a pizza at our favorite place. "It smells
so good," I moaned as we continued on. What was it
about the aroma of hot cheese and tomato sauce?

"Patience, my dear," Kieran said. "We're almost there."

"What if it's cold?" If I were driving my own vehicle—
not the Cortina, which was pristine—I would have torn
into it already. His leather seats were still showroom clean
and I shuddered at the thought of being the one to stain
them.

"We'll heat it up." Traffic was light out here in the
country and Kieran stepped on the gas, probably eager to
feed me and stop my whining.

The way to Hazelhurst House was so familiar by now I
recognized certain houses and trees and bends in the road.
As we pulled down the drive, lights flickered through the
trees. Only a few, as the electric bill must be enormous.
Kieran drove over the bridge and parked in the forecourt.
I carried the pizza and he grabbed his camping lantern for
our expedition to the cemetery.

"Oliver will be joining us," he said as we entered the
house. "He also wants to see Selwyn's writing garret and
take a stab at searching for the second book."

"How's he doing on his own book?" I asked. If he
could have his published at the same time Selwyn's was
rereleased, it would be the literary event of the year.

"Not sure," Kieran said. "I think he's been distracted
lately."

By Thad's murder, the controversy around his teaching, or his relationship with Sophie? All three, probably.

We made our way to the enormous kitchen, where Lady Asha was putting together a meal tray. "Kieran, love. I didn't know you were coming. Hello, Molly."

A nice blend of old and new, the kitchen featured an AGA in an arched niche, a scrubbed table that could seat twenty, banks of cabinets and open shelves, and a butcher-block island.

Kieran greeted his mother with a kiss on the cheek. "We brought our own dinner."

I said hello and placed the cardboard box on the table. Kieran went over to the AGA and turned on an oven.

"How's Dad?" Kieran asked as he dispensed ice from the refrigerator into two glasses.

Once the clatter of ice dropping died down, Lady Asha said, "He's all right. A bit nervous about his appointment in London tomorrow."

I didn't know much about Lord Graham's illness, but had gathered he was waiting to find out if the cancer had gone into remission.

"I'm sure it will go well." Despite his firm tone, doubt flickered in Kieran's eyes. "By the way, I'm going with you."

Lady Asha looked relieved. "Are you? I'm sure your father will appreciate it."

I hoped for everyone's sake that Lord Graham would come through. Although Kieran and I were close, we hadn't talked much about his father's ordeal. Oh, that famous British reticence. I was letting him set the pace regarding the subject.

Lady Asha excused herself with the tray and Kieran slid the pizza into the oven to warm. I pulled out plates and silverware.

We'd chosen a Quattro Stagioni—"four seasons"—which had ham, artichokes, mushrooms, and olives in the Italian four-quadrants style.

"So good," I murmured as I devoured my second piece.

Kieran picked up his third slice. "My favorite."

"Do you want to go to a dance?" I asked. "St. Aelred is having one this weekend, put on by the Gothic Institute."

"A gothic dance, huh? Costumes?" He took a bite, then wiped his mouth with a napkin.

"Yes, which is not my favorite thing. I never know what to wear."

"How about we go as characters from *The Fatal Folio*?" Kieran suggested. "I'll be Matthew and you can be Estella."

"Oh, I like that." I frowned. "Where can I find a dress?" Dresses in the 1840s had natural waistlines and full skirts.

"There's a local place that's pretty good," Kieran said. He pulled out his phone and brought up a site. "Take a look."

Crossing my fingers they would have a dress that was appropriate and in my size, I browsed through the site. To my relief, I found several choices that might work. "I'll have to pop over tomorrow," I said. "Before I come out here to work."

"Why don't we meet at the shop?" he suggested. "We can help each other pick out costumes."

"It's a plan." I handed him his phone back, then surveyed the decimated pizza. "Are we done here?" Then I remembered his cousin was supposed to join us. "Is Oliver still coming?"

Kieran looked at his phone. "Late as usual. We'll go

ahead." After sending a text, presumably to inform Oliver, he tucked his phone away.

Soon after, we stepped outside, Kieran's flashlight the only source of light. Trees whipped in the wind and clouds scudded across the sky, hiding then revealing the moon. Behind us, the walls and towers of Hazelhurst House loomed forbidding and dark, crenellations etched against the sky.

"Good grief," I said as we strolled across the garden bridge. "I feel like we're in a gothic novel."

"We are." He leaned close, speaking in a deep, sonorous voice. "I am luring you to the graveyard, my pretty. I need your, 'blood, your precious blood.'"

I laughed with delighted glee. "Love that quote from *Nosferatu*."

"It's a classic, for sure."

We stepped off the bridge and started to cross the garden, footsteps crunching on gravel. Topiaries and trees made odd shapes in the dark and unseen things rustled in the undergrowth.

I wondered if Selwyn Scott had wandered these paths at night, drawing inspiration from the surroundings. The author didn't have to travel to find a mysterious, brooding landscape and ancient manor. It was all right here.

We turned down a path that took us between head-high hedges. I hadn't been in this corner of the extensive grounds. I was glad to have Kieran guiding me, otherwise I would definitely be lost. We couldn't even see the house lights now.

"It's not much farther," he said. "Honestly."

"I'm glad," I said, shivering. "It's getting cold out." I was grateful for the pair of gloves I'd stuffed in my pocket and the wool socks keeping my feet toasty. Aunt Violet had made them for me.

Kieran put an arm around me. "We'll have to stick close together."

I laughed. "I can live with that."

The hedge ended and we were in the cemetery, a sea of headstones picked out by Kieran's flashlight. Huge trees arched overhead, blocking out the sky.

"No one has been buried here since the late eighteen hundreds," Kieran said as he led me through a gap in a stone wall, leaves rustling as we shuffled along. "We ran out of room." The markers were of various sizes in a jumble of styles, and small mausoleums stood here and there.

"Any idea where to look?" Maybe we should have waited until daylight.

Kieran veered toward the right. "Actually, yes. They're in one of the mausoleums."

"Do we have to go inside?" I had no interest in exploring enclosed spaces after my adventure last summer.

He threw me a look. "Of course not. There are bronze plaques on the outside."

I gave an exaggerated exhale. "Phew. So glad."

We made our way across the clearing, skirting gravestones and plots, dodging edging lifted by frost and markers embedded in the tall grass. Gusts of wind sent leaves spinning down from the trees or propelled them in bursts, as if haunted.

"I wish we could see the stones better," I whispered. It felt wrong to speak in a normal voice out here among the dead, on a dark, cold night. "I like reading the names and dates, and studying the artwork on the stones." Wandering through a cemetery and thinking about those who had come before us was both melancholy and a history lesson.

At some point, I reminded myself, I should visit the

churchyard in Hazelhurst village, where my ancestors had lived. I'd never viewed my grandparents' graves. My mother hadn't gotten along with her parents, who practically drove her away from home. She'd married my American father and moved to Vermont.

"We'll come back," Kieran promised. Moving slowly along, he focused the flashlight on dull metal rectangles fastened to the structure, which was white stone stained with lichens and rust. With the battering of centuries, literally, the plaques were hard to read.

I helped, taking the lower row while he did the upper. "Aha," I said. "I found Alistair." He had died in 1830, at age forty-two.

He moved the light to that square, where we also found Agatha. Her life had spanned 1792 to 1862, so she had reached seventy years of age. "Now the children."

They were on another plaque. Samuel had died in 1886, at age seventy-four. I gasped. Frances had died in 1842, the year *The Fatal Folio* was published.

"Is her death the reason *Among the Ruins* wasn't published?" I mused. "This has me leaning toward Frances as the author."

"It's a possibility," Kieran said. "It doesn't knock her mother and brother out of the running, though."

He was right. The fact that Frances died in 1842 was only one piece of information.

"Look. There's another entry." The final inscription provided another tidbit of information. There had been a third child. His name was Selwyn and he had died at age two, in 1816. "Selwyn Scott. He must have been the reason they chose that as a pen name."

"I'm sure you're right." Kieran traced his fingers over the letters. "Poor little guy. He was only two."

"How sad. They lost so many babies back then." The

sound of leaves shuffling caught my ear and I turned to see a light bouncing along the ground. Instinctively, I moved closer to Kieran. "Someone's coming."

He watched for a moment then called, "Who's there?"

"It's me," came a voice. "Oliver."

I exhaled loudly and Kieran gave me a sidewise glance. "Were you worried?"

"Um, yeah, sort of." How could I share my fear that we might encounter a killer? Though why here and now would certainly be a mystery.

Oliver continued on, muttering to himself when he almost tripped over something. "Hello," he said cheerfully when he got closer. "Doing a spot of grave robbing?"

The remark was ridiculous and we both snorted. Then I noticed Oliver's feet, clearly visible in the beam of his light.

He was wearing orange running shoes—the same style worn by the mysterious runner the night Thad died.

CHAPTER 18

"Those shoes," I blurted, thinking of what Tim had told me.

"They are bright." Kieran shone his own flashlight across them. "What a color."

Didn't he remember? Earlier today, we had discussed the clue of the orange shoes.

Oliver lifted a sneaker with a laugh. "Yeah, they're something, aren't they? I was hoping they might make me visible at night to drivers."

Was Oliver's choice merely a coincidence? Oh, how I hoped so.

"What's up?" Kieran asked. "Molly and I were taking a look at family markers from the Selwyn Scott generation."

"We found Selwyn," I threw in, still bothered about the sneakers. "He died really young."

Oliver came over and studied the bronze plaques with interest. "I'll have to come back in the daytime and get a picture. For my author website."

"Molly found a secret room off the library," Kieran said. "We have a theory that it was Selwyn Scott's writing nook. The author, I mean, not the baby."

"We found a manuscript page on the desk," I added.

In the glow of his flashlight, Oliver's handsome features were almost ghoulish. "Wow. Can you show me?"

"Lady Asha also came up with a great idea," I said as we began walking back across the cemetery. "She wants to have *The Fatal Folio* reprinted. As well as *Among the Ruins*, if we can find it."

"What a crackerjack idea," Oliver said with enthusiasm. "We'll create our own canon of gothic works." He waved his arm, sending the light flashing across the trees. "The Scott novels. Not to be confused with Sir Walter, of course. So, the Scott Gothic Collection. Yes, that works."

Knowing I was feeding the beast, I added, "We also found short stories by Selwyn Scott tucked in a trunk. Published in penny dreadfuls. Nine so far."

"Enough for a collection. That's brilliant, Molly." Oliver picked up the pace. "I can't wait to read them."

"I separated them out," I said. "They're in the closet off the library."

Oliver soon pulled ahead and we let him, watching his light bob across the graveyard and then disappear when he reached the hedges.

"I don't feel like rushing," Kieran said. "All I need is to twist an ankle."

As he said that, my own foot turned in an unexpected divot and I stumbled. "Exactly." I took another step, gingerly testing my ankle. Thankfully it was all right.

Although Oliver was now out of sight, I didn't bring up the sneakers. The topic would have to wait until another time, when I knew for sure that we were alone.

"I'm glad he has the novel to focus on," Kieran said. "Considering the trouble at school." Apparently *he* wasn't concerned about Oliver overhearing us.

●◦●

Oliver was in the library, the penny dreadfuls spread out on a table. Not the table I always used, I was glad to see. Funny how we create habits like that.

"There you are," he said, jumping to his feet. "Can you show me the secret room?"

Kieran bowed. "Molly, will you do the honors? It was your discovery."

"Gentlemen, fire up your flashlights," I said, leading the way into the closet. "No electricity in this section. Go figure."

"I can't imagine when anyone was last in here," Kieran said. He handed me his flashlight so I could venture up the stairs safely. "Nothing's been touched."

"Certainly not the dust." Oliver shone his light on the steps, where our footsteps were plainly visible. The corners still held a thick gray layer.

Up the stairs we went. My heart began to pound, with excitement more than exertion. The hidden chamber really was a fabulous discovery, like something out of a book.

"Oh, man," Oliver said as he shone his light around the room. "I can't believe we never found this place." He stepped around, examining the ceiling, windows, fireplace, and finally, the desk. "Be still my heart." He touched the page on the desk. "Selwyn Scott wrote these words."

"Probably," I said. "Still not sure. The handwriting doesn't match the letters to the publishers."

"Why wouldn't it be the same?" Oliver asked, bending over to read the words.

"I don't know," I admitted. "I've learned not to assume things."

Oliver began to lift the page from the desk. "Hold on," Kieran said. "Leave it here for now."

"If you say so." Oliver took out his phone and snapped a picture. "First thing I'm going to do is analyze the style. You're right, Molly. We shouldn't assume that the same author wrote both books."

"Frances died in 1842," I said. "Her mother or brother might have continued her work." My words slowed. "If she was the original author, that is." I groaned in frustration. "We always end up in the same place." And would, until we found another clue to Selwyn's identity.

"We'll get there," Kieran said. "I hope."

Oliver made the mistake of sitting on the chaise longue, which raised a cloud of dust. "Crikey!" he cried, waving his hand as if to clear the air. "Sorry." He glanced down at the couch. "Thing's hard as a rock anyway."

I had a question for Oliver and I took the opportunity to bring up the topic. "I went on the Gothic tour Amy led. It was very interesting."

"Glad to hear it." Oliver brushed at his pants.

"While we were punting back, I saw you and Sophie on the bank." I forced a laugh. "You probably didn't see us." Kieran shot me a look, no doubt wishing I hadn't brought the subject up.

"Oh, yeah?" Although Oliver didn't sound concerned, his expression was uneasy.

"I didn't know you were dating." I decided to be blunt rather than dance around it. I'd definitely seen them kissing, quite passionately too.

"We're—not really. It was—" His words tumbled over themselves. With a hiss of breath, he stood up straight. "Listen, Molly. Don't say anything about what you saw, all right? Things are a little . . . sticky right now at the college."

Quite an understatement, what with Thad's murder, a missing manuscript, and Oliver's promotion on the line. Sophie was also in the running for the position, he'd said, so they were rivals as well as lovers. Even if the college couldn't forbid adult employees from fraternizing, their involvement muddied the waters, especially if one was promoted over the other.

"I won't say a peep," I promised. "I was just surprised, that's all. I mean, you're both very attractive, it's the situation . . ." Not to mention Sophie's early morning meetings with Thad when they might have been plotting. I hadn't ruled out her involvement in the manuscript theft. It was possible that Oliver's feelings for Sophie had made him more susceptible to being manipulated.

After a rather tense silence, Kieran shifted his stance. "Ready to go down? It's chilly up here."

Oliver gave a last, longing look at the garret. "I'll be back," he said. "In daylight." He touched the page on the desk before following us to the doorway. "I wonder where the rest of it is?"

"So do we," I said. "What a find that would be."

Once downstairs, Kieran suggested we head back to town. Oliver said he was going to stay and read Selwyn's stories.

As soon as we got into the Land Rover, I said, "Kieran. Oliver's shoes."

"What about them?" He turned the key and put the vehicle into gear.

"The runner we saw that night? He was wearing those shoes. According to Tim."

He deftly backed up, turned, and drove across the drawbridge. "The same color shoes. They could be a different brand."

I regarded him with skepticism. "I seriously doubt it. Tim showed me a picture and Oliver's look exactly like them. They're pretty distinctive."

In the light of the dash, I could see him frowning, which gave me a sudden qualm. What was I doing? Pressing him about his cousin's possible guilt was a pretty rash move. Not to mention mean.

"I'm sorry," I said. "I don't think Oliver is guilty. The coincidence just . . . troubles me, that's all."

The lines across his forehead eased. "Yeah, me too. First the jacket, now the shoes . . . why would he wear them? If I killed someone, I'd get rid of the outfit I had on."

"Good to know," I said, which broke the tension. A possibility dawned. "Did someone try to frame him?" Then I remembered Josh. "They also tried to frame Josh, by putting the jacket in his room. Maybe they're framing everyone." I gave a laugh. "Ridiculous, right?"

"Why not fling mud around?" Kieran said. We had reached the end of the drive and we waited to let a vehicle pass. "Something will stick, right?"

I groaned. "It's so confusing." I remembered something else. "I suggested to Tim that he tell the police about the shoes. Just so you know."

"That's fine." He pulled out onto the main road. "Maybe they can figure it out."

"I hope so." We rode in silence for a few minutes. "On another subject, sorry to spring the Sophie thing. I saw an opportunity and grabbed it."

Kieran took his time responding. "Why did you mention it?"

Discomfort churned as I struggled to frame an answer. "Because I'm worried," I finally said, the most palatable reason I could come up with. The last thing I wanted to do was alienate Kieran by voicing additional suspicions regarding his cousin.

"Sophie is a suspect too, at least in my eyes." I told him how she'd met with Thad in his room, which seemed secretive, and how she might have influenced the display of the manuscript. "Oh, and another thing. When I was in Thad's room with Amy, we found a spreadsheet regarding the Institute's finances. Thad made notes, indicating he had questions." He threw me a frown. "Oh, yeah. I didn't mention searching his room, did I?"

Kieran made a rueful scoffing sound. "Nope." A beat and then he asked, "You think something's off with the money?"

"It's a possibility." If Sophie had been skimming from the account and Thad found out, that would definitely give her a motive. The resulting scandal would no doubt lead to her dismissal from the college. "I wonder where she was when Thad was stabbed."

"Wow," Kieran said. "I have no idea. I wonder if she's even on the police's radar."

"Maybe not, with all the other evidence popping up." Evidence that might be successfully obscuring the truth of who killed Thad Devine.

◦◊◦

Early the next morning, I met Kieran outside the bookshop. "Here you are," I said, handing him a to-go cup. "Coffee, the way you like it." To my delight, as a die-hard coffee fanatic, I'd found that English tea shops now sold java. Daisy made it with two methods—pour-over and French press.

We sipped coffee as we walked up Magpie Lane and

through the heart of downtown, dodging pedestrians and cyclists and the occasional delivery vehicle. The air was crisp and clear, the sky so blue it made me ache. Golden sun made the buildings glow.

I sighed with happiness, loving my new home. "Hold on," I said when we walked past Newton's apple tree. I pulled out my phone and took a picture of Kieran with the tree and the medieval windows of Trinity College in the background. Later, I'd post it on social media, mentioning that this tree was grafted from the original at Newton's childhood home. Books we had in stock by Isaac Newton, one of Cambridge's most renowned graduates, would also be mentioned.

"Do I get a modeling fee?" Kieran asked, knowing full well what I was up to.

"That was it." I nodded toward his coffee.

He gave a mock sigh. "I guess it will have to do."

We continued on, soon reaching the costume shop, which was tucked down a side street. "Almost done," I said, drinking the rest of my coffee. "Me and liquids in a store don't mix." He did the same, and we tossed our cups into a trash bin before going inside.

Inside, the shop was tight, with racks of costumes and shelves filled with hats, fake weapons, and other accessories. Since the young woman behind the counter was busy helping someone, we started browsing.

I was checking out Victorian-era dresses when someone tapped me on the shoulder.

Turning, I saw one of those Guy Fawkes masks staring at me. A shriek burst from my mouth. "Kieran. That isn't funny." Especially because Thad and his probable killer had both worn them.

"That's not me," Kieran called from a few racks away.

The wearer pushed up the mask. Wesley Wright, from

St. Aelred. Thad's cousin. "Sorry," he said, grinning. "I couldn't resist."

He was lucky I could resist wringing his neck. "It wasn't funny," I said grumpily. "You startled me. Why do you keep doing that?" Reflexively, I glanced at his shoes. White-and-black sneakers with neon-green laces.

"Sorry," Wesley said again, not sounding the least bit contrite. "Looking for a costume for the dance?"

"I am," I said, turning back to the rack. "Are you going?"

"Uh-huh." He pointed to a black robe draped over his arm. "I'm going as the headless monk." He slid the robe on and draped the huge hood over his face. "I'll put something black over the lower part of my face."

"That is seriously creepy," I said, picturing the full costume.

He laughed with glee as he shrugged off the robe. "Yeah, it is. Can't wait." Still chuckling to himself, he went off to the counter to pay.

Holding a suit on a hanger, Kieran joined me a few minutes later, after Wesley had left the shop. "That was Thad's cousin," I said. "Wesley Wright."

"We've met," he said, not sounding impressed.

"That's right, your family knows Thad's." I had narrowed my choices down to two dresses, one black, the other burgundy. Both had scooped necklines and puffy sleeves and a full skirt below a fitted bodice. I held up the dresses. "Which one?"

He glanced back and forth between the two. "I like both. Very gothic heroine."

"That's the point, right?" I started pushing my way through the racks toward the dressing room. "I'll let you vote."

We decided on the black dress, which fit slightly

better, the neckline not gaping as much. I really didn't want to display the girls for all to see. Kieran's suit was nice, very Dickens with its black frock coat and trousers, and patterned waistcoat.

Outside the store, I realized how close we were to Reginald Dubold's store. "Can you do me a favor?" I asked. "I have another errand down this way. Would you mind taking my costume to the shop for me?"

He reached for the hanger. "Course not." He gave me a quick kiss. "See you later."

"Later." While he set off along the lane with our costumes, I mapped Reginald's address. If I went to the end of this street and turned right, it was only a couple of blocks. I also searched my notes and found the information about Amy's books. While I was there, I'd check if he had the others she wanted. He did have one title.

In this direction, the area was quiet, mostly obscure businesses without storefront windows or blocks of flats. I saw very few pedestrians and one striped orange cat, seated on a windowsill, washing. He paused mid-lick to watch me, leg in the air.

I waved. "Hello, handsome." He stared at me a moment longer and then went back to work. Cats really had it made.

Reginald's shop had a small hanging sign, REGINALD DUBOLD, FINE BOOKS. The bowed window was dusty, with a leaning row of books across the shelf and faded flyers taped on the glass promoting events long past. As a professional bookseller, I found the display less than enticing. However, my profession, like most others, certainly had its share of eccentrics, so inside I went.

A bell rang when I stepped on the mat. The shop was small and poorly lit, with bookshelves and tables placed in no discernable order. It was the kind of shop where you might find a delightful bargain—if you could unearth it from among the jumble.

Nothing stirred, except dust, so I finally called out, "Mr. Dubold?"

"With you in a minute," a man called. "Make yourself right at home, love."

Cringing at the endearment, I stepped into the store, list loaded, trying to decide where to look first. Fiction seemed to be grouped to the right, so I went in that direction. I was edging past a teetering stack when I caught a glimpse of movement at the back.

A short, balding man dressed in a sweater-vest, shirt, and jeans came into view. He wore navy-blue trainers.

Was I going to check everyone's feet for orange running shoes? Maybe. Until they caught Thad's killer, at least.

"Are you looking for anything in particular?" he asked as he went behind a counter piled with stacks of books. He gave me a crooked grin. "Can't keep up with the inventory, it seems."

"I know what you mean." Realizing I should introduce myself, I said, "I'm Molly Kimball, from Thomas Marlowe."

"Yeah?" He lifted one brow. His amiable demeanor fell away and he was all business. "Nice to meet you, Molly. What can I do for you?"

I opened the file on my phone. "I have a customer looking for a particular edition. Your website said you had it, so I'm hoping you do." I read him the particulars.

He thought for a moment, then fired up a computer that was half-hidden on the counter. "Let me see if it's still in stock. Certain books fly right off the shelves. As I'm sure you know."

"I certainly do," I said in a hearty tone. "In and out they go." Sometimes when people acted aloof and rude, I'd be

even friendlier, as if to compensate. Or to annoy them.
Perhaps both.

His compressed lips revealed I'd succeeded in doing
the latter. Fingers clicked on the keys. "I do have the
book." He pointed. "It should be over in that section, filed
alphabetically by author."

My, my. When I had a customer making a special request, I escorted them to the shelf, where I found the
book and placed it in their hands. His bookseller's version of a bedside—shelf-side?—manner left much to be
desired.

"Thanks." I headed off into the maze, hoping I
would be able to locate the book. Despite his promise of
organization, I could tell already that many books had
been misfiled.

I finally found the Brontë titles in a far corner, bookcases looming on both sides and behind me. It was tight
in there and I could barely move without bumping into
something. No wonder Aunt Violet didn't want to deal
with Mr. Dubold. It wasn't the usual pleasant experience
of bonhomie and shoptalk.

The Charlotte Brontë book was as advertised and fairly
priced. He'd evaluated this book accurately, I'd give him
that. That time he tried to cheat Aunt Violet, though . . .
I had to be extra careful.

I took quick pictures of the cover, copyright page,
and title page, and sent them to Amy, asking her if she
wanted me to buy it for her. I gave her the price, assum-
ing I'd get my dealer discount.

That's my book.

Good. I hoped it was the right edition.

*No, I mean—THAT'S MY BOOK! Sorry to shout, but
see the pencil marking on the copyright page?*

I checked the book again and saw the marking she

was referring to, a little scribble that didn't detract greatly from the value.

Thad *had* sold Amy's books.

I'll check for the other ones you want and get back to you.

Her reply was a series of angry emojis. I didn't blame her.

I set the book aside and searched for the other two titles. There they were, Emily Brontë and Daphne du Maurier, sitting snugly on the shelves, the exact conditions and editions she had given me.

I photographed identifying pages from both and sent them. The reply came back immediately.

They're mine too. What do I do now?

If Thad had sold them to Dubold without her permission, then she could involve the police. These particular editions weren't so valuable that Reginald would have asked for provenance or a receipt. It might have been innocent, I reminded myself. Perhaps he gathered a bunch of books to sell and included hers by accident. Either way, she should get her books back. She probably had proof of purchase.

Let me talk to the bookseller. I'll get back to you.

Cradling the books, I sidled through the bookshelves toward the counter. Reginald was standing at the counter, leafing through a tabloid newspaper. I couldn't blame him. Reading trashy stories was more fun than inventory entry.

As I approached, he stopped reading. "Find something you like?"

"I did." I hesitated, wondering how to broach the delicate topic of unauthorized purchases on his part. Provoking his temper was not the result I wanted.

I set the books on the counter, next to a battered copy

of *The Fatal Folio*. Seizing on a side topic, I said, "Selwyn Scott seems to be having a renaissance." Might as well start talking up the author, right, to help Lady Asha and Oliver? "I'm reading that now and I can't believe it isn't more well known."

He studied me for a long moment, staring at me so intently I shifted from foot to foot. I was about to ask him what his problem was when he slapped his palm down onto the newspaper page. "Don't play the innocent with me, 'Vermont lovely.' I know why you're here."

His splayed fingers were resting on a picture of me and Kieran sitting in a pub. Almost every week it seemed someone published a picture of us. The downside of dating someone from British nobility. Plus the lame nicknames.

"Why I'm . . . ?" I gestured at the stack of Amy's books in confusion. Then it sank in. He knew I knew about the theft of the Selwyn Scott manuscript from Hazelhurst House. He thought I was here on a fishing expedition.

Maybe I should cast a line. I pushed that thought right out of my head, fast as it popped in. It wasn't my job to track down stolen manuscripts.

"I really don't understand what you're talking about," I said, playing dumb as I forced a smile onto my face. I touched the stack of books lightly. "I was looking—"

The front door of the shop burst open, the bell in the mat ringing out as Sir Jon and two officers strode in. By the grim expressions on their faces, I guessed they weren't here to browse.

CHAPTER 19

Sir Jon was taken aback to see me, I could tell. Then, with great aplomb, he managed to pretend that we hadn't met. "I'm sorry, miss, you will need to excuse us." He tipped his head toward the door, which I interpreted as meaning, "Please leave now."

I gestured toward my stack of books. "I was here to buy those." Should I share my suspicions with Sir Jon, that they had been stolen? Or at the very least, sold by accident? Noticing that one of the officers was pulling out a search warrant, I decided now was not the time.

"Leave it," Sir Jon said, confirming my decision. "Please."

I put down the books and hurried for the door, wishing I could stay and find out what was going on. Did they think Reginald had the manuscript stolen from Hazelhurst House? Or were they looking for other stolen books?

Aunt Violet had been right about Reginald operating on the margins of the trade. Sir Jon wouldn't question him or serve a search warrant without evidence.

Outside the shop, I glanced around, hoping no one had seen me here. The last thing I wanted was to taint Thomas Marlowe by association, which I should have thought of earlier. I was too impulsive sometimes.

I did find Amy's books, though. That was something. Although, if Reginald was arrested, I wasn't sure how we'd get them back. What was I going to tell her? She was probably waiting for an update.

After pondering this dilemma all the way back to the shop, I decided to call her. This wasn't a conversation to have over text.

I took out my phone as I entered Magpie Lane, planning to sit in one of our outside chairs to talk. The morning sunshine was beaming strongly into the lane, the buildings on both sides capturing and magnifying its meager warmth. With winter looming, I had resolved to savor every minute of good weather.

As I was walking past Spinning Your Wheels, Detective Inspector Sean Ryan exited the front door. "Inspector Ryan. What are you doing here?" Immediately regretting my nosy question, I said, "I mean, hello. How are you?"

He laughed, which made him look much younger and even more handsome. I could see why Mum liked him, even if I would find his profession intimidating.

"I was on my way to see Nina. Is she in?"

"Yes, she is." I threw up a trial balloon. "Were you talking about orange shoes?" I tipped my head toward the bike shop. "In there?" This time I wouldn't mention that Oliver owned the same clothing as the probable killer. I'd done enough damage the first time.

Eyes twinkling, he pursed his lips in amusement. "Maybe. You know I can't share details of a case with you, Molly."

"Even if I'm the one who suggested the report?" He didn't say anything so I shrugged and gave up. "Go ahead in. I have to make a call."

He opened the shop door and I perched on a chair, the

cold from the seat immediately penetrating my jeans. Maybe I wouldn't linger out here after all.

I dialed Amy, who answered right away. "Molly. Did you get them? Did you find out who sold them?"

"Hold on a sec, Amy. I'm sorry to say, the answer is no to both questions."

"What? Why not? You were right there."

"I know I was." I took a breath, debating how to frame my answer. I should tell the truth, I finally decided. It would come out sooner or later, if Reginald was arrested. "I was about to ask the shopkeeper when the police arrived. They booted me out before I could ask him anything."

"The police? What did they want?" Amy sounded confused.

"I'm not sure. They had a search warrant, though."

She didn't say anything for a long moment. "Weird. What now?"

Having never faced this situation before, I had no idea. "I suppose we should wait and see what happens. If he isn't arrested, we can go get your books."

"And if he is?"

"I suppose he'll be out on bail at some point. I'm not sure if they'll let him operate his shop. Or if he'll close it and lay low."

She grunted in frustration. "I want my books back."

"I totally understand." She could file a police report but that might mean the books would then be caught up in red tape. "Why don't we wait and see for now? If we have to, we can file a police report and see if they can help you get them back."

Amy sighed. "I suppose. Thanks for tracking them down. I really appreciate it." She exhaled again. "It's been a day from hell all around. I started digging into the books for the Institute, and wow, what a mess."

"Thad didn't do a good job?" I guessed.

"No, it's not that." She paused. "Some of the numbers don't add up. In other words, money might be missing." She gave a little laugh. "Whoops. Forget I said that, 'kay?"

"Not my business," I said, even though I made a mental note. Did Oliver know? "Good luck. And listen, I'll keep an eye on the Reginald Dubold situation."

"Reginald Dubold?"

"Yes, he's the bookseller I've been talking about." Hadn't I mentioned his name? Thinking back through my messages and this conversation, I might not have. "Do you know him?"

Her answer was a squawk. "Got to go."

I stared at my suddenly dead phone. She'd hung up. Very strange. Why had she reacted so strongly to his name? I'd love to know, though I had a feeling she wouldn't answer if I called back. Next time we spoke, I'd ask her.

Standing, I stretched. My poor bum was frozen solid. Curled in the window in a shaft of sunlight, Clarence opened one eye to regard me with disdain. *You wouldn't catch me out there*, his expression seemed to say.

Smart cat. Moving fast, I nipped into the shop, enjoying the gusts of warm air that enveloped me. Puck ran over to rub against my legs, meowing.

"Tea?" Mum asked. She was seated behind the counter, where Sean Ryan was leaning, mug in hand. Aunt Violet was puttering around the bookshelves.

"I could use one," I said, unbuttoning my coat. "Thanks."

She filled a mug with steaming tea from the teapot

and handed it over. "Like your costume," she said, nodding at my dress, which was hanging on a hook behind the desk.

I smiled at the dress, imagining Kieran and me at the party. "We're going as characters from *The Fatal Folio*."

Did I imagine Sean Ryan's sudden tensing at the mention of the book? I pondered whether to mention my visit to Reginald Dubold's shop. Then I decided, why not? After all, Sir Jon would almost certainly bring it up.

"On the way back from picking out my costume, I stopped by Reginald Dubold's bookshop." The room went utterly still.

Mum looked confused. Sean frowned. Aunt Violet popped out from behind a bookshelf, scowling. "Why on earth did you do that, Molly? The man is a cheat. And worse, no doubt."

"His website said he had a certain book a customer wants. And he did." I paused for dramatic emphasis. "Hers. It was sold to him without her knowledge." All three of them exclaimed in dismay and I put up a hand. "Hold on, I'll explain."

I took them through the situation, starting with Amy retrieving her books from Thad's room. That we'd been in the murder victim's room startled Sean but I didn't stop for his opinion. I explained how Amy wanted to purchase duplicate copies of certain titles and how I'd found one listed by Reginald. Plus, once I was there, found all three books, and Amy asserted that they belonged to her.

"Yet another example of Reginald's dishonesty," Aunt Violet said. "Who sold them to him?"

"Well, to be fair," I said, "they weren't so valuable as to require provenance. I was about to ask him when Sir Jon arrived. With two police officers in tow." After they absorbed that, I added, "I wonder if they were on the trail of the *Fatal Folio* manuscript. The one that was stolen at Hazelhurst House."

One look at Sean told me that yes, he did know about the theft and the task force Sir Jon was leading. "Can you help Amy?" I asked. "She really wants to get her books back. I'm afraid they'll be frozen along with all of Reginald's assets."

"I'll see what I can do," Sean finally said. "Have her send me the information that proves she's the owner of those books."

"Sure thing," I said, relieved. "I have pictures of them in the store. I'm sure she has receipts." Eager to share this progress with Amy, I pulled out my phone and sent her a text, then attached the photos of the books I'd taken.

Put your supporting information together and mail or take it to Detective Inspector Ryan's station. He'll make sure that it gets handled.

Despite this masterful effort on my part, Amy didn't write back, not even to say thank you. That miffed me. Oh, well. The ball was in her court.

Mum and Sean were chatting about various goings-on in Cambridge so I left them to it and went out to the kitchen to make a lunch. I needed to get out to Hazelhurst House and continue the library inventory. Lady Asha had kindly fed me each time, but this afternoon, they were headed to London for medical appointments. I would take care of myself.

∗|∗

One of the staff let me in at Hazelhurst House, which seemed sad and empty without Lady Asha to greet me. Kieran had gone up to London with his parents, so I couldn't ask him to come out and see me either.

The only advantage of working alone without interruption was that I got a lot done. At times I was tempted to linger over a book or two, admiring its rarity, age, and beauty, but I managed to resist. I could revisit them later, once I was finished.

At lunchtime, I carried my sack to the kitchen, where I ate while reading another chapter of *The Fatal Folio*. It was thrilling to realize it had been penned in this house, even if we weren't quite sure yet who the author was. Which reminded me I needed to search for correspondence from any of the Scotts living here during that time— Agatha, Frances, and Samuel. Since they'd written the letters, they would likely be found in collections of the recipient's papers.

The Fatal Folio, cont.

After a sumptuous meal, we were shown to our quarters, large bedrooms on the second floor. Mine had a small balcony and a view of the ruins. In better weather, I would have immediately gone out to survey the landscape, but the storm was still raging.

Mr. Coates and I parted, wishing each other a night of good rest. Although the bed was fine, wide and firm, I wasn't convinced I would get much sleep. In addition to the thunder rumbling through the hills, the villa was eerie at night, full of shadows and mysterious sounds. The tread of footsteps, doors thudding shut. Occasionally something scratching at the window. The thing was, we were alone in this wing. Who or what was making those noises? Several times I peered into the dark corridor, only to see no one. Mr. Coates's door remained firmly shut.

Finally, unable to settle down, I decided to read, having chosen a book from the library. A comfortable armchair was placed in a corner, a table with a lamp close to hand. From here, I could see through the window and keep watch on the storm.

I was soon engrossed in the book, a fine copy of The Castle of Otranto, possibly not the wisest choice under the circumstances. Too many details resembled the situation I found myself in, with the effect that I began to have trouble distinguishing between fact and fancy. Were the flickering shadows, the gloom enveloping me, the sound of footsteps real? Or had I fallen asleep and begun to dream?

I awoke with a start, the clang of a bell still echoing in my ears. It was midnight, according to the clock on the mantel. The book was open on my lap and the lamp still glowed.

The storm was gone, I realized, leaving behind a profound silence. Putting the book aside, I rose—somewhat stiffly—from my chair and went to the balcony door. The air was soft, tinged with moisture still, the hills serene under a sky filled with stars.

The monastery ruins hulked, their shapes impenetrable and forbidding. As I watched, a single light began to glow. At first I thought it might be someone exploring despite the obvious dangers of such an endeavor, but the light didn't move. It remained stationary.

Someone was lurking in the ruins. I couldn't help but wonder: who—and why?

When the light continued to burn, I decided to assuage my curiosity and find out who was there.

What if it were a prowler getting up to mischief? Chasing him off would only improve Estella's estimation of my worth.

The thought forced me to acknowledge that I thought very highly of her, myself. Our conversation over dinner had shown her to be erudite, intelligent, and kind, not to mention beautiful. I had never met such a perfect specimen of womanhood—nor one who was so unobtainable for the likes of me, a humble bookseller from a university town. No, Estella was fated to wed a prince or other nobleman, to rule over this corner of Italy as a benefactress and patron of all that is good.

The fact that she had found only delight in the so-called fatal folio only reinforced my conclusions. In her sweet hands, it was fatal no more.

Was it possible—a faint inkling of the truth knocked at the back of my mind.

The light in the ruins flickered, as though reminding me of its presence, and I thrust aside my speculations. If I was to go, it should be now.

I pulled on my boots and my coat and picked up the lamp. I wasn't going to try to make my journey in the dark. The only danger was that the person in the ruins would see me approaching but it couldn't be helped. The landscape and the tumbled walls were too dangerous to traverse otherwise.

Thinking to bring a companion, I rapped at Mr. Coates's door. He didn't answer, and after a long moment, I tested the knob. It was unlocked. When I pushed the door open, I saw that the room was empty, curtains blowing in the breeze. Was he out on his balcony? When I went to see, I discovered that this was also deserted.

The library. The rascal was probably looking at the folio, perhaps even planning to steal it and leave. I had rarely seen a man so single-minded when it came to a book, and I wasn't without experience in that regard. Collectors could be obsessed, fanatics, even, when it came to the editions they coveted.

Was his inheritance conditional on this gift? I could not think of any other reason why he would go to the trouble and the expense of traveling to this remote place otherwise. Again, the truth knocked, but it was quickly pushed away again in my eagerness to be on my way. Now that I had determined to venture on a quest that would take some effort and time, I naturally longed for my bed. How perverse is man.

Mr. Coates was not in the library as expected, so I continued out to the grounds alone. I exited through the garden doors and passed through what must surely be an enchanting retreat in the daylight hours. Fountains burbled. Flowering hedges released alluring scents. Pebbled paths crunched under my feet.

A gate in the wall led into overgrown fields, the grass wet and up to my knees. Despite the discomfort of this, I kept pressing forward, eager to reach the ruins that always seemed tantalizingly just out of reach.

When I stumbled on a stone hidden in the grass, I knew I had reached the destroyed monastery at last. Thinking it prudent, I stopped to survey the way ahead, my lantern lifted high. Among the tumbled walls, I could see the remains of a courtyard. The wavering light was on the other side, in what looked to be an intact section of the structure.

*With a deep breath of resolve, I continued on.
Whoever was inside the ancient house would soon
be receiving a visitor.*

As I closed the book, deciding to save the reveal for
later, I had another tempting thought. Before I continued
the inventory, I would take another look around the writing garret.

The loose page we'd found nagged at me. Why was it
left behind? Dropped by accident? If so, where was the
rest of the manuscript, and why hadn't it been added at
some point? I hoped the book hadn't been burned. That
would be tragic.

I packed up, making sure I left the kitchen spotless, and
returned to the library. Wary of the door that shut on its
own—or had it?—I propped a chair against it and taped
up a note that said, *I'm in the closet, do not close the
door, please!*

Making sure I had my phone, I climbed the tower
stairs, my heart beating faster with anticipation. Whether
or not I found the lost book, it was a real thrill to explore,
to enter a room untouched for centuries.

Once again, I circuited the room, studying the view out
of every window, which had sills wide enough to sit on.
In one direction, the towers of Cambridge were visible,
and in another, the river wound through the countryside,
patchwork fields bordered with stone on either side. Ignore
the few signs of the modern era and this was what Selwyn Scott had seen. Wind whistled around the tower, a
haunting, melancholy sound. Outside the patches of sunshine, the room was icy cold, making me appreciate my
thick sweater and warm socks.

I took a closer look at the chaise longue. With its rolled
and tufted upholstery header and carved wood trim, it

was a handsome piece. Too bad several metal tacks along the front were hanging loose, along with the frayed gold braid trim in that section.

Hunkering down, I studied the area, wondering how easy it would be to repair. If I owned it, I might carry it downstairs and use it. It might be too valuable, though.

Standing up, I rested my hand on the seat. It didn't give the way it should, as if the cushion had gone hard. Oliver had said the same thing. I pushed down along the seat, trying to see if the whole thing was that way. It wasn't. Other sections, while not exactly soft, gave under my palm.

The firmness of the seat. A section of upholstery that had been tampered with.

I plopped down on the floor, ignoring the thump to my rear, and carefully pushed my fingers up under the fabric.

I touched paper. Holding my breath, barely daring to put my hopes to the test, I found the edges, grabbed it, and pulled. Gently.

A stack of pages flopped down into my lap, dust flying everywhere.

I had found *Among the Ruins*.

CHAPTER 20

For a long moment, I stared at the long-lost manuscript, silently gloating. Well, silently between sneezes. The ancient dust was horrible on my sinuses.

I leafed through the pile to see if all the pages were there, which in this case meant peeking at the last sheet. *The End.* So yes, with the possible addition of the one on the desk, we had the whole book.

The temptation to start reading was almost overwhelming but I managed to choke it back. The Scotts needed to see it first.

As if conjured up by my thoughts, footsteps trod softly on the stairs. Was Kieran back from London already? It didn't seem possible.

Oliver appeared in the doorway. "Molly. There you are." Since I was seated, he loomed over me. "What's that?"

My gaze fastened on the orange sneakers he was wearing once again. Were they a sign of his innocence or guilt?

"I just found *Among the Ruins.*" I patted the chaise longue. "It was under the upholstery where someone stuffed it." Who, when, and why were questions still unanswered.

He trod across the room with careful footfalls, as if approaching some kind of grail. Perhaps it was, to him. He reached out a hand. "Can I see?"

I clutched the pages to my chest. "In a minute. I want to tell Kieran and Lady Asha first." I snapped a couple of pictures and sent them to Kieran, sprinkling the text with excited emojis. Oliver stood over me, watching. "Can you step back, please? You're looming." I had a thought. "Why aren't you at St. Aelred?" When did the man teach? It seemed lately that he was always out here.

He moved back a couple of steps. "Dr. Cutler tore a couple of strips off me this morning. I had to get away for a while."

"Oh no." Text sent, I looked up at him. "I'm sorry. The whole thing is terribly unfair."

Oliver folded his arms. "It certainly is. I wouldn't respond to Thad's blackmail so this is what I get. Unjustly written up and scrutinized. Cutler told me he wants to see all the papers I mark up this term. Then we'll discuss how I graded them."

The blackmail remark spurred a brief thought, one I couldn't quite grasp, so I moved on. "How ridiculous. At this point in your career, you don't need to be monitored like that." I could see it for student teachers, maybe. "Why is he doing this? Why didn't he brush off Thad's complaint? After all, he's—" *Dead.* I stopped myself there.

"Because Thad's parents are big donors. Dr. Cutler wants to stay on their good side. If throwing me under the bus is a suitable sacrifice, he'll do it." His tone was bitter. "He knows my options are limited."

"Unless you do quit and write that bestseller."

"Why do you think I've been obsessed with Selwyn Scott and my own writing? It's saving my sanity."

"I get it." Using the seat, I hoisted myself to my feet. "Why don't we go downstairs where it's a little more comfortable? You can read while I keep going with the inventory." As long as he didn't take the manuscript out of the library, I was sure it would be all right to let him look at it. Not that I really had a say, except that, in the absence of Kieran and his parents, I was the de facto library steward.

I gathered the loose page from the desk and we descended the tower stairs. "Back to work," I said as we entered the library, so warm in comparison to the garret. "This an okay spot?" I set the bundle on a different table.

"Perfect." Oliver pulled out a chair and sat, absorbed within seconds.

We'd need to make copies of that, so it wouldn't get damaged from people handling it. One thing I'd noticed, though, was that the paper was much thicker than our paper today. Made to last.

I got back to work, checking my phone now and then for a text from Kieran, who was probably somewhere without service. Or busy with his father's appointments.

"Knock, knock." We looked over to see Sophie Verona in the doorway, casual but elegant in a black leather jacket, skinny jeans, and ankle boots. Her hair was down around her shoulders, shiny and loose.

Oliver pushed back in his chair. "Sophie. I wasn't sure when you were coming."

She made a face. "Me either. My last tutorial canceled, though. So here I am." She strolled through the room, taking it all in. "I could spend years in this library."

"Me too," I said. "And might be, slow as this inventory is going." I was a little annoyed that she'd shown up and interrupted my streak.

"We're going out to dinner in Hazelhurst," Oliver said,

as if he had to keep me informed. "Kieran knows we're meeting here."

I waved a hand as if to say it didn't concern me, which it did not. Continuing to enter books into the library program, I pretended not to listen, although I couldn't help it.

"What's that?" Sophie asked, taking the seat next to Oliver. She pulled it close, so they were almost touching, thigh to thigh.

"It's another manuscript by my ancestor, Selwyn Scott," Oliver said. "Very exciting find."

Sophie glanced at it then said, "I have some disturbing news."

"What's that?" Oliver sounded alarmed. "Did they figure out who—"

Her headshake was abrupt. "No, no. You know I've had Amy take over the books. For the Institute." She paused for his nod. "She found some irregularities."

Out of the corner of my eye, I saw him pull back, frowning. "Irregularities? Like what?"

"Like missing money." Sophie's tone was vicious. "The little weasel was stealing from us."

"No, really? I can't believe it . . . Why?" Oliver honestly sounded confused. "His family is richer than God."

Sophie shrugged. "Maybe it was a sport to him, you know, see what he could get away with. Anyway, that's where that stands." She sighed heavily. "Want to get out of here? I could use a drink."

Oliver checked his phone. "We can do that. Need to make a call first, though, to one of my students. Hang on." Still staring at the device, he wandered out of the library. A moment later, low tones drifted from the other room.

Sophie glanced over and caught me staring. Her smile was fixed. "Molly. How are you?"

"Fine," I said, trying to sound casual even though my pulse was banging. This was the first time I'd had a chance to talk to Sophie alone. What should I say? Should I plunge right in and talk about Thad?

In the end, caution won. "I've been taking part in the Gothic Institute activities," I said. "It's been really amazing. I went on Amy's Gothic tour, for one." *And saw you kissing Oliver.*

Her face lightened. "I'm so glad to hear that. Putting on an event like that is such an effort and I always worry it won't quite go off."

I rolled my eyes. "Totally hear you. I think the same whenever the bookshop has a reading." *Rapport established.* "Amy said you want to hold it in Paris next year."

Her gaze went down. "Ah. Yes. Well. Perhaps. If we can raise the money."

Amy said you've gotten some big sponsors. Sidestepping, I nodded at the manuscript. "Maybe *Among the Ruins* can be unveiled there. That would be a huge draw. With any luck, it's as good as *The Fatal Folio*." *Unless someone steals that manuscript as well.* Maybe I shouldn't have drawn attention to it.

"Have you read *The Fatal Folio*?" Sophie had an odd, almost mocking expression on her face. "It's one of my class assignments."

"I'm reading it now," I said. "Totally engrossed."

"The core premise of the book raises great debate among my students. Some, including Thad, believe that the notion of retribution from an unseen hand is mere fantasy." I must have looked confused because she added, "Enough said. I don't want to spoil it for you."

The word *retribution* sounded familiar. I'd seen it somewhere recently. Where, though?

Whistling, Oliver strode back into the room. "Ready?"

In answer, Sophie rose to her feet and slung her handbag strap over her shoulder.

As Oliver guided Sophie out, fingertips on her lower back, he said, "Tell Kieran I'll catch up with him later."

"Will do. Have a nice night." I'd learned something new today. Thad's sketchy ventures went beyond selling other people's books. He had embezzled from the Gothic Institute, it sounded like.

Or had he? Convenient that he couldn't defend himself.

I glanced out the window, noticing that dusk was falling. A few more books and I'd head for home. If I came back tomorrow and worked all day, I should be able to make a real dent in the project. That, along with the discovery of *Among the Ruins*, would make my next report a happy one. Before I left, the manuscript was going in the closet and I would hide the key and tell Kieran where it was.

Speaking of Kieran, I still hadn't heard a word, which wasn't like him. He was usually prompt in his responses.

I hope nothing is wrong. Pushing aside a sense of foreboding, I turned to the next book in the pile.

•❦•

The bookshop was closed when I got home, so I dropped my bags and hurried through to the kitchen. Here, all was warmth and good cheer—Aunt Violet busy at the stove, Mum pouring wine into three glasses, and Sir Jon sitting at the table, both cats vying for his attention.

"Sir Jon," I said, taking off my coat and hanging it on a peg. "Good to see you." Inwardly I cringed, hoping he wasn't here to scold me for barging into his investigation. Not that I didn't have legitimate reasons to be at Dubold's.

"Nice to see you as well, Molly." Sir Jon rubbed Clarence under his chin and the old cat purred so loudly we all laughed.

"You have the touch," Aunt Violet said, wiping her hands on her apron. Her cheeks were pink from heat—and dare I say it? Sir Jon's presence. "Potatoes are almost ready."

"What are we having?" I pulled a bottle of brown ale out of the fridge and popped the top. "It sure smells good." Something savory was in the oven.

"Kilmarnock pie," Aunt Violet said. "Beef and gravy." She poked the potatoes with a fork and turned off the gas. "Runner beans and mash."

My mouth was already watering. Aunt Violet made delicious mashed potatoes using lots of milk, butter, salt, and pepper. One of my go-to comfort foods.

"Is there anything I can do?" I asked. Mum, who was setting the table, shook her head, so I went to sit beside Sir Jon and pat cats. And drink beer.

"I was surprised to see you earlier," Sir Jon said dryly. "What brought you to Reginald Dubold's?"

I glanced at Aunt Violet, worried she might get upset again at the mention of the crooked bookseller. She continued to mash potatoes without a hitch so I went ahead and told Sir Jon about Amy's books. "Sean Ryan was here earlier and he promised to help me get them back for Amy," I concluded. "I have a pretty good idea who sold them to him." He looked interested so I went on. "Thad Devine. Amy had lent him the books."

"The student who was murdered?" Sir Jon rubbed his chin. "Hmm. Not to his credit, is it? Selling your friend's books."

"It certainly isn't," Aunt Violet said. "What a low move on his part." She slid mitts on and opened the oven, where four small pastry pies sat on a cookie sheet. Mum went to stand beside her, helping serve the food and ferry it to the table.

After we were all served, Sir Jon said grace and we dug in. After a few bites of potatoes smothered in gravy and tender meat, I said, "Can you share anything about today's raid?"

"Raid?" Aunt Violet asked. Then understanding dawned on her face. "Reginald's crimes finally caught up to him, huh?"

"Nothing gets past you, my dear," Sir Jon murmured. He gave each of us *the look* before saying, "This has to stay here, understand?"

"We understand," we all murmured.

"Reginald Dubold has been on our watch list for a while. We got a tip that he'd started trading under the table again so we went in today."

"Did you find the *Fatal Folio* manuscript?" I asked, my heart leaping with hope. Maybe they also knew who had sold it to Reginald. Who had stolen it right under our noses at Hazelhurst House. It couldn't be Thad, although the connection would tie in with Amy's books, since he was already gone when the theft occurred.

Sir Jon shook his head. "I'm sorry to report that we did not. Other books on the list, yes. Mr. Dubold won't be selling books for a while."

I sagged back in my chair with disappointment. "You didn't? Where can it be?"

"Maybe the thief still has it," Sir Jon suggested. "I'll ask Reginald about it next time we question him. Find out if they approached him."

"I hope they didn't sell it to someone else. Though I can't imagine who." How would university students find a collector content with black market purchases? "I was so sure . . . there's already a connection between Reginald and the students at St. Aelred. Thad had his card, and like I said, Amy's books ended up there."

"We'll find it, Molly," Sir Jon said. "Sooner or later."

At least we had the new manuscript, which I had put in the closet at Hazelhurst House for now. Anxious now about not hearing from Kieran, I took a look at my phone.

Finally a text in my inbox. *Sorry to be out of touch. Dad was admitted today. His blood pressure was too low. Turned out to be electrolytes. Staying overnight.*

Phew. I'm so glad he's going to be OK. I hope you're sitting down. If you aren't then, do.

What? He sent a frightened face emoji.

It's good news. Really, really good news.

Okay, spill, will you?

I found Among the Ruins. It was tucked inside the chaise longue up in the tower.

Oh. I saw the pictures but I didn't quite get it. Too distracted. A comical string of exclamations and emojis followed that made me laugh.

"What's so funny?" Mum asked pointedly.

"Sorry to be rude. Kieran gave me an update on his dad and then I told him the big news. He's pretty excited." I felt a grin break over my face. "I haven't told you either, have I?"

"No," Aunt Violet said with a sniff. "You haven't."

"I found a second Selwyn Scott novel. It's called *Among the Ruins* and was never published. Lady Asha wants to and can, now that we actually located it."

"I didn't know there was a second book," Aunt Violet said. "How did I miss that?"

"No one knew," I said. "I found a reference to it in a letter to Selwyn Scott's publisher. For some reason it was never published. Now it can be."

"What a wonderful discovery," Mum said. "You're a real book detective."

I took my last bite of potato and gravy. "I like the sound of that." Searching out books would probably be a lot safer than the murder investigations I kept stumbling into.

After dinner, Aunt Violet and Sir Jon went to the Magpie to listen to Celtic music. Mum and I stayed in to read more of *The Fatal Folio*.

The Fatal Folio, cont.

I was almost to the lit window when I heard Estella calling out behind me. "Signore Marlboro. Matthew. Wait for me."

What was she doing out here, in the dark, alone? When she arrived at my side, I conveyed these sentiments to her.

"After I saw the light," she explained, "I went out onto my balcony to get a better look. Then, a few minutes later, I saw you leave the house." She put a hand to her chest, trying to catch her breath. "I am as curious as you to find out who it is."

"You've never seen anyone here, at the monastery?"

She shook her head. "Not for a long time. Years. My father always warned me to stay away from the ruins. He said they were dangerous."

"He was right. Stay close so we can look out for each other." Leading the way, I navigated the overgrown grass and tumbled stones.

Soon we reached the window, discovering that the sill was too high for us to peer inside. What now? I scanned the walls, trying to find a way in.

"Lift me," Estella said. "So I can look through the window."

I considered the idea, measuring the distance and her height. It might work. "All right, we can try it. Be careful not to get spotted. Don't say anything."

She regarded me with amusement. "I think I can manage that."

Crouching down, I laced my hands together so she could step onto them. She placed her tiny foot on my palms and I lifted her upward.

Her hands gripped the edge of the window as she strained to see over the stone lip. Then her leg began to waver and she tipped back, forcing me to hastily throw my arms around her to break her fall. Regardless, we both tumbled to the ground.

"Why did you do that?" I whispered, rubbing my elbow and knee.

Instead of answering, she stared up at the window, her mouth agape. Following her gaze, I soon understood her surprise.

A hooded monk stood in the window. "You can come through the door," he said in a deep voice. "It would be easier."

CHAPTER 21

I woke up to a text from Kieran. *Bad news*. My heart began to race.

Your dad? With held breath, I waited for his response. "This stinks, Puck," I said. Lying on my extra pillow, he reached out a paw to touch my arm.

Sorry, I didn't mean to alarm you. I might be late for the dance tonight.

The dance? I don't care about that. I'm just glad that your dad is okay?

He is. Much better. We have another meeting with the doctors today.

Phew. And tell him Puck says get better.

Ha ha. I will. X

Hmm. *X*. Some Brits used *X* as a closing to messages and posts all the time, which gave them a friendly intimacy. Kieran didn't.

X. I thought for a second and upped the ante with a hug. *O*.

He sent a smiley face back.

Well, then. I was awake and might as well get going rather than try to snooze a little longer. I pulled the curtains open to check out the lane, a morning ritual. Today, frost furred the cobblestones, the trash bins, and the roof-tops, which steamed in the rising sun. Lights were on inside Tea & Crumpets and I decided to go have breakfast at Daisy's.

"It's a cold one, Puck," I said, opening a drawer for some woolies. "A real sweater day."

A quick shower later, I was crossing the street to the tea shop. Daisy was clearing a table inside, placing mugs and plates in a dish tub. She looked up when the bells jangled. "Good morning, Molly. Hurry up, close that door."

I wrestled it closed against the wind. "It's frigid out there." The shop was in a lull, which meant Daisy would have time to chat. Only a few tables were occupied with people tapping away on laptops or looking at the phones. Classical music played over the loudspeakers, low enough for private conversation.

Daisy wiped the table before returning to the counter. "What will you have?"

"My usual coffee and something to eat." I scanned the bakery case. "Sausage rolls? Perfect. Two, please."

"Heated?" Daisy put them on a plate.

"Yes, please. I'm planning to eat here." I leaned on the counter and watched as she popped them into the microwave and turned on the kettle. "I have a lot of updates. Oh, and there's a dance tonight at St. Aelred."

"Already on it." Daisy pulled my plate from the microwave. "Tim and I put together costumes. We're going as the leads in *Nosferatu*."

I laughed. "Great. Kieran and I used *The Fatal Folio* as our inspiration. Hopefully he'll make it back from London in time."

"London?" Daisy added napkin-rolled silverware to my tray before deftly pouring boiling water through the coffee cone.

"His father had medical appointments." I waited until she finished pouring. "Can you sit a minute?"

She glanced out the window, at the empty lane. "Sure. Until someone comes." She grabbed a cup of tea and joined me at a table in the corner.

After the first salty, savory bite of sausage roll followed by a rich, delicious sip of coffee, I said, "Feels like I haven't seen you for ages. Not since the tour, right?"

Daisy blew on her tea to cool it. "Feels like months ago."

"Sure does." I swallowed another bite, thinking about where to begin. Why not lead with the best news? "I found *Among the Ruins*."

She let out a squeal loud enough to draw attention. After curious glances, everyone went back their devices. "That's fabulous, Molly. Where was it?"

I told her about my excursion to the garret. "Such fun to make a groundbreaking literary discovery."

"Any progress on Selwyn's identity?"

"Nothing definitive." I showed her the handwriting samples while detailing the trip to the cemetery. That led to a discussion of Oliver's orange shoes, followed by a segue into my trip to Reginald Dubold's and the raid by Sir Jon and his team.

Daisy listened with only occasional prompts and exclamations. "You have had a time of it, haven't you? My goodness." A sip of tea. "And they still don't know who killed Thad, do they?"

"No arrest yet."

"Did they ever find his phone?" Daisy asked.

I started my second sausage roll, which was as good as the first. "Not that I know of. Too bad, because Thad might have been meeting someone at the gate. Wouldn't that be a tidy wrap-up?"

"It would." Daisy's gaze was distant. "So where do we stand?"

I liked how she included herself in my situations. "Jury's still out on Selwyn, though it's got to be Agatha, Frances, or Samuel." An idea struck. "Or two of the three. Maybe they were coauthors." I shelved the concept for later dissection. "Moving on, Thad's case seems stuck right now. The matter of the missing manuscript is too."

"You think it was someone from St. Aelred?"

"Someone who was at Oliver's talk, definitely," I clarified. "Since then, I found out that Thad knew Reginald Dubold, who is in big trouble for illicit book sales. That's probably how Amy's books ended up there. On purpose or not, we don't know. From there, it's a logical step that someone in the group of friends also saw an opportunity to sell the manuscript illegally."

"They didn't find it at the bookstore, you said. Which means . . . ?"

"I don't know, to be honest. Reginald could be lying. He might already have sold it. Or the deal hadn't been finalized. Maybe he was looking for a buyer first." I was spitballing here.

"The last thing you said. Maybe the thief still has it." A gleam shone in Daisy's eyes. "I have an idea, which is probably crazy and due to my binge-watching a detective show last night—"

"The best ideas are out there," I said, nodding to encourage her. "Go on."

"Send texts to the people you suspect, pretending to be Reginald. Say you have a buyer."

"Daisy . . . really? They would see my number."

"Buy a burner phone." Daisy sounded triumphant. "I bet he uses one to do his deals."

"Okay," I said slowly. "What if someone responds? It

won't be admissible." I cringed at the probable reaction I would get from Sean Ryan and Sir Jon. *Yikes*.

"Probably not. But you'll know where the manuscript is. Take it from there."

I would love to know where it was—and rescue the precious document before it was destroyed or lost forever. I thought of a final objection. "I don't have their cell phone numbers."

"Yes, you do," Daisy said. "Look in the packet from Oliver's talk. There was a list of attendees for the conference, complete with cell phone numbers and email addresses." I must have looked disbelieving because she added, "I picked up more than one packet after. People left them."

I still had my handout in my bag, I thought. I hadn't even looked inside the folder.

"You really think I should do that?" What if people found out it was me who sent the text? *How could they with a burner?* "I'll think about it. Want to meet up later? We can walk over to the dance together."

"Sounds like a plan." Daisy rose from the table. "Want a refill to go?"

€

At seven that evening, I was dressed for the dance, Kieran still hadn't returned from London, and I had a burner phone sitting on my bed, staring accusingly up at me.

I'd never bought one of these devices, which were perfectly legal yet felt illicit, probably due to their use by criminals, at least according to the novels I'd read. It had been amazingly inexpensive too.

Sitting beside it was a printout from the packet, which

I had kept. Daisy was right, most attendees had included their email addresses and cell phone numbers. I'd seen such lists before, at library conferences. The aim of the organizers was to help people network. Not set up a sting, I was guessing.

"Molly?" Daisy called up the stairs, followed by the sound of her footsteps. Puck leaped off the bed and went to greet her. When she entered my bedroom, she had him in her arms. "Sweet kitty," she said, stroking his head. "I used to see you lurking in the lane. Now you have a lovely new home." She would have taken him in but cats—and cat hair—weren't allowed in tea shops due to health rules.

"I'm ready." I checked my appearance one more time in front of the mirror. Aunt Violet had found a lacy black shawl that I was wearing over my hair, like a mantilla. It added the perfect touch to my outfit.

"You look gorgeous." Daisy set Puck down and circled a finger. "Turn around."

I obligingly spun for her. "You look beautiful too." She was dressed in a similarly full taffeta dress, a wool shawl over her shoulders pinned with a cameo and her hair hanging in sausage curls.

Daisy patted her hair. "Not bad. I wouldn't want this fuss every day."

"No, we're lucky that way, aren't we?" I searched around for the small handbag I was bringing tonight. "We don't even have to wear underwear if we don't want to."

She laughed. "True." Then she noticed the phone on the bed. "You got a burner." Daisy picked it up and examined it back and front. "Did you text anyone?"

"Not yet." I found the bag and slid my own phone inside. Keys and a tiny wallet with bills and my identification followed.

Daisy plopped down on the bed. "No time like the present. Let's do it."

I stood there, holding the bag, then placed it back on the dresser. "You think we should?"

"Why not? If they're innocent, they'll ignore it. And probably block you. No big deal." Daisy was already flipping through the list. "There are quite a few names here."

I sat beside her. "I know, that's the problem. They weren't all at the talk."

"Maybe Oliver has the list of who actually signed in," Daisy suggested.

"Probably." I hesitated. "I could ask him for it, I suppose. I'd have to tell him why." The fewer people who knew about this, the better. If nothing came of it, it would stay here, in this room, with me, Daisy, and Puck.

"Why don't we start with the main players, then?" Daisy scanned the list. "Half the people who went don't even know who Selwyn Scott is, I bet. The students closest to Oliver definitely do."

I laughed. "Yeah, I'm sure he makes sure to mention the connection." I moved closer to look over her shoulder. "So, Amy, Josh, and Wesley. We'll text them. Oh, Sophie Verona too." I couldn't quite bring myself to include Oliver. If Kieran found out—

Daisy didn't press me. "Okay. What shall we say?"

"Something simple." I thought for a minute. "How about: 'I have a buyer. Text me back if you want to proceed.'"

"I like it. Short and simple, doesn't reveal anything. Josh first." Daisy entered his number and began typing in the text box.

"You know, Amy had quite the reaction when she found out Reginald Dubold was under investigation." As

Daisy worked on the text, I told her how shocked Amy had been when I said his name.

"She might not answer, then," Daisy said. "If she thinks it's the police texting her."

"True." That would mean another dead end. Not much lost, though, except a few minutes on our end. And a few pounds. Maybe I could resell the phone and recoup some.

Daisy sent the text to the three students, then handed me the phone. "Bring this with you in case one of them answers."

"Hold on. Why don't we send Sophie one?" I flipped the list pages so I could see the beginning. Sophie, Oliver, and Thad were listed as conference contacts.

Thad. I thought of his missing cell phone. The killer might have tossed it somewhere—into a trash can or the river; hopefully not. Or run it over with a car.

What if they'd kept it? Purely on impulse, I sent the same text to Thad's number. Sophie's as well. "There. All done."

Hopefully we would get an answer from someone.

I couldn't help but think of *The Fatal Folio*, and how greed led to so many problems. Thad hadn't been content with what he had, which by all accounts was a generous amount. Whoever had stolen the rare manuscript had been overcome by the temptation to make money through a criminal act. Worst of all, Thad's greed—for money, Amy's attention, and no doubt other things unknown as of this moment—had led to his death. Or so I believed.

The Fatal Folio, cont.

The monk directed us to a doorway I hadn't noticed, and met us there with his lamp. Most consid-

erate of him, and I have to admit being surprised
by his welcome. Anyone who lurked in a ruined
monastery was most likely a hermit, I would have
thought.

"I knew your father well," he said to Estella as
we traversed a half-ruined corridor. "I am very
sorry for your loss."

She inclined her head in acknowledgement.
"When did you meet my father?"

"We had various encounters over the years,"
was the cryptic answer. "He was very opinionated
in some ways and we would debate. Iron sharpens
iron, you know." He lifted the lamp a little higher,
illuminating the room that was our destination.

Besides a table and chair, it held a pallet on the
floor and a satchel or two.

"My donkey is housed in the stable," he explained as he set the lamp on the table. "I pilgrim-
age from place to place as I am led."

I imagined him traveling through Italy from ruin
to ruin. Surely not. He must stop at monasteries
that were still inhabited.

"What leads you here?" I boldly asked. Despite
the beauty and grandeur of the situation, there was
nothing of comfort to be found here. Why didn't he
come to the manor and seek shelter? He wouldn't
be the first holy man to do so.

Estella had the same thought. "Why didn't you
come to me? We would gladly have taken you in."

The monk shook his head. "A kind offer to be
sure, signorina. However, I need to be alone while
writing." He gestured to the table, where an inkpot
and loose pages were placed. He inhaled deeply,

gazing around the bare stone room. "This very room was where The Ramblings of a Monk *was penned. I draw inspiration from this seminal work, even if my own efforts pale in comparison."*

I certainly hoped they would, since the original book was known for its unfortunate effects on its owners.

"My father owned that book," Estella said. "Now it is mine." She sighed. "I already have offers to buy it. Including from Mr. Marlboro's companion."

The monk regarded her with eyes that glittered deep within the shelter of his hood. "Does he realize it is not merely a pretty book to place upon a shelf? It has a mysterious power that can be dangerous."

"Surely not." Estella laughed. "I find it delightful."

"You have read it?" The monk seemed to stand even taller as he loomed over her petite form. "You opened the cover and looked at the pages?"

She drew back, her expression puzzled. "Of course I did. How else do you read a book?" She mimed the movements one used while reading.

Seeming to realize that his aspect was overbearing, he pulled back, staring into space as if lost in thought. Then, muttering to himself, he began to pace, hands clasped behind his back.

Estella and I exchanged glances. When she shivered, the shawl she wore entirely inadequate in the chilly room, I offered her my coat. As a gentleman would. She smiled at me with gratitude as I draped it around her shoulders.

"I have never read the book myself," he said. "I was afraid to."

Estella cocked her head. "I don't understand."

"You wouldn't, fair lady. You are obviously blameless and pure of heart." He stared down at her for a long moment as if he could peer right into her soul. "I hesitate to tell you the rest, in light of your own father's death."

"Why?" Estella cried. "I don't understand. The book belongs to me and I need to know the truth about it."

I had an inkling now, a mere theory only, but rather than voice it, I waited for the monk to make it plain. No wonder the author was considered mad. Who would believe it? The deaths were all coincidences, people would say. The way any object gains a reputation of being haunted—or cursed.

The monk closed his eyes and took a deep breath. I had the impression he was girding himself to reveal what he knew. As if once said, the words and their consequences could not be erased.

"Come on, man," I urged him, perhaps without the respect due a cleric. "From what I can gather, it's a matter of life and death." Literally, it seemed.

With a sharp inhale, he squared his shoulders. "All right. I will tell you. After you promise not to call me a liar or otherwise assault me or my character."

"I promise," Estella said. "Although that is quite a disclaimer."

"You will understand why in a moment." Another hesitation, during which time I felt the urge to throttle the man to get him to speak. That would indeed be unbecoming behavior toward a man in holy orders. I might even be arrested.

The silence was fraught. Neither of us breathed. Finally the monk spoke.

"The book has an uncanny power. Each reader discovers a different story."

"You mean they interpret it differently, according to their own thinking?" I asked.

He shook his head. "No. Different tales entirely. The book reflects back to each reader the state of his or her soul. That is why so many have died while perusing it. They are stricken by the blatant and unavoidable depiction of their hidden sins."

CHAPTER 22

Downstairs, I was thrilled to see George seated at the kitchen table, having a cup of tea with Mum and Aunt Violet. "Hello, stranger," I said, going to give him a hug. I hadn't seen George since the tour.

He chuckled and blushed. "Don't you two look a treat? Is that the latest in club wear?"

We burst out laughing. "Not hardly," I said, twirling for the full effect. Daisy copied me. "We're going to the gothic dance at St. Aelred." Seeing that we had a few minutes before meeting Tim, I decided to give George an update. I told him about Reginald Dubold and Amy's books, Sophie's discovery of a different sort of books being cooked, and Oliver's orange shoes. I mentioned finding *Among the Ruins* but not that Daisy and I had set up a sting. I wasn't ready to admit that to anyone yet.

He took it all in with nods and occasional interjections. "It all revolves around Thad, doesn't it? He had the bookseller's card and he was doing the association books."

"Not surprising, I suppose," I said. "It seems he was always short of money. He even borrowed from his cousin, who has far fewer resources."

"So someone took a leaf out of his book and stole the manuscript?" George suggested. "It does seem likely that the thief knew Thad."

Daisy and I exchanged looks. That had been our theory too. I thought uneasily of Amy's reaction when I said Reginald's name. I didn't want her to be guilty, which meant I wasn't being totally objective.

"You think Thad's murder was related to money?" Mum asked.

"Could be," I said. "He also harassed Amy, who was his ex-girlfriend. Her new boyfriend, who was also Thad's friend, was pretty upset about it. That's Josh, who the police questioned. They also found a bloodstained jacket in Josh's room."

"They didn't arrest him?" George asked. "That must mean they didn't have quite enough evidence, even with the jacket."

Aunt Violet mimed someone using a magnifying glass. "The forensic evidence probably didn't match Josh. Lucky for him."

I remembered the shooting in Scotland. "There might have been a first attempt on Thad's life." I explained how Thad had been hunting grouse and almost hit by a stray bullet.

"Who was there?" George asked. "Any of our players?"

"Josh and Wesley were hunting. Amy was there, sitting by the fire with the old aunts, she said."

George sipped tea absently. "It's a puzzler, all right."

"No kidding. That's probably why the police case has stalled." I sighed, having hoped George might offer some pithy insight that solved everything.

"Did you see the email tonight?" he asked. "I got on the St. Aelred mailing list somehow and there's been an announcement. Dr. Sophie Verona has been promoted to full professor."

"Oh no," I groaned. "Oliver was hoping to get that promotion. What a disappointment for him." I wondered if he would quit teaching, as he said. "Thad again. His complaint obviously succeeded in blocking Oliver's progress."

Although I believed George, I checked the St. Aelred site for the announcement. There it was. Seeing it in print struck me almost as strongly as if Oliver were my own cousin. Scanning the notice, I saw that Sophie had been commended for scholarly papers on English novelists. One on retribution as theme, with a focus on *The Fatal Folio*, had received a prize.

There was that word again. Retribution.

"I'm sorry Thad was killed," George said. "But I must say, he doesn't sound like a most agreeable chap."

"No, he was not." He'd run roughshod over the people he knew until someone got sick of it. I looked at the clock. "We'd better scoot. It's time to meet Tim and head to the dance."

Followed by a chorus of "have fun," and "be careful," Daisy and I donned coats, hats, and gloves and stepped into the chilly evening.

❧

Tim emerged from the bike shop right as we arrived at the front door, sporting a Victorian suit, derby hat, and silver-headed cane.

"Good timing," Daisy said, giving him a quick kiss. "You look very dapper."

"I was watching for you," he said, twirling the cane. "May I escort you lovely ladies to the ball?"

"You may, kind sir," I said with a curtsey. "Lord Scott sends his regrets." Referring to Kieran by this title was a joke, because his brother was next in line. They took it that way and laughed.

"I understand Lord Scott is detained deep in the dark belly of London Town." Tim kept up the joke. "May he escape unscathed."

"May he indeed," I replied. "I await his return to the wilds of Cambridgeshire with the eagerness of a pining heart." I fluttered my hand as if overcome.

Daisy gripped my arm. "Pray do not faint, milady. The cobblestones are not a suitable bed for your fair form."

Bantering in this vein, we linked arms and sauntered up the lane and out onto Trinity Street, where our unusual attire garnered quite a few glances. Tim especially hammed it up, tipping his hat to other pedestrians and wishing them a good evening.

"This is fun," Daisy said when someone whistled at us. "We should do it more often."

"We could even earn a little extra money." Pulling away, Tim began to dance a jig and sing, then held his hat out to passersby. When one man reached into his pocket, he clapped the hat back on his head. "You're in luck," he said. "Performance is free tonight."

The man strode away with his companions, shaking his head. "Takes all kinds," drifted back to us. "It's a college town. What do you expect?" one of his friends said.

The three of us linked arms again and danced down the road, laughing. I felt like we were Dorothy, the lion, and the tin man, on their way to see the wizard.

We signed in at the main gate, listing our destination as the dance. The elderly porter smiled as he took in our costumes. "I haven't seen the like since I was a boy," he jested.

"Surely you haven't been here that long?" Daisy joked back with a shake of her curls.

"Almost it seems, at times." He pushed a campus map forward. "Go in the dining hall entrance and follow the signs. The dance is in the cellars."

"That sounds appropriately creepy," I said. "Thank you for your help."

"You're very welcome. Have a nice evening." He turned to the next visitors.

We emerged into the main court. "Where now?" Tim asked.

"I forgot you haven't been here." Daisy tugged on his sleeve. "This way."

As we crossed the path to the building, others in costume joined us. Ghosts. Women in white. Count—and Countess—Dracula. The mood was lively and festive, with much horseplay, chasing each other, and shouting. A fair amount of pregaming had gone on, I guessed, adding to the freedom of donning a new persona.

We pushed through the doors into the building, where, as promised, signs pointed to the staircase down. Beside the stairs, two students sat at a table selling tickets, next to the cloakroom. Taking a closer look at the one dressed in a black fitted coat and feather-trimmed hat from the 1930s, I recognized Amy underneath a thick layer of makeup.

"Rebecca, I presume?" I said. "Great outfit."

Amy glanced up with surprise, easing into a smile when she recognized me. "Good guess." She touched her hair, set into rippling waves. "Bit fussier than I'm used to, but Josh likes it. He's dressed as Max." De Winter. Her eyes scanned my outfit. "I love your costume too. Very gothic."

"Thanks. I'm Estella from *The Fatal Folio*." Was I imagining it or did her lips press together at my mention of the book? "My boyfriend, Kieran, was going to be Matthew Marlboro. Unfortunately he hasn't made it back from London yet."

While we were chatting, Tim had bought three tickets from the other student. He handed me one. "Oh, thanks." I glanced behind me. "Sorry. I'm holding up the line." Clutching the ticket, I moved aside. "See you later, Amy." She was already helping the next person.

"After we drop our coats, let's stop by the ladies'," Daisy said. "Tim, meet you by the stairs?"

He agreed to that and we got into line for the facilities, which moved slowly. I opened my bag to check the burner phone, curious if anyone had responded.

"Anything?" Daisy asked.

"No notifications." I opened the message program to check there. A couple of messages were still in the outbox. "Oh no. They didn't send."

"Do it now," Daisy advised. "There won't be service in the cellar, I'm guessing."

Probably not, if we were underground in a stone-lined vault. Which also meant leaving to check for answers now and then. I wouldn't get any texts in the cellar, I guessed. I sent again, this time waiting until I heard the little sound that meant they were airborne before putting the phone away.

That chore done, I people-watched while the line inched along. The costumes were really fun, showing much creativity. A hooded monk wearing a black mask that made them appear faceless pushed through the entrance doors. "There's Wesley," I said. "He said he was coming as a monk." Then I glanced at his feet.

Orange sneakers. I must have flinched because Daisy said, "What's wrong?"

"I didn't know Wesley owned orange sneakers."

Daisy frowned in confusion. "Maybe it isn't Wesley. A lot of people own those trainers, Tim said."

I barely heard her, my mind already leaping ahead. I pictured Wesley killing his cousin and then running past us, secure in his costume, and entering the college through a different gate. Then up to his room, where he quickly stripped off the jacket, shoes, and mask. He could have done it. St. Aelred wasn't a large college.

Why would he wear the sneakers again? Why not ditch them as he had the jacket?

Then I understood. Shoes wouldn't work to frame someone—unless the person wore the same size. So he'd kept them and now wore them around, practically flaunting them in people's faces.

Daisy elbowed me firmly, interrupting my descent into the rabbit hole. "Cut it out. After we're done here, we'll track that monk down and find out who it is."

"You know me too well," I said ruefully, thinking it had to be Oliver. I sent him a text. *Are you coming to the dance? Look for Estella from The Fatal Folio. Kieran can't make it. Hope to see you.*

After I put away the phone, a shock raced through me. Which phone had I used? Phew. My own. Using two devices was confusing. How did criminals do it? I imagined a dealer sending drop deets to his mom. That would be hard to explain.

As we finally arrived at the restroom door, my phone pinged. Oliver was at the dance and would look for us. *Cool costume. I'm the monk from the book.*

Maybe he was wearing the orange shoes.

"Sorry to make you wait so long," Daisy told Tim when we joined him at the staircase. "That took forever."

"No problem," he said. "I've been having fun watching the action." He let us start down and then followed. "I wonder what they used this for," he asked, his voice echoing as we went down the stone steps.

"Wine cellar? Dungeon for naughty students?" I suggested. We laughed, the sound echoing along with our footsteps.

Rock music grew louder the farther down we went. At the bottom, we were confronted with a thick wooden door, which thankfully opened easily. And then we were in. The party was being held in a huge, cavernous room with arched stone supports. A band thrashed and clashed at one end, while at the other, tables had been set up with food and drink. We headed there first.

"Punch or brew?" Tim shouted above the noise.

A huge vat of red punch sat on the table. I bet it was spiked. Two kegs of beer also sat on the table, with a man in a skeleton suit dispensing. A handwritten label read, *Monk's Head Ale*.

"Brew," I said. "Can you pour me one?" I asked the skeleton.

He threw me a look. "I was getting my own, but sure." He poured me a beer and then two others for Daisy and Tim. We thanked him before he rushed off, carrying two beers.

"Cheers," Tim said, touching his plastic cup to ours. "We made it."

After the first refreshing sip, we browsed the food offerings, which were hilarious. A cheese ball with ham "skin" shaped like a face. Deviled egg eyes. Shrimp in aspic shaped like a brain. Gelatin worms. Fun to look at—and to me, appetite-killing. Others around us didn't think so as they devoured the treats.

I took a cracker and a square of cheese. "Oliver said he's here, in a monk costume."

"Costume of the day, looks like." Tim pointed out another monk nearby.

"I can see why," Daisy said. "It's simple and comfortable and you can throw it on over regular clothes." She tugged at her waist, grimacing. "Unlike this thing. It has built-in boning."

"Suffering for beauty," I said, rolling my eyes. How had women put up with it for so long? I was thankful for light underwear and stretchy clothing.

Yet another monk wove through the crowd, coming right toward us. Once closer, he pushed back his hood and black mask to reveal a head of red curls. Wesley. He was beaming.

I immediately looked at his feet. Black sneakers, not orange. There went my earlier theory.

"Hey," he said. "Glad you could make it." He held up his beer cup to salute mine. Bobbing his head to the music, he glanced around. "Great turnout."

"It is." I sipped my beer, glad to see him in a good mood. He'd usually been either morose or mischievous, such as when he tried to scare me in the shop. "Is Josh here? I saw Amy selling tickets."

Wesley nodded toward the crowded dance floor. After a moment, I saw Josh waving his top hat as he boogied. He too seemed much happier than the last time I'd seen him. Maybe the scars from being hauled off by the police were fading.

Daisy and Tim joined the dancers, almost immediately lost to view.

"Want to dance?" Wesley asked me.

"Not really," I said. "Maybe later. Thanks, though."

Instead of looking for another partner, Wesley hung out with me, not saying much. He kept looking at his phone, which was in his habit pocket. The third time, he caught me noticing. "Expecting a message back."

"You know how it is. A watched phone never pings."

He grinned as he put the phone away. "True. I should give it up."

His vigilance made me itch to check my two phones. I certainly didn't feel comfortable doing that here, in front of him. "You might not have reception down here," I pointed out. "I'm going upstairs to check my messages. Expecting to hear from my boyfriend." *And a manuscript thief.* I pointed to the exit. "Excuse me."

I had to push my way through densely packed bodies to reach the stairs. What was the capacity down here, anyway? By all indications, it had been met.

The upstairs hall was deserted, Amy and her fellow ticket-seller gone. There wasn't a line to the restroom anymore so I went in there, figuring I would have privacy. Inside a stall, I opened my bag and took out my phone. Nothing new from Kieran. I sent a message. *At the dance, missing you. Hope all is well.*

A response came right back. *On my way home. Good news. Will try to make the dance before midnight. Wait before getting into the pumpkin.*

Good news must mean that his father was all right. I was beyond relieved. *Hurray on all counts. Look for my shoe, Prince, and you'll find me.* For good measure, I snapped a picture of my boot and sent it. A thumbs-up came back.

Now for the burner phone. My pulse began to beat faster as I brought the screen to life. Realizing I was holding my breath, I inhaled.

I had a message. Which number was it from? My heart thumped when I recognized the last four digits as Thad's. I had been right. Someone had taken his phone.

The killer? Were the killer and the thief the same person?

Calm down and open the message.

It said: *Great to hear. What was the price they accepted?*

Uh-oh. I had no idea what had been discussed between Dubold and the thief. What should I say? Finally I settled on something vague. *Actually more than we discussed. They're very anxious.*

Awesome. When can we talk? I'd like to hear more—in person.

Now what? I could pretend to be Reginald Dubold in a text message. In real life, not so much.

Although I could watch and see who arrived for this imaginary meeting.

Finally I hit upon a plan. *Meet me outside the Master's Lodge Gate at St. A. Fifteen minutes?*

Fifteen it is.

Now I had fifteen minutes to inform Daisy and Tim what was up before making my way to the gate. I would watch from a distance and see who showed up.

I forwarded the text messages to my regular phone, as backup. Then I debated. Should I send the messages to Sean Ryan? At the very least, he should know that Thad's phone was being used. I thought of sending them to Sir Jon as well, since he was investigating stolen manuscripts.

A couple of things stopped me from sending the messages to Sir Jon, besides the fact he might not appreciate me wading into his investigation. I wasn't one hundred percent sure it was the manuscript Dubold had been trying to sell. Or that Dubold had been the contact. I was making assumptions here. All I knew for sure was that someone had used Thad's phone. I'd made a wild-ass guess about the rest, as they said in Vermont.

I did forward them to Sean, with a note. *Found out by accident that someone is using Thad's phone. Thought you should know. Don't worry. I'm not going to confront them in person.* Now that his phone was on, maybe they could ping it and triangulate, whatever tech magic they did to find cell phones.

Rather than wait for his response, which would probably be scorching, I put away the phones and zipped my bag. I needed to go find Daisy and Tim. They probably were wondering what had happened to me.

They were still on the dance floor, and when she spotted me, Daisy danced her way over. "Come on, Molly." She reached for my hand.

"Later." I bent close to speak into her ear. "I got a response to the text. Thad's."

"What?" She cupped a hand around her ear.

I patted my bag. "Thad's phone." She nodded. "Spying on them. Master's Gate."

She drew back, a frown creasing her brow.

I put circled fingers to my eyes then slashed a finger across my lips, as if zipping them.

She stopped dancing, hands on hips. "I'm coming with you."

I shook my head. Leaning close, I spoke into her ear. "It will blow my cover." I could see the three of us—me, Daisy, and Tim—trying to hide behind a tree. "I won't talk to them, promise."

Daisy gripped my arm. "Be careful," she said. "If you're not back in ten . . ."

Backing away, I nodded. She stared at me for a few seconds before plunging back into the mass of dancers.

After stopping in the cloakroom for my coat, I slipped outside with five minutes to spare. The Master's Lodge Gate was in the next court so I went in that direction, cutting diagonally across the green, which brought me past the bell tower.

Near the gate, I found a spot behind a hedge, a location where I could clearly see the gate area and anyone approaching.

Wind rattled in the bushes and clouds crept across the moon, making it even darker in the shadowed, poorly lit court. The setting was Gothic for sure and when a tall figure in a monk's robe came gliding along the path, I had to suppress a shiver at how perfectly creepy it all was.

I suppressed a groan as the unfortunate truth set in. The monk's hood was up, hiding the wearer's face. Now what? I pushed through the bushes, straining for a glimpse of a nose, a mouth, anything.

The monk glided on, robes swaying gently. They were almost at the gate. A minute or two more and they would be through.

There was nothing for it. Despite my promise to Daisy, I'd have to reveal myself and speak to the monk.

They fumbled at the gate, preparing to open it. Pretending not to have come out of the bushes, I darted to the path about ten feet from the gate.

"Hold on," I called. "Wait. Are you going out?" My ploy was to pretend that I didn't know if the gate was locked from the inside. Visitors were supposed to go through the staffed main gate.

The monk whirled around, making the hood drop back. Red curls caught the dim light from a lamppost.

Wesley.

CHAPTER 23

The Fatal Folio, cont.

My first thought after the monk's extraordinary revelation was that I would never read The Ramblings of a Monk. *Although I tried to do what was right, I was uncomfortably aware of my imperfections. The last thing I needed was to see them on full display, in black and white, as it were.*

I also understood why Estella had read the book without harm. She was an innocent soul, inclined to think the best of people.

"What did my father do?" she asked now, her expression troubled. She began to tremble. "It must have been horrific if facing his sins brought death."

"That is not for us to know or judge," the monk said, wisely I thought. Pursuing this line of inquiry would only cause Estella grief. Her father was gone and there was nothing to be done now. "Your father is in God's hands."

Estella put a hand to her mouth. "I hope so. Rather than the . . . alternative."

The monk put a hand on his shoulder. "Pray for his soul, dear one. That is all we can do."

The obstinate part of my nature reared its contrary head. "Surely this is all a fable. How can a mere book wield such power?"

His response was to stare into me with a burning gaze. "Dare you put it to the test? Why have so many perished after coming into possession of this cursed tome?"

"Perhaps they died of fright, knowing the book's reputation," I argued. "They brought it upon themselves with their expectation."

He shook his head sadly. "One poor soul lived long enough to pen a letter detailing the experience. He had been entranced by the book's beauty until he looked further. He said he saw his misdeeds plainly written, with details only he would know. He died soon after, begging his family for forgiveness."

To me that spoke of delusions brought about by a fevered state of mind. Rather than argue, I decided to leave the monk to his solitary discomfort and return to the villa.

"We will bid you good night," I said, picking up my lamp. "I hope you slumber well."

He watched us as we moved toward the door. "Your skepticism is understandable. In this case, I urge you not to try to prove me wrong. If I could, I would prevent that book from taking more lives. While man's greed is ascendant, that will never happen, I am afraid."

At first I almost shot back a retort, stating that greed had nothing to do with my interest in the book. Then I was forced to revise that hasty conclusion.

Hadn't I traveled all this distance in company with Mr. Coates because of the commission promised? Although I was fascinated by this rare and storied tome, I would not have journeyed so far without compensation.

If not for the promised fee, I would be safely at home in Cambridge right now, tucked in my own bed and fast asleep. How I wished it were so.

Except . . . Estella reached for my arm as we traversed the dark corridor. "Are you worried about Mr. Coates?" she asked. "I am."

To my shame, I had not considered him at all during this last adventure. Once I found that he wasn't in his room, I had blithely made my way here, to the ruins, without giving him further thought.

"Why do you say that, signorina?"

"Estella." Her grip tightened. "After what we have been through together, I consider you my friend."

"Matthew," I said, my throat thick. I was honored by her acceptance and hoped that I might prove worthy of it. Already I was falling short, I realized with chagrin. Witness my lack of concern for the well-being of Mr. Coates.

I helped her out of the building, using fallen blocks for steps. Then we set off across the overgrown field, which held many traps for the unwary. Although the wind was fresh and cold, it was exhilarating, as were the stars spanning the heavens above.

We paused to rest about halfway to the villa garden. "I don't go outside often enough at night," I said, tipping my head back. "Although it is a different matter in the city, the lights and smoke often veil the sky. The cold there is damp and bone-chilling, creeping up from the river with its fogs."

Estella shivered. "I think I would stay inside. It sounds horrid."

"Oh, England has its beauties. And so does Cambridge." I described the halls of learning, the quaint streets, and markets full of the best goods. I found myself wanting to impress her with the desirability of my city.

"That doesn't sound so terrible," she said, pulling the shawl more tightly around her shoulders. "Shall we continue on? It is getting chilly."

As we approached the villa, I noticed that the lights were on in the library. That is where we would find Mr. Coates, I was sure. The shelves of rare and fine books certainly exerted a siren call to those susceptible. I had found it difficult to tear myself away earlier, sure that there were more treasures waiting to be discovered.

When we entered the house, I said, "I'm going by the library before retiring to my chamber. I believe Mr. Coates is there."

"I'm coming with you," she said. "Perhaps he is in need of sustenance." She glanced at me. "I can prepare a hot drink or something to eat if you would like."

Although I was deeply chilled and a hot toddy would not have gone amiss, I declined, not wanting to burden Estella. The breakfast hour would come soon enough.

Other lamps had been left burning so mine was no longer required to find our way to the library. I left it by the staircase for my return.

Estella gasped as we entered the library. My

gaze followed hers and I saw Mr. Coates sprawled back in a chair, a book open upon his lap.

A terrible certainty gripped me. Mr. Coates had found the fatal folio and had made the mistake of reading it.

We rushed to his side. "Take the book, Estella." I averted my gaze, afraid that even a glance might injure me. Or rather, bring the justice that I so richly deserved. She lifted the book and slapped the covers shut while I bent over my employer.

His chin was lowered to his chest, eyes closed, so I was able to check his neck for a pulse. I found one, faint and thready. "He's alive." I put my hand on his shoulder and shook it gently. "Mr. Coates. Mr. Coates? Can you hear me?" To Estella, I said, "Fetch the doctor."

"It means sending to the village, but I will do it." She rushed from the room, no doubt to rouse one of the servants.

His head lolled back and his eyes opened a crack. "Mr. Marlboro? I can barely see you. Everything is dark . . . so dark."

"Calm yourself, man. Rest. The doctor will soon be here."

Eyes closed again, he licked his lips. "A doctor cannot save me. This is an illness of the soul." His brief smile was crooked and wry. "I am caught in the trap I hoped to set."

I immediately caught his meaning. "You wanted to kill your uncle with the book, so you would inherit."

It all made sense now. Mr. Coates had searched out a gift that would flatter the old goat with its rarity and price, while knowing that a mere glimpse would send the rapacious earl to his reward. I'd heard the stories, even isolated in my book-lined lair. The Earl was the worse of what England had to offer, a stain on the term "of noble birth." There was nothing noble or honorable about him.

Now Mr. Coates had been hoist by his own petard. The temptation to look inside the book had been too much for him. Perhaps he thought, after Estella's experience, that the rumors had been greatly exaggerated and the deaths were merely coincidences.

His hand reached out and gripped my sleeve. "Mr. Marlboro. I urge you." A pause as he labored for breath. "Do not give that book to my uncle. Or to anyone else. I have made a grave mistake and it will cost me my life."

"Surely not," I said, hoping that somehow he would pull through. I didn't like the man very much but still, I did not wish for an untimely death to befall him.

He didn't speak again. He sat with chin resting on his chest, his breathing becoming ever more labored. The clock ticked on the mantel, marking the minutes while we waited for help.

His breathing slowed. I paced the carpet, urgency gripping me. When would the doctor arrive? The journey down to the village and back was sure to be difficult in the dark. And after a storm? There might be rocks and other debris strewn upon the path.

I have never felt so helpless as I did while waiting in that illustrious library for help to come.

Beyond the tall windows, the sky lightened toward dawn, paling into gray and then tinged with rose along the horizon.

Mr. Coates still sat in his chair, unmoving, his breaths irregular. Horribly, he reminded me of a clock winding down, the movement of the hands slower and slower until they finally halt at the final time.

So too do our years and hours slow and stop, when we do not know yet it is inevitable. Standing vigil with Mr. Coates, I couldn't help but reflect on my own life, on how satisfied I would be if I died right now. My fear of opening the fatal folio told me all I needed to know.

During whatever time I had left, I must strive to do what was right, to make amends where I could and seek forgiveness where I could not. Perhaps, I thought fancifully, exhausted and swaying on my feet, the book could be used as a cautionary tale. If you are afraid to read it, take heed. Search your heart and repent.

The sun was gilding the horizon when I heard footsteps in the hall. The doors burst open and a man carrying a medical bag bustled in, followed by Estella and the manservant.

While the doctor attended to his patient, Estella came to my side. "I am sorry to desert you. I had to travel to the village myself, in company with the manservant. I was afraid that the proper urgency would not be conveyed."

It was more likely that the doctor could have easily refused a request from a servant. From the lady of the villa? No, he would not want to lose her patronage.

"Help me move him," the doctor ordered, indicating a couch nearby.

Between the manservant and myself, we were able to shift Mr. Coates to a supine position. Estella hovered, asking what she could do.

"I'm afraid there is nothing that can be done," the doctor said. *"I only seek to make him comfortable in his last moments. His heart has suffered a great shock and he will not see noon."*

Estella gave a little gasp. "I am so sorry to hear that. Please, do whatever you can to make him comfortable."

The doctor's brow lifted. "Perhaps call a priest. To give him the last rites."

The fatal folio had claimed another victim. I resolved that it would be the last.

CHAPTER 24

Wesley's mouth dropped when he recognized me. "Molly. What are you doing here?"

Then, as if aware how that sounded, he amended, "I thought you were having fun at the dance."

"I was." My mind spun as I tried to decide what to say. "Um, I'm going to go meet someone. At the pub. Then go back to the dance."

He didn't question that, lame as it sounded. This gate was closer to the Headless Monk. After a moment, he pulled the gate open. "Out you go."

Now what? I wanted so badly to question him about Thad's phone. Why he had it. Where he got it. Not to mention *The Fatal Folio*'s whereabouts. He wasn't wearing orange trainers, I'd noticed. Did that mean he hadn't killed his cousin? Or had it only been a red herring, a clue in my own mind? An orange red herring, I thought nonsensically.

The gate swung close behind us. Wesley glanced up and down the alley in between sending looks toward me. I had the distinct feeling he wanted me to leave.

"Waiting for someone?" I asked. It wasn't my business and it was foolish to prod the bear.

"Why do you ask?" His tone was sharp. "What if I am?"

"No reason." Definitely defensive. He was the one, all

right, I was almost positive. "See ya." I strode off down the lane, leaving him standing alone under the streetlight. Was the pub this way? *Yes.* Phew.

A distance away, I stopped and pulled out my phone, acting as if I'd gotten a message or call. I sent Thad's number a text. *Delayed. Be there ASAP.*

The notification sound from Wesley's phone was audible. He began to furiously peck at the screen.

Now my phone bleeped. *I'll give you five.*

Good for Wesley. He wasn't going to let the bookdealer, fictional as he was, push him around.

Unfortunately he had also heard my phone—er, the burner—go off. I could feel the accusation in his glare from here.

Adrenaline flooded my body but I couldn't move. My limbs had that leaden, rooted-to-the ground sensation so common in nightmares.

He took big strides down the lane toward me. "What are you playing at, Molly?"

I squared up, clenching my fists. "What are *you* playing at?" Best defense was good offense, right? I sent off my one and only shot. "Detective Inspector Ryan has your messages. So be careful. Be *very* careful."

His big foot actually paused mid-step. "Wha— Detective Inspector—you . . ." Then the foot went down and the hands went up. "I didn't kill him. I swear."

"Why should I—I mean, the inspector, believe you? You have Thad's phone. You've had it all along. Why didn't you turn it in, if you're innocent?"

He lowered his chin. "I thought I could help," he mumbled. "Figure out who killed him, I mean."

His excuse was out-there enough to be plausible. I moved a few steps closer. "Did you take it off his . . . person?" That would be gruesome—and indicate that he hadn't called for help after the attack. We had been the ones to do it and the phone was already missing by then.

He shook his head. "No way. You really think— He left it in his room. Plugged into the charger. I saw it sitting there and grabbed it, before the police came to search. I thought I might find clues on it. Find out who he was meeting. Who killed him."

"Did he say he was meeting anyone?" If Wesley knew all this and hadn't shared . . . I wouldn't want to be in his shoes when Sean Ryan caught up with him. Not that Ryan was going to be happy with me either. I decided not to think about that right now.

Wesley folded his arms. "He didn't tell me anything. He said he was going to the common for the bonfire." He tipped his head back enough that the streetlight shone on his face. "He asked me to go and I said no." He began to blink rapidly. Was he crying? "If I had . . ." His voice, husky now, almost broke. "Maybe—"

Compassion flooded my heart. I knew that helpless feeling of losing someone all too well. "Oh, Wesley."

He cleared his throat. "Anyway. Yeah, I have his phone."

"Any idea who killed him?" I asked. Maybe this bumbling student had made some progress, unlike the police and me.

"It all started with the hunting lodge," he said. "Someone tried then."

"I thought that too," I said, excited. "An accidental shooting that wasn't."

"Josh was with me the whole time," he said. "So it wasn't him. Thad was off by himself, still in line, though. He knew better than that, to get ahead of the shooters." He pointed to his right, as if imagining the scene. "The shot came from the east. If it had been someone in the hunt, it would have come from the opposite direction."

"Did you share that with anyone? His parents? The police?"

Wesley's shoulders slumped. "I tried. Everyone was invested in the idea of an accident. Anything else sounded too far out." He toed his sneaker into the cobblestones. "Not much fun being right sometimes."

"I hear that," I said. "What did Thad think?"

He thought for a moment. "He was pretty freaked out. He dragged us to a hotel in Edinburgh where we drank ourselves sick before taking the train back."

"I can't blame him. Or you." Edinburgh. Where had I heard that mentioned? Never mind. This wasn't the time or place to start pondering.

Wesley's head lifted. "So you sent my messages to the police. What does that mean, exactly?"

I knew he'd get around to this question at some point. I tried to break it to him gently. "Reginald Dubold isn't coming. There's no buyer for the manuscript." And the police and I knew he was involved in the theft. That part remained unspoken.

In response, Wesley literally rocked back on his heels. Then he spun around, unlocked the gate, and fled inside.

He sure could move fast when he wanted to. "Wait," I called out. "Wesley." I leaped forward, grabbing the gate before it clicked shut. I could have bitten my tongue. Hard. Was he going to get rid of the manuscript? Maybe even destroy it? Heartsick, cursing my big mouth, I picked up my skirts and ran, chasing him.

To my relief, he didn't head for his staircase, where I assumed he kept the stolen book. Instead he kept going, in the direction of the main court. Was he going back to the dance?

I lost him near the arched entrance to the main court.

Not seeing anywhere else he could have gone, I plunged through the passage.

As I emerged at the other end, I saw a monk striding away. There he was. I committed the sin of cutting across the grass so as to shorten the distance.

On he went, and as he passed under a light, I saw the shoes. Huh. Orange. Maybe it was *Oliver* I was following now. Oh, the absurdity of people everywhere dressed like monks. I pictured them crisscrossing the courts, hands in their sleeves.

As they had centuries ago, no doubt. With a huff at my own unruly brain, I watched as the monk approached the bell tower. The bottom of this edifice was open, with arches supporting the upper part housing the bell. As I got closer, I saw the monk with orange shoes step inside. Another person emerged from the shadows. Wesley.

"The jig is up," Wesley said.

The other monk laughed and I could tell it was a woman. "What are you talking about?"

Wesley gestured and the other monk pushed back her hood with an impatient gesture. *Sophie Verona.* When she moved to stand beside him, I noticed they were very similar in height and build. *And she was wearing orange shoes.* "We sold a lot of that style," Tim had said. Men's and women's both.

Was Sophie the masked runner we believed had killed Thad? They worked together in the Institute, which had funky bookkeeping, according to Amy. Sophie had let Thad redo his paper for a better grade.

And Sophie had probably been in Edinburgh at the conference with Oliver the day Thad was shot at while hunting.

"So," Wesley was saying, "I got a text from Reginald tonight saying he had a buyer."

"Really? That's wonderful. Did he say how much?"

Sophie and Wesley had worked together to steal the manuscript. I had no doubt that Wesley had carried out the actual dirty work. That seemed like her style.

Wesley lowered the phone. "Let me finish." After a pause, he went on. "The messages weren't from him. Someone used a burner phone."

I was impressed that he hadn't mentioned me by name. Trying to keep me out of the line of fire? That was nice of him.

"It was a prank?" Sophie barked. "But who would know to send you that message?"

"Exactly," Wesley said. "They know we stole *The Fatal Folio*. That's not the worst of it. The police have these texts now."

"*The police?*" Sophie shrieked. She began to swear at him while slapping at his head and shoulders.

"Hey." Wesley ducked away, trying to fend her off. "Cut it out."

I called 999 to report an assault, speaking low under the shouts and protests. My hope was that when they questioned Sophie about this altercation, she would confess to Thad's murder.

Wesley managed to get away from her flailing arms and he bolted from the bell tower, robe flying. I was still in the middle of the call. Was Sophie going to run as well?

No, she stayed in the bell tower, pacing around. I'd keep an eye on her, I decided, to make the police's job easier.

I had barely hung up, officers supposedly on their way, when footsteps sounded on the path. Half expecting to see Wesley returning for a final word, I wasn't surprised to see a monk costume.

Then he pushed back the hood. Oliver. "Sophie?" he

called. "I've been looking for you." He entered the bell tower and went over to her. "What's the matter?"

She had turned her back on him. "Nothing. I had an argument with someone, that's all. I'll be okay in a minute."

"Why don't we go back to the dance? We can have a drink and celebrate your promotion."

"You're something else," she said, admiration in her tone. "I thought you'd be all bitter and angry."

"I am," he said with a laugh. "But not at you. Dr. Cutler is a different matter."

As the pair hesitated, I saw an opportunity to clarify some matters. Putting my phone on record, I approached the bell tower. "Hey, Oliver," I called. "There you are." They turned to face me, dressed identically in habits and orange shoes. I laughed. "Did you notice that you're both wearing the same shoes?"

Oliver lifted one sneaker and glanced at Sophie's feet. "I guess we are. These are my favorite trainers."

"Mine too," she said. "Great minds, right?" She snuggled closer, taking his arm.

"Congratulations, Dr. Verona," I said. "I read about your promotion." She inclined her head to accept the kudos. "I have to say, the Institute this week has only increased my interest in gothic literature. Plus I've been enjoying *The Fatal Folio*. I'd love to read your paper, Dr. Verona. The one on *retribution*." I turned to Oliver, acting innocent. "You presented on that in Edinburgh too, right?"

"We were co-presenters," Oliver said. He nudged her with an elbow. "Which was a good thing. I had to start without you."

She sighed. "And I pride myself on being prompt."

"Where were you?" I asked. Temptation trembled on

my tongue and I gave into it. "Doing a spot of hunting, perhaps?"

Her eyes went wide. "What? How did—"

"Wild guess," I said. "You decided to take a potshot at Thad, using the conference as a cover. Or you made the plan after you learned his lodge was so close to the city? It didn't work, so you tried again. So clever, Sophie, pointing the finger at the other students with a grudge against him."

"Molly," Oliver said, sounding confused. "What are you talking about?"

Sophie tried to make a break for it, which required pushing past Oliver and me.

"You can run but you can't hide," I said. "The police are on their way." As if in answer, blue-and-white lights flashed outside the main gate, reflecting off the buildings.

She ran anyway, of course, shoving us both aside. Oliver stared at me. "What's going on?"

"She killed Thad. And she helped steal *The Fatal Folio*." Noticing movement at the main gate door to the court, I went over to the bell rope. "Cover your ears."

I pulled the rope and the bell pealed out, once, twice, three times. That would attract their attention. Thad Devine was going to get justice. And with any luck, we would soon be restoring the *Fatal Folio* manuscript to the Hazelhurst House library.

CHAPTER 25

Two weeks later

"All done," I said aloud, my voice startling in the quiet library. Sighing in satisfaction, I sat back from the computer and flexed my fingers. All one thousand two hundred and three books were now entered into the catalogue.

Including the original manuscripts for *The Fatal Folio* and *Among the Ruins*. Wesley had returned the manuscript with the hope that it would lower his sentence for theft. He'd been crafty enough not to hand the precious document over to Dubold before getting a sale lined up.

Sophie was taking the main fall, though. She had masterminded the theft and convinced Wesley to actually steal the book. He'd had no idea Sophie killed his cousin and it had been his idea to use Thad's number when visiting Dubold's, unbeknownst to Sophie, figuring it was wiser than using his own.

Money was the motive for both of them. Wesley was perpetually short of cash, especially with his cousin borrowing from him, and Sophie needed to make up shortfalls in the Institute bank accounts. Yes, she had been the embezzler, something Thad and then Amy figured out.

Poor Oliver had been oblivious, to the theft and to Sophie's true nature as a conniving and manipulative killer. Sophie had confessed to taking the knife from Thad's room and waiting for him near the gate, wearing the Guy Fawkes mask. Outside, she'd stabbed him, then left him for dead.

Her motive? Thad was going to turn her in for embezzling despite the blackmail he'd already extorted by forcing her to write his papers, including the one on retribution. Being totally without remorse, Thad had laughed at the idea of retribution for his misdeed, Sophie mentioned during her confession. She'd decided to teach him a lesson while ridding herself of a burden once and for all, especially with the promotion in the balance. She had also worked covertly to sway Dr. Cutler against Oliver.

Speaking of Oliver, he'd been at the Headless Monk during Thad's murder, in response to an urgent message from Sophie. Enamored with her, he hadn't been able to resist blowing off dinner with us. She'd sent him there to keep him out of the way.

As for the mysterious music in Thad's room and the hooded figure watching us on the tour, that had been Wesley. He'd hoped to learn more by scaring Amy and Josh, who he thought had killed his cousin. Sophie had planted the bloody jacket in Josh's room to muddy the waters. She was well aware of the conflicts between Thad and the others, the reason she tried to shoot Thad while he and his friend were at the lodge.

Oliver had finally gotten the promotion to full professor. After the truth came out about Sophie actually writing Thad's papers, the student's complaint was considered null and void. Dr. Cutler was required to backtrack and award Oliver his due. Though I wasn't sure it made up for the knowledge that his girlfriend was a killer.

I'd finally caught up to Amy to ask about her strong reaction to hearing Dubold's name. She said that she'd warned Thad about Dubold, having heard that he'd dealt unfairly with other students selling books. She took him selling her own precious novels to the crooked dealer as an insult and it had upset her. By the way, Amy got back all her books.

Lady Asha popped her head around the door. "Ready for a break?"

"More like a celebration," I said, rising to my feet. "I'm finished."

She clasped her hands together. "I'm so glad." Her gaze surveyed the shelves. "It was a big job, wasn't it?"

"It was," I admitted. "And I loved every minute of it. What a spectacular collection. The catalogue will help you manage it generations into the future."

"That's the plan." She waited by the door for me to join her. "Kieran's joining us, as is Graham."

Her husband and Kieran's father. "How is he today?"

We set off down the corridor. "Doing much better. The report that his cancer is in remission has put a new spring in his step for sure."

"I'll bet." Despite the scare with the low electrolytes, caused by medication, the overall report from the London doctors had been good. Lord Graham was on the mend.

As usual, tea was in the small sitting room. When we entered, Lord Graham and Kieran, already waiting, rose to their feet.

"Molly has good news," Lady Asha said, going to her seat behind the tea tray. She lifted the pot and began to pour. "The inventory is done."

"Hurray," Kieran said. "Well done, you," Lord Graham added.

I made a small bow to accept their accolades before taking a seat beside Kieran. Cups of tea went around, as did a platter of lemon curd tarts. I thought of the email I'd received earlier and saved for when we got together. "We finally have progress regarding Selwyn Scott's identity." Stubbornly refusing to give up, I'd tried several different avenues and had finally met success.

They all turned to me with expressions of surprise.

"I didn't know you were still trying to figure it out," Kieran said.

With a shrug, I said, "I didn't say anything in case it was another dead end." I explained that I'd found letters from Agatha Scott to her sister, Lady Amelia Birtwistle, in a collection at Oxford University. "A very kind librarian made digital copies for us so we can compare her handwriting to the manuscript and publisher letters." I picked up my phone. "She also said that the one written in January 1843 would definitely be of interest." I hadn't opened the attachment yet, so I was as excited and curious as my audience.

Bringing it up, I began to read aloud, thankful the handwriting was legible.

Dearest Amelia,

I do hope you had a nice Christmas. Ours, I'm afraid to say, was rather dismal without our dear Frances. We do miss her so.

There is a bright spot, however. Although Samuel put off the wedding when his sister died, we will host it in the spring. I hope that Hazelhurst House will soon ring with young voices and laughter again.

As to the other matter, I have decided not to continue writing. Without the inspiration and help

*Frances provided, I can't see my way clear to pro-
ceeding with the second book.*

I decided to pause at this point. "I think we've solved
our mystery. Frances and Agatha must have worked together. That explains the different handwriting."

The writing in this letter was the same as the letters
to the publisher, I could already tell. Which must mean
that the manuscripts themselves had been penned by
Frances.

"*The Fatal Folio.*" Lady Asha waved her hand to
demonstrate. "By Agatha and Frances Scott. Originally
published under the name Selwyn Scott." She lifted her
teacup. "Cheers, Molly. You did it."

"With lots of help." I tapped Kieran's knee. "Especially
from you."

"We make a good team, don't we?" he said. "Mum,
we'll credit *Among the Ruins* the same way, right?"

"Absolutely," Lady Asha said. "Did I show you mock-
ups of the covers?" She got up and went to the desk in the
corner and rummaged around, then returned with two
cardboard sheets in hand. "We'll have them change the
author name."

The covers captured the eerie, haunting feel that was
the hallmark of both novels. I imagined the two authors,
alone much of the time in this isolated yet beautiful
manor. They had made good use of the inspiration the setting provided, with a touch of fantastical and exotic. I
wondered if they had ever traveled to Italy. *Among the
Ruins* was set in England, in Yorkshire.

As I passed the covers to Kieran, I thought that the
writing team would have loved them. *This is for you, Agatha and Frances. May your work live on.*

THE FATAL FOLIO, CONCLUSION

Mr. Coates was interred in the villa graveyard, there being no point in trying to send the body home. After notifying his uncle, his only relation, a generous gift arrived to provide an appropriate burial stone and to assist with maintenance. This alone redeemed the Earl somewhat in my eyes. Whether it would in Heaven's view was not mine to determine.

After much discussion along these lines, Estella and I decided to destroy the fatal folio. No more lives would it claim, either accidentally or as part of a nefarious plot such as Mr. Coates had planned.

With the help of Estella's servants, a huge bonfire was built in the field. With great ceremony, she and I placed the book right in the center, in a place where it could not move or be dislodged.

"Please, dear Matthew, do the honors," she said, indicating the servant should hand me the torch.

I hesitated briefly at the edge of the stack, knowing that what I was about to do was irrevocable.

Once the book burned, it would be gone forever. The monk's ramblings would be silenced at last.

Then I thought of Estella's father and Mr. Coates, who while far from perfect, would be with us still if not for that infernal tome.

With determination and a lightness of heart, I bent and touched the flame to the kindling. As the fire caught, flames running along the brittle sticks and licking at the logs, I saw a figure in the distance, watching.

It was the monk from the ruins. After a long moment, he nodded then turned and glided away. We never saw him again.

Estella and I stayed up until the fire had burned itself out. During those sweet hours, I asked her to become my wife, and to my great joy, she accepted. Our plan was to live here, where I will still collect and sell books, able to scour Europe and even beyond for the finest and rarest specimens. I will take on a partner in the Cambridge bookshop and Estella and I will visit, with our children, so I can share my England with them.

Or so we dreamed during that long night under the stars as the huge fire crackled and leaped, burning lower and lower until it was finally ash.

And out of that ash, our new lives have begun.

THE END